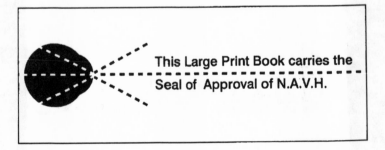

LIKE A LAMB TO SLAUGHTER

LAWRENCE BLOCK

with an Introduction by Joe Gores

WHEELER
PUBLISHING

Published in 2006 by arrangement with Baror International, Inc.

Wheeler Large Print Softcover.

The text of this Large Print edition is unabridged.
Other aspects of the book may vary from the original edition.

Set in 16 pt. Plantin by Christina S. Huff.

Printed in the United States on permanent paper.

Library of Congress Cataloging-in-Publication Data

Block, Lawrence.
    Like a lamb to slaughter / by Lawrence Block ; with an
introduction by Joe Gores. — Large print ed.
      p. cm.
    ISBN 1-59722-207-0 (lg. print : sc : alk. paper)
    1. Fantasy fiction, American.   2. Large type books.
I. Title.
PS3552.L63L55 2006
  813′.54—dc22   2005036171

This is for
Ann, Bern, Bonnie, Brenna,
Cathy, Charlotte, the three Davids,
Ellie, Geoffrey, Jack, Joyce,
Kenna, Laurie, Lilli, Lolly,
Patrick John, Peggy Ann,
Philip, Rick, Roger, Susan and Wendy.

It's also for
Alex and Gayle, Jay and Claudia,
Peter and Meg, Robert and Doreen,
Ron and Miri and, of course,
Bob and Mallie.

But most of all,
and with all my love,
it's for Lynne.

As the Founder/CEO of NAVH, the only national health agency solely devoted to those who, although not totally blind, have an eye disease which could lead to serious visual impairment, I am pleased to recognize Thorndike Press* as one of the leading publishers in the large print field.

Founded in 1954 in San Francisco to prepare large print textbooks for partially seeing children, NAVH became the pioneer and standard setting agency in the preparation of large type.

Today, those publishers who meet our standards carry the prestigious "Seal of Approval" indicating high quality large print. We are delighted that Thorndike Press is one of the publishers whose titles meet these standards. We are also pleased to recognize the significant contribution Thorndike Press is making in this important and growing field.

Lorraine H. Marchi, L.H.D.
Founder/CEO
NAVH

* Thorndike Press encompasses the following imprints: Thorndike, Wheeler, Walker and Large Print Press.

ACKNOWLEDGMENTS

The author wishes to acknowledge with gratitude the magazines in which these stories initially appeared. "The Books Always Balance," "Change of Life," "Click!," "If This Be Madness," "Like a Lamb to Slaughter" (originally "A Candle for the Bag Lady"), "The Most Unusual Snatch," "That Kind of a Day," "Weekend Guests" and "With a Smile for the Ending" were first published in *Alfred Hitchcock's Mystery Magazine.* "The Dangerous Business" (originally "The Dangerous Game") and "The Ehrengraf Experience" were first published in *Ellery Queen's Mystery Magazine.* "The Ehrengraf Appointment" first appeared in *Mike Shayne's Mystery Magazine*; "You Could Call It Blackmail" in *For Women Only*; and "The Boy Who Disappeared Clouds" in *The Magazine of Fantasy and Science Fiction.* "Hot Eyes, Cold Eyes" and "A Little Off the Top" were first published in *Gallery.*

"Death of the Mallory Queen" and "Leo Youngdahl, R.I.P." have never been published before.

CONTENTS

INTRODUCTION
by Joe Gores

Across from the Algonquin Hotel on West Forty-fourth Street in New York, where the famed literary coterie that called itself the Round Table used to meet in the 1930s, is the Royalton Hotel. Here, in the 1960s, another literary group started meeting. It never got famous, and what was bandied about the table instead of wit — or in addition to wit — was money. It was called, with admirable brevity, "The Poker Game."

The Poker Game eventually disintegrated: people got married, got divorced, got rich, got bored, went broke, went away. But in its heyday some damned fine poker was played, and one could emerge an occasional four-figure winner. Or loser. Regulars in The Game included some of the finest young professional writers in the country — men such as Brian Garfield, Donald E. Westlake, Justin Scott and Larry Block.

During one marathon eighteen-hour session of The Game, for instance, a novel was written. Each player would, in turn, sit out a few hands in the next room where he would type a chapter of The Book. He could read only the last page of the previous chapter written by the previous player. The one who wrote the first chapter also wrote the last, bringing the book back together again in *la ronde* fashion.

An agent who regularly sat in on the game sold the novel as a paperback original for a thousand bucks. The players split the pot. I don't know if the agent took his 10 percent or not.

A professional writer is just that: a person who writes for a living. Under this definition, people who write for newspapers are still newspeople, and people who teach school and write at night are still schoolteachers. The professional writer writes. It is what he does, as laying bricks is what a bricklayer does. He is always a craftsman, occasionally an artist, and he is not a hack; he does the very best job he can, every time, on whatever writing job is at hand.

Almost anyone who is literate can write a short story. But to write a *good* short story . . . Aye, there's the rub, as Hamlet once remarked. The short story is right up there next to poetry in the demands it places on the writer. It is not just a short novel; it is, say, a battle rather than a war. A moment, not a lifetime. It marks some vivid instant that forever alters the life of its protagonist, rather than depicting the slow evolutional effect of time and events on a group of people.

It is unforgiving. There is very little room for artistic maneuvering and none at all for self-indulgence. Every word, every phrase, every nuance, is vital. The short story can teach a beginning writer the elements of his craft — along with precision, discipline and grace. Unfortunately, in today's world of depleted markets, where people who used to be readers turn too often to television to scratch their story-hearing itch, it can also break him financially. Any professional writer turning out short stories today does it from sheer love of the game.

Larry Block has written the stories in this volume because he loves to write short stories. And he knows how to do it. He knows what a short story is, what the form demands. His best work is very good in-

13

deed, almost shockingly better than it would have to be merely for publication.

Lovers of the Chip Harrison novels will find here the first-ever Chip Harrison short story. Because the Harrison stories parody Rex Stout's Nero Wolfe stories, "Death of the Mallory Queen" is full of name puns and impossibly complicated formal mystery plotting. It is a froth, a meringue, a joy, as light and entertaining as a story can be.

At the far end of the spectrum is the somber and superb "Like a Lamb to Slaughter," featuring Matt Scudder, the recurring protagonist of some of Block's best novels. This novelette has all the virtues of the longer Scudders: realism, compassion, beautifully crafted dialogue that evokes the rich tapestry of New York street life, and a resolution of the violence at the core of the story that is at once satisfying and moving.

The contrast between the two stories could not be more telling; together, they illuminate the range, depth, color and shading of Block's storytelling genius.

In between are stories with a rare ability to move us outside ourselves — and knock us slightly off balance at the same time — such as "The Boy Who Disappeared Clouds" and "With a Smile for the End."

14

There are macabre stories such as "Hot Eyes, Cold Eyes" and "Click!" The final sentence of each tale carries the reader that little bit farther into the bizarre that his imagination refuses to go unguided. One is not all that sure that one wanted to get there — but Block writes stories that are very hard to put down. A remarkable bonus is a brace of Martin Ehrengraf stories, about that dapper little defense attorney who calls himself a "corrector of destinies" and whose clients "are always innocent . . . in the sense that they are not guilty."

Ehrengraf is unique; a formidable genius whose endlessly fertile schemes suggest that his creator might also possess the greatest noncriminal criminal mind of our day. But we cannot ever be totally sure that Ehrengraf is really behind his clients' ineluctable innocence, which is what always leaves us mentally pleading for just one more revelation at the end of the story. Ehrengraf, always entertaining and shocking, merits being both collected on his own and having a serious doctoral dissertation written about him.

This is as rich a collection of short fiction as one is likely to find, in turn shocking, amusing, moving, sexy, funny, compassionate, frightening. And always entertaining. Always lifting us out of our own world into that special world of Larry Block, where (to quote Christopher Smart of Bedlam, one of Ehrengraf's favorite poets) "the rankle-dankle fish with hands."

The Boy Who Disappeared Clouds

Jeremy's desk was at the left end of the fifth row. Alphabetical order had put him in precisely the desk he would have selected for himself, as far back as you could get without being in the last row. The last row was no good, because there were things you were called upon to do when you were in the last row. Sometimes papers were passed to the back of the room, for example, and the kids in the last row brought them forward to the teacher. In the fifth row you were spared all that.

And, because he was on the end, and the left end at that, he had the window to look out of. He looked out of it now, watching a car brake almost to a stop, then accelerate across the intersection. You were supposed to come to a full stop but hardly anybody ever did, not unless there were other cars or a crossing guard around. They probably figured nobody was looking, he thought, and he liked the idea that they were unaware that he was watching them.

He sensed that Ms. Winspear had left her desk and turned to see her standing a third of the way up the aisle. He faced forward, paying attention, and when her eyes reached his he looked a little off to the left.

When she returned to the front of the room and wrote on the blackboard, he shifted in his seat and looked out the window again. A woman was being pulled down the street by a large black and white dog. Jeremy watched until they turned a corner and moved out of sight, watched another car not quite stop for the stop sign, then raised his eyes to watch a cloud floating free and untouched in the open blue sky.

"Lots of kids look out the window," Cory Buckman said. "Sometimes I'll hear myself, standing in front of them and droning on and on, and I'll wonder why they're not all lined up at the windows with their noses pressed against the glass. Wouldn't you rather watch paint dry than hear me explain quadratic equations?"

"I used to know how to solve quadratic equations," Janice Winspear said, "and now I'm not even sure what they are. I know lots of kids look out the window. Jeremy's different."

"How?"

"Oh, I don't know." She took a sip of coffee, put her cup down. "You know what he is? He's a nice quiet boy."

"That has a ring to it. Page five of the *Daily News*: ' "He was always a nice quiet boy," the neighbors said. "Nobody ever dreamed he would do something like this." ' Is that the sort of thing you mean?"

"I don't think he's about to murder his parents in their beds, although I wouldn't be surprised if he wanted to."

"Oh?"

She nodded. "Jeremy's the youngest of four children. The father drinks and beats his wife and the abuse gets passed on down the line, some of it verbal and some of it physical. Jeremy's at the end of the line."

"And he gets beaten?"

"He came to school in the fall with his wrist in a cast. He said he fell and it's possible he did. But he fits the pattern of an abused child. And he doesn't have anything to balance the lack of affection in the home."

"How are his grades?"

"All right. He's bright enough to get C's and B's without paying attention. He never raises his hand. When I call on him he knows the answer — if he knows the question."

"How does he get along with the other kids?"

"They barely know he exists." She looked across the small table at Cory. "And that's in the sixth grade. Next year he'll be in junior high with classes twice the size of mine and a different teacher for every subject."

"And three years after that he'll be in senior high, where I can try teaching him quadratic equations. Unless he does something first to get himself locked up."

"I'm not afraid he'll get locked up, not really. I'm just afraid he'll get lost."

"How is he at sports?"

"Hopeless. The last one chosen for teams in gym class, and he doesn't stay around for after-school games."

"I don't blame him. Any other interests? A stamp collection? A chemistry set?"

"I don't think he could get to have anything in that house," she said. "I had his older brothers in my class over the years and they were monsters."

"Unlike our nice quiet boy."

"That's right. If he had anything they'd take it away from him. Or smash it."

"In that case," Cory said, "what you've got to give him is something nobody can take away. Why don't you teach him how to disappear clouds?"

"How to — ?"

"Disappear clouds. Stare at them and make them disappear."

"Oh?" She arched an eyebrow. "You can do that?"

"Uh-huh. So can you, once you know how."

"Cory —"

He glanced at the check, counted out money to cover it. "Really," he said. "There's nothing to it. Anybody can do it."

"For a minute there," she said, "I thought you were serious."

"About the clouds? Of course I was serious."

"You can make clouds disappear."

"And so can you."

"By staring at them."

"Uh-huh."

"Well," she said, "let's see you do it."

He looked up. "Wrong kind of clouds," he announced.

"Oh, right. It figures."

"Have I ever lied to you? Those aren't

individual clouds up there; that's just one big overcast mess blocking the sun."

"That's why we need you to work your magic, sir."

"Well, I'm only a journeyman magician. What you need are cumulus clouds, the puffy ones like balls of cotton. Not cumulonimbus, not the big rain clouds, and not the wispy cirrus clouds either, but the cumulus clouds."

"I know what cumulus clouds look like," she said. "It's not like quadratic equations, it stays with you. When the sky is full of cumulus clouds, what will your excuse be? Wrong phase of the moon?"

"I suppose everyone tells you this," he said, "but you're beautiful when you're skeptical."

She was sorting laundry when the phone rang. It was Cory Buckman. "Look out the window," he ordered. "Drop everything and look out the window."

She was holding the receiver in one hand and a pair of tennis shorts in the other, and she looked out the window without dropping either. "It's still there," she reported.

"What's still there?"

"Everything's still there."

"What did you see when you looked out the window?"

"The house across the street. A maple tree. My car."

"Janice, it's a beautiful day out there!"

"Oh. So it is."

"I'll pick you up in half an hour. We're going on a picnic."

"Oh, don't I wish I could. I've got —"

"What?"

"Laundry to sort, and I have to do my lesson plans for the week."

"Try to think in terms of crusty french bread, a good sharp cheese, a nice fruity Zinfandel and a flock of cumulus clouds overhead."

"Which you will cause to disappear?"

"We'll both make them disappear, and we'll work much the same magic upon the bread and the cheese and the wine."

"You said half an hour? Give me an hour."

"Split the difference. Forty-five minutes."

"Sold."

"You see that cloud? The one that's shaped like a camel?"

"More like a llama," she said.

"Watch."

She watched the cloud, thinking that he

was really very sweet and very attractive, and that he didn't really need a lot of nonsense about disappearing clouds to lure her away from a Saturday afternoon of laundry and lesson plans. A grassy meadow, air fresh with spring, cows lowing off to the right, and —

A hole began to open in the center of the cloud. She stared, then glanced at him. His fine brow was tense, his mouth a thin line, his hands curled up into fists.

She looked at the cloud again. It was breaking up, collapsing into fragments.

"I don't believe this," she said.

He didn't reply. She watched, and the process of celestial disintegration continued. The hunks of cloud turned wispy and, even as she looked up at them, disappeared altogether. She turned to him, open-mouthed, and he sighed deeply and beamed at her.

"See?" he said. "Nothing to it."

"You cheated," she said.

"How?"

"You picked one you knew was going to disappear."

"How would I go about doing that?"

"I don't know. I'm not a meteorologist, I'm a sixth-grade teacher. Maybe you used math."

"Logarithms," he said. "Cumulus clouds are powerless against logarithms. You pick one."

"Huh?"

"You pick a cloud and I'll disappear it. But it has to be the right sort of cloud."

"Cumulus."

"Uh-huh. And solitary —"

"Wandering lonely as a cloud, for instance."

"Something like that. And not way off on the edge of the horizon. It doesn't have to be directly overhead, but it shouldn't be in the next county."

She picked a cloud. He stared at it and it disappeared.

She gaped at him. "You really did it."

"Well, I really stared at it and it really disappeared. You don't have to believe the two phenomena were connected."

"You made it disappear."

"If you say so."

"Could you teach my nice quiet boy? Could you teach Jeremy?"

"Nope. I don't teach sixth graders."

"But —"

"*You* teach him."

"But I don't know how to do it!"

"So I'll teach you," he said. "Look, Jan, it's not as remarkable as you think it is.

Anybody can do it. It's about the easiest ESP ability to develop. Pick a cloud."

"You pick one for me."

"All right. That one right there, shaped like a loaf of white bread."

"Not like any loaf I ever saw." Why was she quibbling? "All right," she said. "I know which cloud you mean."

"Now let me tell you what you're going to do. You're going to stare at it and focus on it, and you're going to send energy from your Third Eye chakra, that's right here —" he touched his finger to a spot midway between her eyebrows "— and that energy is going to disperse the cloud. Take a couple of deep, deep breaths, in and out, and focus on the cloud, that's right, and talk to it in your mind. Say, 'Disappear, disappear.' That's right, keep breathing, focus your energies —"

He kept talking to her and she stared at the loaf-shaped cloud. *Disappear,* she told it. She thought about energy, which she didn't believe in, flowing from her Third Eye whatsit, which she didn't have.

The cloud began to get thin in the middle. *Disappear,* she thought savagely, squinting at it, and a hole appeared. Her heart leaped with exultation.

"Look!"

"You got it now," he told her. "Keep on going. Put it out of its misery."

When the cloud was gone (gone!) she sat for a moment staring at the spot in the sky where it had been, as if it might have left a hole there. "You did it," Cory said.

"Impossible."

"Okay."

"I couldn't have done that. You cheated, didn't you?"

"How?"

"You helped me. By sending your energies into the cloud or something. What's so funny?"

"You are. Five minutes ago you wouldn't believe that I could make clouds disappear, and now you figure I must have done this one, because otherwise you'd have to believe *you* did it, and you know it's impossible."

"Well, it is."

"If you say so."

She poured a glass of wine, sipped at it. "Clearly impossible," she said. "I did it, didn't I?"

"Did you?"

"I don't know. Can I do another?"

"It's not up to me. They're not my clouds."

"Can I do that one? It looks like — I don't know what it looks like. It looks like a cloud."

"That's what it looks like, all right."

"Well? Can I do the cloud-shaped one?"

She did, and caused it to vanish. This time she could tell that it was her energy that was making the cloud disperse. She could actually feel that something was happening, although she didn't know what it was and couldn't understand how it worked. She did a third cloud, dispatching it in short order, and when it fell to her withering gaze she felt a remarkable surge of triumph.

She also felt drained. "I've got a headache," she told Cory. "I suppose the sun and the wine would do it, but it doesn't feel like the usual sort of headache."

"You're using some mental muscles for the first time," he explained. "They say we only use a small percentage of the brain. When we learn to use a new part, it's a strain."

"So what I've got is brain fatigue."

"A light case thereof."

She cocked her head at him. "You think you know a person," she said archly, "and then you find he's got hitherto undreamt-of talents. What else can you do?"

"Oh, all sorts of things. Long division, for example. And I can make omelets."

"What other occult powers have you got?"

"Thousands, I suppose, but that's the only one I've ever developed. Oh, and sometimes I know when a phone's about to ring, but not always."

"When I'm in the tub," she said, "that's when my phone always rings. What a heavenly spot for a picnic, incidentally. And private, too. The ants didn't even find us here."

She closed her eyes and he kissed her. *I have psychic powers,* she thought. *I knew you were going to do that.*

She said, "I'll bet you make inhibitions disappear, too. Can't you?"

He nodded. "First your inhibitions," he said. "Then your clothes."

The hardest part was waiting for the right sort of day. For a full week it rained. Then for two days the sky was bright and cloudless, and then it was utterly overcast. By the time the right sort of clouds were strewn across the afternoon sky, she had trouble trusting the memory of that Saturday afternoon. Had she really caused clouds to break up? Could she still do it?

And could she teach her Jeremy, her nice quiet boy?

Toward the end of the last class period she walked to the rear of the room, moved over toward the windows. She had them writing an exercise in English composition, a paragraph on their favorite television program. They always loved to write about television, though not as much as they loved to watch it.

She watched over Jeremy's shoulder. His handwriting was very neat, very precise.

Softly she said, "I'd like you to stay a few minutes after class, Jeremy." When he stiffened, she added, "It's nothing to worry about."

But of course he would worry, she thought, returning to the front of the room. There was no way to stop his worrying. No matter, she told herself. She was going to give him a gift today, a gift of self-esteem that he badly needed. A few minutes of anxiety was a small price for such a gift.

And, when the room had cleared and the others had left, she went again to his desk. He looked up at her approach, not quite meeting her eyes. He had the sort of undefined pale countenance her southern relatives would call po-faced. But it was, she thought, a sweet face.

She crouched by the side of his desk. "Jeremy," she said, pointing, "do you see that cloud?"

He nodded.

"Oh, I don't know," she said, thinking aloud. "The glass might be a problem. You used to be able to open classroom windows, before everything got climate-controlled. Jeremy, come downstairs with me. I want to take you for a ride."

"A ride?"

"In my car," she said. And when they reached her car, a thought struck her. "Your mother won't worry, will she? If you're a half hour or so late getting home?"

"No," he said. "Nobody'll worry."

When she stopped the car, on a country road just past the northern belt of suburbs, the perfect cloud was hovering almost directly overhead. She opened the door for Jeremy and found a patch of soft grass for them both to sit on. "See that cloud?" she said, pointing. "Just watch what happens to it."

Sure, she thought. Nothing was going to happen and Jeremy was going to be convinced that his teacher was a certifiable madwoman. She breathed deeply, in and out, in and out. She stared hard at the center of the cloud and visualized her energy as a beam of white light running from her Third Eye chakra, directly into the cloud's middle. *Disappear,* she thought. *Come on, you. Disappear.*

Nothing happened.

She thought, *Cory, damn you, if you set me up like this to make a fool of myself* — She pushed the thought aside and focused on the cloud. *Disappear, disappear* —

The cloud began to break up, crumbling into fragments. Relief flowed through her like an electric current. She set her jaw and concentrated, and in less than a minute not a trace of the cloud remained in the sky.

The other clouds around it were completely undisturbed.

She looked at Jeremy, whose expression was guarded. She asked him if he'd been watching the cloud. He said he had.

"What happened to it?" she asked.

"It broke up," he said. "It disappeared."

"I made it disappear," she said.

He didn't say anything.

"Oh, Jeremy," she said, taking his hand in both of hers, "Jeremy, it's *easy!* You can do it. You can make clouds disappear. I can teach you."

"I —"

"I can teach you," she said.

"I think he's got a natural talent for it," she told Cory.

"Sure," he said. "Everybody does."

"Well, maybe his strength is as the strength of ten because his heart is pure. Maybe he has the simple single-mindedness of a child. Whatever he's got, the clouds of America aren't safe with him on the loose."

"Hmmm," he said.

"What's the matter?"

"Nothing. I was just going to say not to expect miracles. You gave him a great gift, but that doesn't mean he's going to be elected class president or captain of the football team. He'll still be a basically shy boy with a basically difficult situation at home and not too much going for him in the rest of the world. Maybe he can disappear clouds, but that doesn't mean he can move mountains."

"Killjoy."

"I just —"

"He can do something rare and magical," she said, "and it's his secret, and it's something for him to cling to while he grows up and gets out of that horrible household. You should have seen his face when that very first cloud caved in and gave up the ghost. Cory, he looked transformed."

"And he's still a nice, quiet boy?"

"He's a lovely boy," she said.

The window glass was no problem.

She'd thought it might be, that was why they'd gone all the way out into the country, but it turned out the glass was no problem at all. Whatever it was that got the cloud, it went right through the glass the same way your vision did.

She was in the front of the room now, thrusting a pointer at the pulled down map of the world, pointing out the oil-producing nations. He turned and looked out the window.

The clouds were the wrong kind.

A tree surgeon's pickup truck, its rear a jumble of sawn limbs, slowed almost to a stop, then moved on across the intersection. Jeremy looked down at the stop sign. A few days ago he'd spent most of math period trying to make the stop sign disappear, and there it was, same as ever, slowing the cars down but not quite bringing them to a halt. And that night he'd sat in his room trying to disappear a sneaker, and of course nothing had happened.

Because that wasn't how it worked. You couldn't take something and make it stop existing, any more than a magician could really make an object vanish. But clouds were masses of water vapor held together by — what? Some kind of energy, probably. And the energy that he sent out warred with the energy that held the water vapor particles together, and the particles went their separate ways, and that was the end of the cloud. The particles still existed but they were no longer gathered into a cloud.

So you couldn't make a rock disappear. Maybe, just maybe, if you got yourself tuned just right, you could make a rock crumble into a little pile of dust. He hadn't been able to manage that yet, and he didn't know if it was really possible, but he could see how it might be.

In the front of the room Ms. Winspear indicated oil-producing regions of the United States. She talked about the extraction of oil from shale, and he smiled at the mental picture of a rock crumbling to dust, with a little stream of oil flowing from it.

He looked out the window again. One of

the bushes in the foundation planting across the street had dropped its leaves. The bushes on either side of it looked healthy, but the leaves of the one bush had turned yellow and fallen overnight.

Two days ago he'd looked long and hard at that bush. He wondered if it was dead, or if it had just sickened and lost its leaves. Maybe that was it, maybe they would grow back.

He rubbed his wrist. It had been out of the cast for months, it never bothered him, but in the past few days it had been hurting him some. As if he was feeling pain now that he hadn't allowed himself to feel when the wrist broke.

He was starting to feel all sorts of things.

Ms. Winspear asked a question, something about oil imports, and a hand went up in the fourth row. Of course, he thought. Tracy Morrow's hand always went up. She always knew the answer and she always raised her hand, the little snot.

For a moment the strength of his feeling surprised him. Then he took two deep breaths, in and out, in and out, and stared hard at the back of Tracy's head.

Just to see.

If This Be Madness

St. Anthony's wasn't a bad place at all. There were bars on the windows, of course, and one couldn't come and go as one pleased, but it might have been a lot worse. I had always thought of insane asylums as something rather grim. The fictional treatment of such institutions leaves a good deal to be desired. Sadistic orderlies, medieval outlook, all of that. It wasn't like that, though.

I had a room to myself, with a window facing out on the main grounds. There were a great many elms on the property, plus some lovely shrubs which I would be hard pressed to name. When I was alone I would watch the groundskeeper go back and forth across the wide lawn behind a big power mower. But of course I didn't spend all of my time in the room — or cell, if you prefer it. There was a certain amount of social intercourse — gab sessions with the other patients, interminable ping pong matches, all of that. And the occupational therapy which was a major concern at St. Anthony's. I made these foolish little ceramic tile plates, and I wove baskets, and I made potholders. I suppose this was of some value. The simple idea of concentrating very intently on something which is essentially trivial must have some therapeutic value in cases of this nature — perhaps the same value that hobbies have for sane men.

Perhaps you're wondering why I was in St. Anthony's. A simple explanation. One cloudless day in September I left my office a few minutes after noon and went to my bank, where I cashed a check for two thousand dollars. I asked for — and received — two hundred crisp new ten-dollar bills. Then I walked aimlessly for two blocks until I came to a moderately busy street corner. Euclid and Paine, as I remember, but it's really immaterial.

There I sold the bills. I stopped passersby and offered the bills at fifty cents apiece, or traded them for cigarettes, or gave them away in return for a kind word. I recall paying one man fifteen dollars for his necktie, and it was spotted at that. Not surprisingly, a great many persons refused to have anything to do with me. I suspect they thought the bills were counterfeit.

In less than a half hour I was arrested. The police, too, thought the bills were counterfeit. They were not. When the police led me off to the patrol car I laughed uproariously and hurled the ten-dollar bills into the air. The sight of the officers of the law chasing after these fresh new bills was quite comic, and I laughed long and loud.

In jail, I stared around blindly and refused to speak to people. Mary appeared in short order with a doctor and a lawyer in tow. She cried a great deal into a lovely linen handkerchief, but I could tell easily how much she was enjoying her new role. It was a marvelous experiment in martyrdom for her — loving wife of a man who has just managed to flip his lid. She played it to the hilt.

When I saw her, I emerged at once from my lethargy. I banged hysterically on the bars of the cell and called her the foulest names imaginable. She burst into tears and they led her away. Someone gave me a shot of something — a tranquilizer, I suspect. Then I slept.

I did not go to St. Anthony's then. I remained in jail for three days — under observation, as it were — and then I began to return to my senses. Reality returned. I was quite baffled about the entire experience. I asked guards where I was, and why. My memory was very hazy. I could recall bits and pieces of what had happened but it made no sense to me.

There were several conferences with the prison psychiatrist. I told him how I had been working very hard, how I had been under quite a strain. This made considerable sense to him. My "sale" of the ten-dollar bills was an obvious reaction of the strain of work, a symbolic rejection of the fruits of my labors. I was fighting against overwork by ridding myself of the profits of that work. We talked it all out, and he took elaborate notes, and that was that. Since I had done nothing specifically illegal, there were no charges to worry about. I was released.

Two months thereafter, I picked up my typewriter and hurled it through my office window. It plummeted to the street below, narrowly missing the bald head of a Salvation Army trumpet player. I heaved an ashtray after the typewriter, tossed my pen out the window, pulled off my necktie and hurled it out. I went to the window and was about to leap out after my typewriter and necktie and ashtray and pen when three of my employees took hold of me and restrained me, at which point I went joyously berserk.

I struck my secretary — a fine woman, loyal and efficient to the core — in the teeth, chipping one incisor rather badly. I kicked the office boy in the shin and belted my partner in the belly. I was wild, and quite difficult to subdue.

Shortly thereafter, I was in a room at St. Anthony's.

As I have said, it was not an unpleasant place at all. At times I quite enjoyed it. There was the utter freedom from responsibility, and a person who has not spent time in a sanitarium of one sort or another could not possibly appreciate the enormity of this freedom. It was not merely that there was nothing that I had to *do*. It goes considerably deeper than that.

Perhaps I can explain. I could *be* whomever I wished to be. There was no need to put up any sort of front whatsoever. There was no necessity for common courtesy or civility. If one wished to tell a nurse to go to the devil, one went ahead and did so. If one wished, for any reason at all, to urinate upon the floor, one went ahead and did so. One needed to make no discernible effort to appear sane. If I had been sane, after all, I would not have been there in the first place.

Every Wednesday, Mary visited me. This in itself was enough reason to fall in love with St. Anthony's. Not because she visited me once a week, but because for six days out of every seven I was spared her company. I have spent forty-four years on this planet, and for twenty-one of them I have been married to Mary, and her companionship has grown increasingly less tolerable over the years. Once, several years ago, I looked into the possibility of divorcing her. The cost would have been exorbitant. According to the lawyer I consulted, she would have wound up with house and car and the bulk of my worldly goods, plus monthly alimony sufficient to keep me permanently destitute. So we were never divorced.

As I said, she visited me every Wednesday. I was quite peaceable at those times; indeed, I was peaceable throughout my stay at St. Anthony's aside from some minor displays of temper. But my hostility toward her showed through, I'm afraid. Periodically I displayed some paranoid tendencies, accusing her of having me committed for one nefarious motive or other, calling her to task for imagined affairs with my friends (as if any of them would want to bed down with the sloppy old bitch) and otherwise being happily nasty to her. But she kept returning, every Wednesday, like the worst of all possible pennies.

The sessions with my psychiatrist (not mine specifically, but the resident psychiatrist who had charge of my case) were not at all bad. He was a very bright man and quite interested in his work, and I enjoyed spending time with him. For the most part I was quite rational in our discussions. He avoided deep analysis — there was no time for it, really, as he had a tremendous work load as it was — and concentrated instead in trying to determine just what was causing my nervous breakdowns and just how they could be best controlled. We worked things out rather well. I made discernible progress, with just a few minor lapses from time to time. We investigated the causes of my hostility toward Mary. We talked at length.

I remember very clearly the day they released me from St. Anthony's. I was not pronounced cured — that's a rather difficult word to apply in cases of this particular nature. They said that I was readjusted, or something of the nature, and that I was in condition to rejoin society. Their terminology was a bit more involved than all that. I don't recall the precise words and phrases, but that's the gist of it.

That day, the air was cool and the sky was filled with clouds. There was a pleasant breeze blowing. Mary came to pick me up. She was noticeably nervous, perhaps afraid of me, but I was quite docile and perfectly friendly toward her. I took her arm. We walked out of the door to the car. I got behind the wheel — that gave her pause, as I think she would have preferred to do the driving just then. I drove, however, I drove the car out through the main gate and headed toward our home.

"Oh, darling," she said. "You're all better now, aren't you?"

"I'm fine," I said.

I was released five months ago. At first it was far more difficult on the outside than it had been within St. Anthony's heavy stone walls. People did not know how to speak with me. They seemed afraid that I might go berserk at any moment. They wanted to talk normally with me, yet they did not know how to refer to my "trouble." It was all quite humorous.

People warmed to me, yet at the same

time they never entirely relaxed with me. While I was normal in most respects, certain mannerisms of mine were unnerving, to say the least. At times, for instance, I was observed mumbling incoherently to myself. At other times I answered questions before they were asked of me, or ignored questions entirely. Once, at a party, I walked over to the hi-fi, removed a record from the turntable, sailed it out of an open window, and put another record on. These periodic practices of mine were bizarre, and they set people on edge, yet they caused no one any real harm.

The general attitude seemed to be this — I was a little touched, but I was not dangerous, and I seemed to be getting better with the passage of time. Most important, I was able to function in the world at large. I was able to earn a living. I was able to live in peace and harmony with my wife and my friends. I might be quite mad, but it hurt no one.

Saturday night Mary and I are invited to a party. We will go to the home of some dear friends whom we have known for at least fifteen years. There will be eight or ten other couples there, all of them friends of a similar vintage.

It's time, now. This will be it.

You must realize that it was very difficult at first. The affair with the ten-dollar bills, for example — I'm essentially frugal, and such behavior went very much against the grain. The time when I hurled the typewriter out of the window was even harder. I did not want to hurt my secretary, of whom I have always been very fond, nor did I want to strike all those other people. But I did very well, I think. Very well indeed.

Saturday night, at the party, I will be quite uncommunicative. I will sit in a chair by the fireside and nurse a single drink for an hour or two, and when people talk to me I will stare myopically at them and will not answer them. I will make little involuntary facial movements, nervous twitches of one sort or another.

Then I will rise abruptly and hurl my glass into the mirror over the fireplace, hard enough to shatter either the glass or the mirror or both. Someone will come over in an attempt to subdue me. Whoever it is, I will strike him or her with all my might. Then, cursing violently, I will hurry to the side of the hearth and will pick up the heavy cast-iron poker.

I will smash Mary's head with it.

The happy thing is that there will be no nonsense about a trial. Temporary insanity may be difficult to plead in some cases, but it should hardly be a problem when the murderer has a past record of psychic instability. I have been in the hospital for a nervous breakdown. I have spent considerable time in a mental institution. The course is quite obvious — I shall be arrested and shall be sent forthwith to St. Anthony's.

I suspect they'll keep me there for a year or so. This time, of course, I can let them cure me completely. Why not? I don't intend to kill anyone else, so there's nothing to set up. All I have to do is make gradual progress until such time as they pronounce me fit to return to the world at large. But when that happens, Mary will not be there to meet me at the gate. Mary will be quite dead.

Already I can feel the excitement building within me. The tension, the thrill of it all. I can feel myself shifting over into the role of the madman, preparing for the supreme moment. Then the glass crashing into the mirror, and my body moving in perfect synchronization, and the poker in my hand, and Mary's skull crushed like an eggshell.

You may think I'm quite mad. That's the beauty of it — that's what everyone thinks, you see.

The Dangerous Business

When she heard his car in the driveway she hurried at once to the door and opened it. Her first glimpse of his face told her all she wanted to know. She'd grown used to that expression over the years, the glow of elation underladen with exhaustion, the whole look foreshadowing the depression that would surely settle on him in an hour or a day or a week.

How many times had he come home to her like this? How many times had she rushed to the door to meet him?

And how could he go on doing this, year after year after year?

She could see, as he walked toward her now, just how much this latest piece of work had taken out of him. It had drawn new lines on his face. Yet, when he smiled at her, she could see too the young man she had married so many years ago.

Almost thirty years, and she treasured all

those years, every last one of them. But what a price he'd paid for them! Thirty years in a dangerous, draining business, thirty years spent in the company of violent men, criminals, killers. Men whose names were familiar to her, men like Johnny Speed and Bart Callan, men he had used (or been used by) on and off throughout his career. And other men he would work with once and never again.

"It's finished," she said.

"All wrapped up." His smile widened. "You can always tell, can't you?"

"Well, after all these years. How did it go?"

"Not bad. It's gone better, but at least it's finished and I got out of it alive. I'll say this for it, it's thirsty work."

"Martini?"

"What else?"

She made a pitcher of them. They always had one drink apiece before dinner, but on the completion of a job he needed more of a release than came with one martini. They would drain the pitcher, with most of the martinis going to him, and dinner would be light, and before long they would be in bed.

She stirred at the thought. He would want her tonight, he would need her. Their pleasure in each other was as vital as ever after almost thirty years, if less frequently taken, and they both lived for nights like this one.

She handed him his drink, held her own aloft. "Well," she said.

"Here's to crime," he said. Predictably.

She drank without hesitating but later that evening she said, "You know, I like our toast less and less these days."

"Well, get a new toaster. We can afford it. They have models now that do four slices of bread at a time."

"I mean *Here's to crime.* You knew what I meant."

"Of course I knew what you meant. I don't know that I like it much myself. *Here's to crime.* Force of habit, I guess."

"It takes so much out of you, darling. I wish —"

"What?"

She lowered her eyes. "That you could do something else."

"Might as well wish for wings."

"You're really that completely locked in?"

"Of course I am, baby. Now how many times have we been over this? I've been doing this my whole life. I have contacts, I have a certain reputation, there are some people who are kind enough to think I'm good at what I do —"

"You'd be good at anything you did."

"That's a loyal wife talking."

"It's still true."

He put his hand on hers. "Maybe. Sometimes I like to think so. And other times it seems to me that I was always cut out for this line of work. Crime and violence and sudden death."

"You're such a gentle, gentle man."

"Don't let the word get out, huh? Not that anyone would be likely to believe you."

"Oh, baby —"

"It's not such a bad life, kid. And I'm too old to change now. Isn't it funny how I get older all the time and you stay the same? It's my bedtime already, an old man like me."

"Some old man. But I guess you're tired."

"I said bedtime. I didn't say anything about being tired."

But in the days that followed she knew just how tired he was, and there was a brooding quality to his exhaustion that frightened her. Often at such times he liked to get away, and they would flee the city and spend a couple of weeks un-winding in unfamiliar terrain. This time, when his depression failed to pass, she suggested that they go away for a while. But he didn't want to go anywhere. He didn't even want to leave the house, and he passed the daytime hours sitting in front of the television set or turning the pages of books and magazines. Not *watching* the television, not *reading* the books and magazines.

At one point she thought he might want to talk about his work. In their first years together he had been excited about what he did, and at times she had felt herself a participant. But with the passage of time and with his growing discontent about his profession he tended to keep more and more of it to himself. In a sense she was grateful; it alienated her, the corruption and violence, the wanton killing, and it was easier for her to love him if she let herself dissociate the man from his work. And yet she wondered if this didn't make the burden on his shoulders that much heavier for the lack of anyone to share it.

So she made an effort. "You've hardly talked about it," she said one afternoon. "It went well, you said."

"Well enough. Won't make us rich, but it

went quite smoothly. Hit a couple of snags along the way but nothing serious."

"Who was in this one? Johnny Speed?"

"No."

"Callan?"

"I don't think I'm going to be able to use Callan any more. No, none of the regulars came into it this time. Let's say I put it together with a cast of unknowns. And there was nobody in it I'd care to work with again." He chuckled mirthlessly. "Hardly anybody got out of it alive, as a matter of fact."

"Then it was very violent."

"You might say that."

"I thought so. I can tell, you know."

"You've said that before. It's hard to believe, but I guess I believe you."

"If there were just a way to avoid the violence, the awful bloodshed —"

He shook his head. "Part of the game."

"I know, but —"

"Part of the game."

She let it go.

His mood lifted, of course. The depression had been deeper than usual and had lasted longer than usual, but it was not nearly so deep or so enduring as some he — and she — had been forced to live through in the past. Some years previously drinking had become a problem. Alcoholism was virtually an occupational illness in his profession, and of course it made efficient functioning impossible. He'd gone on the wagon for several years, then found he was able to drink normally again. A single martini before the evening meal, a pitcher of them at the conclusion of a job, an occasional beer with lunch when he was resting up between jobs. But drinking never became a problem again, and she thanked God for that, even as she prayed to God that he could get into a line of work that didn't take so much out of him.

She raised the subject again one evening. He'd begun to talk about going back to work, not right away but before too long, and she wondered how he could face it so soon.

"You don't have to work so much," she said. "The kids are grown and gone. You and I have everything we want and money in the bank. You don't have to drive yourself."

"It's not a matter of driving myself. I can't sit idle too long. It gets to me."

"I know, but —"

"Rather wear out than rust out. Trite but true."

"Couldn't you try something else some of the time? Couldn't you try doing what you really want to do?"

He looked at her for a long moment, then turned his eyes aside and gazed off into space. Or, perhaps, into time.

"I've tried that," he said at length.

"I didn't know that."

"I didn't really want to talk about it. It didn't work out." Now he turned to face her again, and the expression on his face was enough to break her heart. "Maybe there was once something else I wanted to do. Maybe at some stage in my life I had the potential to do other things, to be somebody other than the man I turned into."

But I love the man you turned into, she thought. *I love the man you are, the man you've always been.*

"I may have the dreams," he said. "But that's all they ever were, baby. Dreams. You know what happens to dreams when you wake up. They go where smoke goes, into the air. Maybe I was born to do what I do. Maybe I just trained myself and wound up painting myself into a corner. But I'm an old man now —"

"You are like hell an old man!"

"— and it's all I know how to do and all I even seem to want to do. I've spent my whole life with crooks and grifters and strong-arm men, and I'll spend the rest of it with the same awful types, and yes, there'll be violence, but I guess I can go on living with that."

He smiled suddenly, and not merely with his mouth. "It's not so bad," he said. "It's depressing when I think of what might have been, but the hell with that, kid. I'm doing what I was cut out for. That's a hard thing to admit to yourself and it hurts, I'll say it hurts, but once you make yourself believe it, then it becomes a liberating thing."

She thought for a moment. "Yes," she said. "Yes, I suppose that's true."

And so she was prepared a week later when he told her he was ready to go back to work. He'd been restless for a day or two, pacing back and forth across the living-room rug, jotting incomprehensible notes on long yellow pads of paper, even mumbling and muttering to himself. Then on Monday morning he looked at her over the brim of his second cup of coffee and told her.

"Well, the signs were there," she said. "You're sure you don't want more time off?"

"Positive."

"And you know what you want to do?"

"Uh huh. I'm going to use Johnny again."

"Johnny Speed. How many times have you used him?"

"I don't know. Too many, I guess. He's got a lot of miles on the clock but I guess he's good for another go-round."

"How long do you think it'll take?"

"Couple of weeks."

"Be careful."

He looked at her. "Oh, come on," he said. "The violence never touches me, baby. You know that."

"Oh, but it does."

"Come off it."

"It's a dangerous business."

"Dangerous business," he said, tasting the phrase. "I kind of like that."

"Well, it is."

"I like the phrase," he said. "I don't know that it fits my life —"

"I think it does."

"— but it certainly fits the current project. *Dangerous Business. A Dangerous Business.* Which do you prefer?"

"I don't know. *The Dangerous Business?*"

"You know, that's best of all. *The Dangerous Business.* I think I'm going to use it."

"Don't you have to make sure nobody's used it already?"

"Doesn't matter. There's no such thing as copyright on titles. I thought you knew that."

"I must have forgotten."

"*The Dangerous Business.* A Johnny Speed Mystery. Yes, by God, I'm going to use it. It has a nice ring to it and it fits the plot I've got in mind."

"It fits, all right," she said. But he was caught up in the book he'd start that morning and didn't even notice the tone of her voice.

A Little Off the Top

"Consider the gecko," the doctor said, with a gesture toward the wall at my left. There one of the tiny lizards clung effortlessly, as if painted. "Remarkable for its rather piercing cry, the undoubted source of its name. Remarkable as well for the suction cups at the tips of its fingers and toes, which devices enable it to scurry across the ceiling as readily as you or I might cross a floor. Now a Darwinian would point to the gecko and talk of evolution and mutation and fitness to survive, but can you honestly regard such an adaptation as the result of random chance? I prefer to see the fingerprints of the Creator in the fingertips of that saurian. It would take a God to create a gecko, and a whimsical fun-loving God at that. The only sort, really, in whom one would care to believe."

The doctor's name was Turnquist. He was an Englishman, an anomaly on an island where the planters were predominantly Dutch with a scattering of displaced French. He had just given me the best dinner I'd had since I left the States, a perfectly seasoned curried goat complemented by an even dozen side dishes and perhaps as many chutneys. Thus far in my travels I'd been exposed almost exclusively to Chinese cooks, and not one of them could have found work on Mott Street.

Dr. Turnquist's conversation was as stimulating as his cook's curry. He was dressed in white, but there his resemblance to Sidney Greenstreet ended. He was a short man and a slender one, with rather large and long-fingered hands, and as he sat with his hands poised on the white linen cloth, it struck me that there was about him a quality not dissimilar to the gecko. He might have been clinging to a wall, waiting for a foolish insect to venture too close.

There was a cut crystal bell beside his wineglass. He rang it, and almost immediately a young woman appeared in the kitchen doorway. "Bring the brandy," he told her, "and a pair of the medium-sized bell glasses."

She withdrew, returning moments later with a squat-bodied ship's decanter and a pair of glasses. "Very good, Leota," he said. "You may pour a glass for each of us."

She served me first, placing the glass on the tablecloth at my right, pouring a generous measure of cognac into it. I watched the procedure out of the corner of my eye. She was of medium height, slender but full-figured with a rich brown skin and arresting cheekbones. Her scent was heavy and rich in the tropical air. My eyes followed her as she moved around the table and filled my host's glass. She left the bottle on the table. He said, "Thank you, Leota," and she crossed to the kitchen door.

My eyes returned to the doctor. He was holding his glass aloft. I raised mine. "Cheers," he said, and we drank.

The cognac was excellent and I said as much. "It's decent," he allowed. "Not the best the French ever managed, but good enough." His dry lizard eyes twinkled. "Is it the cognac you admired? Or the hand that poured it?"

"Your servant is a beautiful woman," I said, perhaps a little stiffly.

"She's a Tamil. They are an attractive race, most especially in the bloom of youth. And Leota is particularly attractive, even for a Tamil." His eyes considered me carefully. "You recently ended a marriage," he said.

"A relationship. We weren't actually married. We lived together."

"It was painful, I suppose."

I hesitated, then nodded.

"Then I daresay travel was the right prescription," the doctor said. "Your appetites are returning. You did justice to your dinner. You're able to appreciate a good cognac and a beautiful woman."

"One could hardly do otherwise. All three are quite superb."

He lifted his glass again, warmed its bowl in his palm, inhaled its bouquet, took a drop of the liquid on his tongue. His eyes closed briefly. For a moment I might have been alone in the high-ceilinged dining room.

His eyes snapped open. "Have you," he demanded, "ever had a cognac of the comet year?"

"I beg your pardon?"

"Eighteen thirty-five. Have you ever tasted an eighteen thirty-five cognac?"

"Not that I recall."

"Then you very likely have not, because you would recall it. Have you ever made love to a virgin? Let me rephrase that.

Have you ever embraced a virgin of mixed ancestry, Tamil and Chinese and Scandinavian? You needn't answer. A rhetorical question, of course."

I took a small sip of cognac. It was really quite excellent.

"I could tell you a story," Dr. Turnquist said. "Of course you'd want to change the names if you ever decided to do anything with it. And you might take care to set it on some other island."

"I wouldn't have to name the island at all," I said.

"No," he said. "I don't suppose you would."

There were, it seemed, two brothers named Einhoorn. One, Piet, was a planter, with large and valuable holdings in the southern portion of the island. The other, Rolf, was a trader with offices in the capital city on the island's eastern rim. Both were quite prosperous, and each had survived the trauma of the island's metamorphosis from colony to independent nation.

Both had been married. Piet's wife had died years ago, while delivering a stillborn child. Rolf's wife deserted him at about the same time, leaving on a Europe-bound freighter with whose captain Rolf had traded for years. The ship still called at the island from time to time, and Rolf still did business with her captain. The woman was never a subject of conversation between them.

Although he saw them infrequently, Dr. Turnquist got along well enough with both of the Einhoorn brothers. He thought them coarse men. They both had a hearty appetite for the pleasures of the flesh, which he approved, but it seemed to him that they lacked refinement. Neither had the slightest taste for art, for music, for literature. Neither gave any evidence of having a spiritual dimension. Both delighted in making money, in drinking brandy, and embracing young women. Neither cared much for anything else.

One evening, Rolf, the trader, appeared at the doctor's door. The doctor had already finished his dinner. He was sitting on the enclosed veranda, sipping a postprandial brandy and reading, for the thousandth time, a sonnet of Wordsworth's, the one comparing the evening to a nun breathless with adoration. A felicitous phrase, he had thought for the thousandth time.

He set the book aside and put his guest in a wicker chair and poured him a brandy.

Rolf drank it down, pronounced it acceptable, and demanded to know if the doctor had ever had an 1835 cognac. The doctor said that he had not.

"The comet year," Rolf said. "Halley's Comet. It came in eighteen thirty-five. It was important, the coming of the comet. The American writer, Mark Twain. You know him? He was born in that year."

"I would suppose he was not the only one."

"He thought it significant," Rolf Einhoorn said. "He said he was born when the comet came and would die when it reappeared. He believed this, I think. I don't know if it happened."

"Twain died in nineteen ten."

"Then perhaps he was right," the trader said, "because the comet comes every seventy-five years. I think it is every seventy-five years. It will be due again in a couple of years, and that is when I intended to drink the bottle."

"The bottle?"

"Of eighteen thirty-five cognac." Rolf rubbed his fleshy palms together. "I've had it for two years. It came off a Chinese ship. The man I bought it from didn't know what he had but he knew he had something. Cognac of the comet year is legendary, my dear Turnquist. I couldn't guess at its value. It is not like a wine, changing with the years, perhaps deteriorating beneath the cork. Brandies and whiskeys do not change once they have been bottled. They neither ripen nor decay. A man may spend a thousand pounds buying a rare wine at a London auction house only to find himself the owner of the world's most costly vinegar. But a cognac — it will no more spoil with age than gold will rust. And a cognac of eighteen thirty-five —"

"A famous cognac."

"A legend, as I've said." He put down his empty glass, folded his hands on his plump stomach. "And I shall never taste it."

The silence stretched. A fly buzzed against a lightbulb, then flew off. "Well, why not?" the doctor asked at length. "You haven't sworn off drinking. I don't suppose you've lost your corkscrew. What's the problem?"

"My brother is the problem."

"Piet?"

"Have I another brother? One is sufficient. He wants the cognac, the Comet Year cognac."

"I daresay he does. Who wouldn't? But why should you give it to him?"

"Because he has something I want."

"Oh?"

"You know his ward? She's called Freya."

"I've heard of her," the doctor said. "A half-caste, isn't she?"

"Her mother was half Tamil and half Chinese. Her father was a Norwegian seaman, captain of a freighter that docked here once and has never returned. You haven't seen Freya?"

"No."

"She is exquisite. Golden skin that glows as if lighted from within. A heart-shaped face, cheekbones to break your heart, and the most impossible blue eyes. A waist you could span with your hands. Breasts like, like —"

The man was breathless with adoration, Dr. Turnquist thought, though not like a nun. "How old is this goddess?" he asked.

"Fifteen," Rolf Einhoorn said. "Her mother died five years ago. Piet took her into his household, made a home for her. People credit him with an act of charity. My brother has never performed an act of charity in his life."

"He makes sexual use of her?"

"Not yet. The bastard's been *saving* her."

"Ah," said the doctor. "Even as you have

been saving your cognac. Waiting, you might say, for the reappearance of the comet."

"Piet has been waiting for her sixteenth birthday. Then he will make her his mistress. But he wants my cognac."

"And you want — I've forgotten her name."

"Freya. He has offered a trade. Her virginity for my bottle."

"And you have accepted?"

"I have accepted."

The doctor raised his eyebrows.

"It seems unfair," Rolf said. The doctor noted a crafty light in his eyes. "Piet will have every drop of my precious cognac. He may drink it all in one night or stretch it out over a lifetime, and if he wishes he may shatter the bottle when he has drained it. And what will I have in return? One night with this beauty. Her maidenhead will be mine, but when I return her to him she will be a far cry from an empty bottle. She will be his to enjoy for as long as he wants her, and I will be left with the memory of her flesh and not even the memory of the cognac. Does it seem fair to you?"

"Can't you get out of the deal?"

"I could," Rolf said. "And yet there

ought to be a better solution, don't you think? The little angel's birthday is two months from tomorrow. That is when the exchange will take place." He lowered his eyes deliberately. "Piet has seen my bottle. He has examined the seal."

"Ah."

"You are a clever man. A doctor, good with your hands. Perhaps there is a way to remove the contents from a sealed bottle, eh?"

"You would have to bring me the bottle," the doctor said, "and I should have to see what I could do."

Piet turned up later that week. Coincidentally, Dr. Turnquist was reading another sonnet of Wordsworth's at the moment of his arrival, the one about the world being too much with us. Old Wordsworth, he thought, had a knack.

Piet, not surprisingly, told essentially the same story as his brother. He spoke quite eloquently of the legendary perfection of the 1835 cognac, then spoke at least as eloquently of his ward. "She has spent five years under my roof," he said. "She is like a daughter to me."

"I'm sure."

"And now I've traded her to my

70

verdammte brother for a bottle of brandy. Five years, doctor!"

"The brandy's been around for almost a century and a half. Five years seems a short time in comparison."

"You know what I mean," Piet said. "I wonder."

"What is it that you wonder?"

"I wonder what virginity is," Piet mused. "A virgin's embrace is nothing so special, is it? Ordinarily one wants one's partner to be schooled, able. With a virgin, one delights in her incompetence. What is so special, eh, about a tiny membrane?"

The doctor kept silent.

"You are a doctor," Piet Einhoorn said. "One hears tales, you know. Exotic bordellos whose madams sell a virginity ten times over, tightening the passage with alum, restoring the maidenhead. One hears these things and wonders what to believe."

"One cannot believe everything one hears."

"Oh," Piet said.

"Still, there is something that can be done if the girl is a virgin in the first place."

"I have not had her, if that is what you are implying."

"I implied nothing. Even if she hasn't

71

been with a man, she could have lost her hymen in any of a dozen ways. But if it's intact —"

"Yes?"

"You want to be with her once, is that right? You want to be the first man to have her."

"That is exactly what I want."

"If the hymen were surgically detached before the first intercourse, and if it were subsequently reattached *after* intercourse has taken place —"

"It is possible?"

"Bring the child," the doctor said. "Let me have a look at her, eh?"

Two days later Rolf returned to the doctor's house. This time his visit was expected. He carried a small leather satchel, from which he produced a bottle that fairly shouted its age. The doctor took it from him, held it to the light, examined its label and seal, turned it this way and that.

"This will take careful study," he announced.

"Can you do it?"

"Can I remove the contents without violating the seal? I think not. There is a trick of removing a tablecloth without disturbing the dishes and glasses resting atop it. One gives an abrupt all-out pull. That would not do in this case. But perhaps the seal can be removed and ultimately restored without its appearance being altered in any way." He set the bottle down. "Leave it with me. There is lead foil here which will not be readily removed, paper labels which might yield if the glue holding them can be softened. It is a Chinese puzzle, Einhoorn. Come back Saturday. If it can be done, it shall be done that day in front of your eyes."

"If my brother suspects —"

"If it cannot be done safely it will not be done at all. So he will suspect nothing. Oh, bring a bottle of the best cognac you can find, will you? We can't replace cognac of the comet year with rotgut, can we now?"

The following day it was Piet's turn. He brought with him not a leather satchel but an altogether more appealing cargo, the girl Freya.

She was, the doctor noted, quite spectacular. Rolf's cognac had looked like any other cognac, possessed of a good enough color and a perfect clarity but otherwise indistinguishable from any other amber liquid. Freya, her skin a good match for the cognac, looked like no other young woman the doctor had ever seen. Three races had blended themselves to perfection in her lithe person. Her skin was like hot velvet, while her eyes made one wonder why blue had ever been thought a cool color. And, thought Dr. Turnquist, a man could impale himself upon those cheekbones.

"I'll want to examine her," he told Piet. "Make yourself comfortable on the veranda."

In his surgery, Freya shucked off her clothing without a word, and without any trace of embarrassment. He placed her on his table, put her feet in the stirrups, and bent to his task. She was warm to the touch, he noted, and after a moment or two she began to move rhythmically beneath his fingers. He looked up from his work, met her eyes. She was smiling at him.

"Why, you little devil," he said.

He left her there, found Piet on the veranda. "You've very fortunate," he told the planter. "The membrane is intact. It hasn't yielded to horseback riding or an inquisitive finger."

"Have you detached it?"

"That will take some time. It's minor surgery, but I'd as soon sedate her all the same. It would be best if she didn't know the nature of the procedure, don't you think? So she can't say anything that might find its way to your brother's ear."

"Good thinking."

"Come back in the morning," the doctor told him. "Then you may enjoy her favors tomorrow night and bring her back to me the next morning for repair. Or restoration, if you prefer."

Piet came in the morning to reclaim his ward. As he led her to his car, the doctor thought not for the first time what a coarse, gross man the planter was.

Not that his brother was any better. Rolf arrived scarcely an hour after Piet had left — there was an element of French farce in the staging of this, the doctor remembered thinking — and the doctor led him into his study and showed him the bottle. Its neck was bare now, the wax and lead foil and paper labels carefully removed.

"Please notice," he said, "that the cork is quite dry. If this bottle held wine it would only be fit for pouring on a salad."

"But since it is brandy —"

"It is presumably in excellent condition. Still, if one attempts to remove this cork it will at once crumble into dust."

"Then —"

"Then we must be inventive," said the doctor. He brought forth an oversized hypodermic needle and plunged it in a single motion through the cork. As he drew back its plunger the syringe filled with the amber liquid.

"Brilliant," the trader said.

The doctor drew the syringe from the bottle, squirted its contents into a beaker, and repeated the process until the bottle was empty. Then he took the bottle that Rolf had brought — an excellent flask of twenty-year-old Napoleon brandy — and transferred its contents via the syringe into the ancient bottle. It was the work of another hour to replace the various sealing materials, and when he was done the bottle looked exactly as it had when the trader first obtained it from the Chinese seaman who'd been its previous owner.

"And now we'll employ a funnel," Dr. Turnquist said, "and pour your very old cognac into a much newer bottle, and let's not spill one precious drop, eh?" He sniffed appreciatively at the now empty beaker. "A rich bouquet. You'll postpone your enjoyment until the return of Halley's Comet?"

"Perhaps I'll have one glass ahead of

schedule," Rolf Einhoorn said, grinning lewdly. "To toast Freya's sixteenth birthday."

The conversation took a similar turn when Piet collected his ward after the surgical restoration of her physical virginity. "I have had my cake," the planter said, smacking his lips like an animal. "And in less than a month's time I shall eat it, too. Or drink it, more precisely. I will be sipping cognac of the comet year while my fool of a brother makes do with —" And here he employed a Dutch phrase with which the doctor was not familiar, but he later was able to translate loosely as *sloppy seconds.*

Piet left, taking Freya with him. The doctor stood for a moment at the front door, watching the car drive out of sight. Then he went looking for his volume of Wordsworth.

"It's a beautiful story," I told him. "A classic, really. I assume the exchange went according to plan? Freya spent the night of her sixteenth birthday with Rolf? And Piet had the brandy in exchange?"

"All went smoothly. As smooth as old cognac, as smooth as Freya's skin."

"Each had his cake," I said, "and each ate it, too. Or thought he did, which amounts to the same thing, doesn't it?"

"Does it?"

"I should think so. If you are thinking you're drinking a legendary cognac, isn't that the same as drinking it? And if you think you're a woman's first lover, isn't that the same as actually being the first?"

"I would say it is *almost* the same." He smiled. "In addition, these brothers each enjoyed a third pleasure and perhaps it was the most exquisite of all. Each had the satisfaction of having pulled something over on the other. So the whole arrangement could hardly have been more satisfactory."

"A beautiful story," I said again.

He leaned forward to pour a little more cognac into my glass. "I thought you would appreciate its subtleties," he said. "I sensed that about you. Of course, there's an element you haven't considered."

"Oh?"

"You raised a point. Is the illusion quite the same as the reality? Was Piet's experience in drinking the cognac identical to Rolf's?"

"Except insofar as one cognac was actually better or worse than the other."

"Ah," the doctor said. "Of course in this instance both drank the same cognac."

"Because they believed it to be the same?"

He shook his head impatiently. "Because it *was* the same," he said. "The identical brand of twenty-year-old Napoleon, and that's not as great a coincidence as it might appear, since it's the best brandy available on this island. It's the very same elixir you and I have been drinking this very evening."

"Piet and Rolf were both drinking it?"

"Of course."

"Then what happened to the real stuff?"

"I got it, of course," said the doctor. "It was easy to jab the hypodermic needle straight through the cork, since I'd already performed the procedure a matter of hours earlier. That part was easy enough. It was softening the wax without melting it altogether, and removing the lead foil without destroying it, that made open-heart surgery child's play by comparison."

"So you wound up with the Comet Year cognac."

"Quite," he said, smiling. And, as an afterthought, "And with the girl, needless to say."

"The girl?"

"Freya." He looked down into his glass. "A charming, marvelously exciting creature. Genetics can no more explain her perfection than can Darwin account for the gecko's fingertips. A benevolent Creator was at work there. I detached her hymen, had her during the night she spent here, then let her go off to lose her already-lost virginity to Piet. And then he brought her back for hymenal restoration, had me lock up the barn door, if you will, after I'd galloped off on the horse. And now Rolf has had her, gathering the dear thing's first fruits for the third time."

"Good Lord."

"Quite. Now if the illusion is identical to the reality, then Piet and Rolf have both gained everything and lost nothing. Whereas I have gained everything and lost nothing whether the illusion is equal to the reality or not. There are points here, I suspect, that a philosopher might profitably ponder. Philosophical implications aside, I thought you might enjoy the story."

"I love the story."

He smiled, enjoying my enjoyment. "It's getting late. A pity you can't meet Freya. I'm afraid my description has been woefully inadequate. But she's with Piet and he's never welcomed visitors. Still, if you

80

don't mind, I think I'll send Leota to your room. I know you fancy her, and I saw the look she was giving you. She's not Freya, but I think you'll enjoy her acquaintance."

I muttered something appreciative.

"It's nothing," he said. "I wish, too, that I could let you have a taste of the Comet Year cognac. From the bouquet, it should turn out to be quite nice. It may not be all that superior to what we've been drinking, but think of the glamour that accompanies it."

"You haven't tasted it yet?"

He shook his head. "Those two brothers have probably finished their bottles by now. I shouldn't doubt it. But I think I'd rather hold out until the comet comes up again. If you're in this part of the world in a couple of years, you might want to stop in and watch the comet with me. I suppose one ought to be able to turn up a telescope somewhere, and we could raise a glass or two, don't you think?"

"I'm sure we could."

"Quite." He winked slowly, looking more than ever like an old gecko waiting for a fly. He lifted the crystal bell, rang. "Ah, Leota," he said, when the Tamil woman appeared. "My guest's the least bit tired. Perhaps you could show him to his room."

The Ehrengraf Experience

"Innocence," said Martin Ehrengraf. "There's the problem in a nutshell."

"Innocence is a problem?"

The little lawyer glanced around the prison cell, then turned to regard his client. "Precisely," he said. "If you weren't innocent you wouldn't be here."

"Oh, really?" Grantham Beale smiled, and while it was hardly worthy of inclusion in a toothpaste commercial, it was the first smile he'd managed since his conviction on first-degree murder charges just two weeks and four days earlier. "Then you're saying that innocent men go to prison while guilty men walk free. Is that what you're saying?"

"It happens that way more than you might care to believe," Ehrengraf said softly. "But no, it is not what I am saying."

"Oh?"

"I am not contrasting innocence and guilt, Mr. Beale. I know you are innocent of murder. That is almost beside the point. All clients of Martin Ehrengraf are innocent of the crimes of which they are charged, and this innocence always emerges in due course. Indeed, this is more than a presumption on my part. It is the manner in which I make my living. I set high fees, Mr. Beale, but I collect them only when my innocent clients emerge with their innocence a matter of public record. If my client goes to prison I collect nothing whatsoever, not even whatever expenses I incur on his behalf. So my clients are always innocent, Mr. Beale, just as you are innocent, in the sense that they are not guilty."

"Then why is my innocence a problem?"

"Ah, *your* innocence." Martin Ehrengraf smoothed the ends of his neatly trimmed mustache. His thin lips drew back in a smile, but the smile did not reach his deeply set dark eyes. He was, Grantham Beale noted, a superbly well-dressed little man, almost a dandy. He wore a Dartmouth green blazer with pearl buttons over a cream shirt with a tab collar. His slacks were flannel, modishly cuffed and pleated and the identical color of the shirt. His silk tie was a darker green than his jacket and sported a design in silver and bronze thread below the knot, a lion battling a unicorn. His cufflinks matched his pearl blazer buttons. On his aristocratically small feet he wore highly polished seamless cordovan loafers, unadorned with tassels or braid, quite simple and quite elegant. Almost a dandy, Beale thought, but from what he'd heard the man had the skills to carry it off. He wasn't all front. He was said to get results.

"*Your* innocence," Ehrengraf said again. "Your innocence is not merely the innocence that is the opposite of guilt. It is the innocence that is the opposite of experience. Do you know Blake, Mr. Beale?"

"Blake?"

"William Blake, the poet. You wouldn't know him personally, of course. He's been dead for over a century. He wrote two groups of poems early in his career, *Songs of Innocence* and *Songs of Experience*. Each poem in the one book had a counterpart in the other. 'Tyger, tyger, burning bright, In the forests of the night, What immortal hand or eye Could frame thy fearful symmetry?' Perhaps that poem is familiar to you, Mr. Beale."

"I think I studied it in school."

"It's not unlikely. Well, you don't need a poetry lesson from me, sir, not in these depressing surroundings. Let me move a little more directly to the point. Innocence versus experience, Mr. Beale. You found yourself accused of a murder, sir, and you knew only that you had not committed it. And, being innocent not only of the murder itself but in Blake's sense of the word, you simply engaged a competent attorney and assumed things would work themselves out in short order. We live in an enlightened democracy, Mr. Beale, and we grow up knowing that courts exist to free the innocent and punish the guilty, that no one gets away with murder."

"And that's all nonsense, eh?" Grantham Beale smiled his second smile since hearing the jury's verdict. If nothing else, he thought, the spiffy little lawyer improved a man's spirits.

"I wouldn't call it nonsense," Ehrengraf said. "But after all is said and done, you're in prison and the real murderer is not."

"Walker Murchison."

"I beg your pardon?"

"The real murderer," Beale said. "I'm in prison and Walker Gladstone Murchison is free."

"Precisely. Because it is not enough to be guiltless, Mr. Beale. One must also be able to convince a jury of one's guiltlessness. In

85

short, had you been less innocent and more experienced, you could have taken steps early on to assure you would not find yourself in your present condition right now."

"And what could I have done?"

"What you *have* done, at long last," said Martin Ehrengraf. "You could have called me immediately."

"Albert Speldron," Ehrengraf said. "The murder victim, shot three times in the heart at close range. The murder weapon was an unregistered handgun, a thirty-eight-caliber revolver. It was subsequently located in the spare tire well of your automobile."

"It wasn't my gun. I never saw it in my life until the police showed it to me."

"Of course you didn't," Ehrengraf said soothingly. "To continue. Albert Speldron was a loan shark. Not, however, the sort of gruff-voiced neckless thug who lends ten or twenty dollars at a time to longshoremen and factory hands and breaks their legs with a baseball bat if they're late paying the vig."

"Paying the what?"

"Ah, sweet innocence," Ehrengraf said. "The vig. Short for vigorish. It's a term used by the criminal element to describe the ongoing interest payments which a debtor must make to maintain his status."

"I never heard the term," Beale said, "but I paid it well enough. I paid Speldron a thousand dollars a week and that didn't touch the principal."

"And you had borrowed how much?"

"Fifty thousand dollars."

"The jury apparently considered that a satisfactory motive for murder."

"Well, that's crazy," Beale said. "Why on earth would I want to kill Speldron? I didn't hate the man. He'd done me a service by lending me that money. I had a chance to buy a valuable stamp collection. That's my business, I buy and sell stamps, and I had an opportunity to get hold of an extraordinary collection, mostly U.S. and British Empire but a really exceptional lot of early German States as well, and there were also — well, before I get carried away, are you interested in stamps at all?"

"Only when I've a letter to mail."

"Oh. Well, this was a fine collection, let me say that much and leave it at that. The seller had to have all cash and the transaction had to go unrecorded. Taxes, you understand."

"Indeed I do. The system of taxation makes criminals of us all."

"I don't really think of it as criminal," Beale said.

"Few people do. But go on, sir."

"What more is there to say? I had to raise fifty thousand dollars on the quiet to close the deal on this fine lot of stamps. By dealing with Speldron, I was able to borrow the money without filling out a lot of forms or giving him anything but my word. I was quite confident I would triple my money by the time I broke up the collection and sold it in job lots to a variety of dealers and collectors. I'll probably take in a total of fifty thousand out of the U.S. issues alone, and I know a buyer who will salivate when he gets a look at the German States issues."

"So it didn't bother you to pay Speldron his thousand a week."

"Not a bit. I figured to have half the stamps sold within a couple of months, and the first thing I'd do would be to repay the fifty thousand dollars principal and close out the loan. I'd have paid eight or ten thousand dollars in interest, say, but what's that compared to a profit of fifty or a hundred thousand dollars? Speldron was doing me a favor and I appreciated it. Oh, he was doing himself a favor too, two percent interest per week didn't put him in the hardship category, but it was just good business for both of us, no question about it."

"You've dealt with him before?"

"Maybe a dozen times over the years. I've borrowed sums ranging between ten and seventy thousand dollars. I never heard the interest payments called vigorish before, but I always paid them promptly. And no one ever threatened to break my legs. We did business together, Speldron and I. And it always worked out very well for both of us."

"The prosecution argued that by killing Speldron you erased your debt to him. That's certainly a motive a jury can understand, Mr. Beale. In a world where men are commonly killed for the price of a bottle of whiskey, fifty thousand dollars does seem enough to kill a man over."

"But I'd be crazy to kill for that sum. I'm not a pauper. If I was having trouble paying Speldron all I had to do was sell the stamps."

"Suppose you had trouble selling them."

"Then I could have liquidated other merchandise from my stock. I could have mortgaged my home. Why, I could have raised enough on the house to pay Speldron off three times over. That car they found the gun in, that's an Antonelli Scorpion. The car alone is worth half of what I owed Speldron."

"Indeed," Martin Ehrengraf said. "But this Walker Murchison. How does he come into the picture?"

"He killed Speldron."

"How do we know this, Mr. Beale?"

Beale got to his feet. He'd been sitting on his iron cot, leaving the cell's one chair for the lawyer. Now he stood up, stretched and walked to the rear of the cell. For a moment he stood regarding some graffito on the cell wall. Then he turned and looked at Ehrengraf.

"Speldron and Murchison were partners," he said. "I only dealt with Speldron because he was the only one who dealt in unsecured loans. And Murchison had an insurance business in which Speldron did not participate. Their joint ventures included real estate, investments and other activities where large sums of money moved around quickly with few records kept of exactly what took place."

"Shady operations," Ehrengraf said.

"For the most part. Not always illegal, not *entirely* illegal, but, yes, I like your word. Shady."

"So they were partners, and it is not unheard of for one to kill one's partner. To dissolve a partnership by the most direct means available, as it were. But why this partnership? Why should Murchison kill Speldron?"

Beale shrugged. "Money," he suggested. "With all that cash floating around, you can bet Murchison made out handsomely on Speldron's death. I'll bet he put a lot more than fifty thousand unrecorded dollars into his pocket."

"That's your only reason for suspecting him?"

Beale shook his head. "The partnership had a secretary," he said. "Her name's Felicia. Young, long dark hair, flashing dark eyes, a body like a magazine centerfold and a face like a Chanel ad. Both of the partners were sleeping with her."

"Perhaps this was not a source of enmity."

"But it was. Murchison's married to her."

"Ah."

"But there's an important reason why I know it was Murchison who killed Speldron." Beale stepped forward, stood over the seated attorney. "The gun was found in the boot of my car," he said. "Wrapped in a filthy towel and stuffed in the spare tire well. There were no fingerprints on the gun and it wasn't registered to me but there it was in my car."

"The Antonelli Scorpion?"

"Yes. What of it?"

"No matter."

Beale frowned momentarily, then drew a breath and plunged onward. "It was put there to frame me," he said.

"So it would seem."

"It had to be put there by somebody who knew I owed Speldron money. Somebody with inside information. The two of them were partners. I met Murchison any number of times when I went to the office to pay the interest, or vigorish as you called it. Why do they call it that?"

"I've no idea."

"Murchison knew I owed money. And Murchison and I never liked each other."

"Why?"

"We just didn't get along. The reason's not important. And there's more, I'm not just grasping at straws. It was Murchison who suggested I might have killed Speldron. A lot of men owed Speldron money and there were probably several of them who were in much stickier shape financially than I, but Murchison told the police I'd had a loud and bitter argument with Speldron two days before he was killed!"

"And had you?"

"*No!* Why, I never in my life argued with Speldron."

"Interesting." The little lawyer raised his hand to his mustache, smoothing its tips delicately. His nails were manicured, Grantham Beale noted, and was there colorless nail polish on them? No, he observed, there was not. The little man might be something of a dandy but he was evidently not a fop.

"Did you indeed meet with Mr. Speldron on the day in question?"

"Yes, as a matter of fact I did. I made the interest payment and we exchanged pleasantries. There was nothing anyone could mistake for an argument."

"Ah."

"And even if there had been, Murchison wouldn't have known about it. He wasn't even in the office."

"Still more interesting," Ehrengraf said thoughtfully.

"It certainly is. But how can you possibly prove that he murdered his partner and framed me for it? You can't trap him into confessing, can you?"

"Murderers do confess."

"Not Murchison. You could try tracing the gun to him, I suppose, but the police tried to trace it to me and found they couldn't trace it at all. I just don't see —"

"Mr. Beale."

"Yes?"

"Why don't you sit down, Mr. Beale. Here, take this chair, I'm sure it's more comfortable than the edge of the bed. I'll stand for a moment. Mr. Beale, do you have a dollar?"

"They don't let us have money here."

"Then take this. It's a dollar which I'm lending to you."

The lawyer's dark eyes glinted. "No interest, Mr. Beale. A personal loan, not a business transaction. Now, sir, please give me the dollar which I've just lent to you."

"Give it to you?"

"That's right. Thank you. You have retained me, Mr. Beale, to look after your interests. The day you are released unconditionally from this prison you will owe me a fee of ninety thousand dollars. The fee will be all inclusive. Any expenses will be mine to bear. Should I fail to secure your release you will owe me nothing."

"But —"

"Is that agreeable, sir?"

"But what are you going to do? Engage detectives? File an appeal? Try to get the case reopened?"

"When a man engages to save your life, Mr. Beale, do you require that he first outline his plans for you?"

"No, but —"

"Ninety thousand dollars. Payable only if I succeed. Are the terms agreeable?"

"Yes, but —"

"Mr. Beale, when next we meet you will owe me ninety thousand dollars plus whatever emotional gratitude comes naturally to you. Until then, sir, you owe me one dollar." The thin lips curled in a shadowy smile. " 'The cut worm forgives the plow,' Mr. Beale. William Blake, *The Marriage of Heaven and Hell*. 'The cut worm forgives the plow.' You might think about that, sir, until we meet again."

The second meeting of Martin Ehrengraf and Grantham Beale took place five weeks and four days later. On this occasion the lawyer wore a navy two-button suit with a subtle vertical stripe. His shoes were highly polished black wing tips, his shirt a pale blue broadcloth with contrasting white collar and cuffs. His necktie bore a half-inch wide stripe of royal blue flanked by two narrower strips, one gold and the other a rather bright green, all on a navy field.

And this time Ehrengraf's client was also

95

rather nicely turned out, although his tweed jacket and baggy flannels were hardly a match for the lawyer's suit. But Beale's dress was a great improvement over the shapeless gray prison garb he had worn previously, just as his office, a room filled with jumbled books and boxes, a desk covered with books and albums and stamps in and out of glassine envelopes, two worn leather chairs and a matching sagging sofa — just as all of this comfortable disarray was a vast improvement over the spartan prison cell which had been the site of their earlier meeting.

Beale, seated behind his desk, gazed thoughtfully at Ehrengraf, who stood ramrod straight, one hand on the desk top, the other at his side. "Ninety thousand dollars," Beale said levelly. "You must admit that's a bit rich, Mr. Ehrengraf."

"We agreed on the price."

"No argument. We did agree, and I'm a firm believer in the sanctity of verbal agreements. But it was my understanding that your fee would be payable if my liberty came about as a result of your efforts."

"You are free today."

"I am indeed, and I'll be free tomorrow, but I can't see how it was any of your doing."

"Ah," Ehrengraf said. His face bore an expression of infinite disappointment, a disappointment felt not so much with this particular client as with the entire human race. "You feel I did nothing for you."

"I wouldn't say that. Perhaps you were taking steps to file an appeal. Perhaps you engaged detectives or did some detective work of your own. Perhaps in due course you would have found a way to get me out of prison, but in the meantime the unexpected happened and your services turned out to be unnecessary."

"The unexpected happened?"

"Well, who could have possibly anticipated it?" Beale shook his head in wonder. "Just think of it. Murchison went and got an attack of conscience. The bounder didn't have enough of a conscience to step forward and admit what he'd done, but he got to wondering what would happen if he died suddenly and I had to go on serving a life sentence for a crime he had committed. He wouldn't do anything to jeopardize his liberty while he lived but he wanted to be able to make amends if and when he died."

"Yes."

"So he prepared a letter," Beale went on. "Typed out a long letter explaining just why he had wanted his partner dead and how the unregistered gun had actually belonged to Speldron in the first place, and how he'd shot him and wrapped the gun in a towel and planted it in my car. Then he'd made up a story about my having had a fight with Albert Speldron, and of course that got the police looking in my direction, and the next thing I knew I was in jail. I saw the letter Murchison wrote. The police let me look at it. He went into complete detail."

"Considerate of him."

"And then he did the usual thing. Gave the letter to a lawyer with instructions that it be kept in his safe and opened only in the event of his death." Beale found a pair of stamp tongs in the clutter atop his desk, used them to lift a stamp, frowned at it for a moment, then set it down and looked directly at Martin Ehrengraf. "Do you suppose he had a premonition? For God's sake, Murchison was a young man, his health was good, and why should he anticipate dying? Maybe he did have a premonition."

"I doubt it."

"Then it's certainly a remarkable coincidence. A matter of weeks after turning this letter over to a lawyer, Murchison lost control of his car on a curve. Smashed right through the guard rail, plunged a couple of hundred feet, exploded on impact. I don't suppose the man knew what had happened to him."

"I suspect you're right."

"He was always a safe driver," Beale mused. "Perhaps he'd been drinking."

"Perhaps."

"And if he hadn't been decent enough to write that letter, I might be spending the rest of my life behind bars."

"How fortunate for you things turned out as they did."

"Exactly," said Beale. "And so, although I truly appreciate what you've done on my behalf, whatever that may be, and although I don't doubt you could have secured my liberty in due course, although I'm sure I don't know how you might have managed it, nevertheless as far as your fee is con-cerned —"

"Mr. Beale."

"Yes?"

"Do you really believe that a detestable troll like W. G. Murchison would take pains to arrange for your liberty in the event of his death?"

"Well, perhaps I misjudged the man. Perhaps —"

"Murchison *hated* you, Mr. Beale. If he

found he was dying his one source of satisfaction would have been the knowledge that you were in prison for a crime you hadn't committed. I told you that you were an innocent, Mr. Beale, and a few weeks in prison has not dented or dulled your innocence. You actually think Murchison wrote that note."

"You mean he didn't?"

"It was typed upon a machine in his office," the lawyer said. "His own stationery was used, and the signature at the bottom is one many an expert would swear is Murchison's own."

"But he didn't write it?"

"Of course not." Martin Ehrengraf's hands hovered in the air before him. They might have been poised over an invisible typewriter or they might merely be looming as the talons of a bird of prey.

Grantham Beale stared at the little lawyer's hands in fascination. "*You* typed that letter," he said.

Ehrengraf shrugged.

"You — but Murchison left it with a lawyer!"

"The lawyer was not one Murchison had used in the past. Murchison evidently selected a stranger from the Yellow Pages, as far as one can determine, and made contact with him over the telephone, explaining what he wanted the man to do for him. He then mailed the letter along with a postal money order to cover the attorney's fee and a covering note confirming the telephone conversation. It seems he did not use his own name in his discussions with his lawyer, and he signed an alias to his covering note and to the money order as well. The signature he wrote, though, does seem to be in his own handwriting."

Ehrengraf paused, and his right hand went to finger the knot of his necktie. This particular tie, rather more colorful than his usual choice, was that of the Caedmon Society of Oxford University, an organization to which Martin Ehrengraf did not belong. The tie was a souvenir of an earlier case and he tended to wear it on particularly happy occasions, moments of personal triumph.

"Murchison left careful instructions," he went on. "He would call the lawyer every Thursday, merely repeating the alias he had used. If ever a Thursday passed without a call, and if there was no call on Friday either, the lawyer was to open the letter and follow its instructions. For four Thursdays in a row the lawyer received a phone call, presumably from Murchison."

"Presumably," Beale said heavily.

"Indeed. On the Tuesday following the fourth Thursday, Murchison's car went off a cliff and he was killed instantly. The lawyer read of Walker Murchison's death but had no idea that was his client's true identity. Then Thursday came and went without a call, and when there was no telephone call Friday either, why the lawyer opened the letter and went forthwith to the police." Ehrengraf spread his hands, smiled broadly. "The rest," he said, "you know as well as I."

"Great Scott," Beale said.

"Now if you honestly feel I've done nothing to earn my money —"

"I'll have to liquidate some stock," Beale said. "It won't be a problem and there shouldn't be much time involved. I'll bring a check to your office in a week. Say ten day at the outside. Unless you'd prefer cash?"

"A check will be fine, Mr. Beale. So long as it's a good check." And he smiled his lips to show he was joking.

The smile chilled Beale.

A week later Grantham Beale remembered that smile when he passed a check across Martin Ehrengraf's heroically disorganized desk. "A good check," he said. "I'd never give you a bad check, Mr. Ehrengraf. You typed that letter, you made all those phone calls, you forged Murchison's false name to the money order, and then when the opportunity presented itself you sent his car hurtling off the cliff with him in it."

"One believes what one wishes," Ehrengraf said quietly.

"I've been thinking about all of this all week long. Murchison framed me for a murder he committed, then paid for the crime himself and liberated me in the process without knowing what he was doing. 'The cut worm forgives the plow.' "

"Indeed."

"Meaning that the end justifies the means."

"Is that what Blake meant by that line? I've long wondered."

"The end justifies the means. I'm innocent, and now I'm free, and Murchison's guilty, and now he's dead, and you've got the money, but that's all right, because I made out fine on those stamps, and of course I don't have to repay Speldron, poor man, because death did cancel that particular debt, and —"

"Mr. Beale."

"Yes?"

103

"I don't know if I should tell you this, but I fear I must. You are more of an innocent than you realize. You've paid me handsomely for my services, as indeed we agreed that you would, and I think perhaps I'll offer you a lagniappe in the form of some experience to offset your colossal innocence. I'll begin with some advice. Do not, under any circumstances, resume your affair with Felicia Murchison."

Beale stared.

"You should have told me that was why you and Murchison didn't get along," Ehrengraf said gently. "I had to discover it for myself. No matter. More to the point, one should not share a pillow with a woman who has so little regard for one as to frame one for murder. Mrs. Murchison —"

"Felicia framed me?"

"Of course, Mr. Beale. Mrs. Murchison had nothing against you. It was sufficient that she had nothing *for* you. She murdered Mr. Speldron, you see, for reasons which need hardly concern us. Then having done so she needed someone to be cast as the murderer.

"Her husband could hardly have told the police about your purported argument with Speldron. He wasn't around at the time. He didn't know the two of you had met, and if he went out on a limb and told them, and then you had an alibi for the time in question, why he'd wind up looking silly, wouldn't he? But *Mrs.* Murchison knew you'd met with Speldron, and she told her husband the two of you argued, and so he told the police in perfectly good faith what she had told him, and then they went and found the murder gun in your very own Antonelli Scorpion. A stunning automobile, incidentally, and it's to your credit to own such a vehicle, Mr. Beale."

"Felicia killed Speldron."

"Yes."

"And framed me."

"Yes."

"But — why did you frame Murchison?"

"Did you expect me to try to convince the powers that be that *she* did it? And had pangs of conscience and left a letter with a lawyer? Women don't leave letters with lawyers, Mr. Beale, anymore than they have consciences. One must deal with the materials at hand."

"But —"

"And the woman is young, with long dark hair, flashing dark eyes, a body like a magazine centerfold and a face like a Chanel ad. She's also an excellent typist and most cooperative in any number of ways which we needn't discuss at the moment. Mr. Beale, would you like me to get you a glass of water?"

"I'm all right."

"I'm sure you'll be all right, Mr. Beale. I'm sure you will. Mr. Beale, I'm going to make a suggestion. I think you should seriously consider marrying and settling down. I think you'd be much happier that way. You're an innocent, Mr. Beale, and you've had the Ehrengraf Experience now, and it's rendered you considerably more experienced than you were, but your innocence is not the sort to be readily vanquished. Give the widow Murchison and all her tribe a wide berth, Mr. Beale. They're not for you. Find yourself an old-fashioned girl and lead a proper old-fashioned life. Buy and sell stamps. Cultivate a garden. Raise terriers. The West Highland White might be a good breed for you but that's your decision, certainly. Mr. Beale? Are you *sure* you won't have a glass of water?"

"I'm all right."

"Quite. I'll leave you with another thought of Blake's, Mr. Beale. 'Lilies that fester smell worse than weeds.' That's also from *The Marriage of Heaven and Hell*, another of what he calls Proverbs of Hell, and perhaps some day you'll be able to interpret it for me. I never quite know for sure what Blake's getting at, Mr. Beale, but his things do have a nice sound to them, don't they? Innocence and experience, Mr. Beale. That's the ticket, isn't it? Innocence and experience."

Weekend Guests

We hadn't been in the house more than five minutes when Pete called. We were in the living room and I was trying to get Roz to calm down when the phone rang. I put her on the couch and went over to answer it.

"I can't talk to you," I told him. "We just this minute walked in and we got a little shock. It seems we had company."

"What do you mean?"

"I mean somebody came calling while we were spending the weekend at the lake. Forced the front door and turned the place upside down. Everything's a mess and Roz is hysterical and I'm not too happy myself."

"That's terrible, Eddie. They get much?"

"I don't even know what's missing. I told you, we just walked in. I have to run around now and start taking inventory and they left such a mess I don't even know where to start. You know, drawers upside down, that kind of thing."

"That's terrible, it really is. Look, you

got things to do and I don't want to keep you. I just called to check that we're set for tonight."

I glanced over at the couch. "She's pretty shaky," I said, "but what the hell, she can always stay with friends if it bothers her to stay here alone."

"How about if I pick you up around nine-thirty?"

"Fine," I said. "I'll be waiting."

I was waiting out in front when he drove up in a large white panel truck. He pulled over to the curb and I opened the door and swung up onto the seat beside him.

"Well, you look real good," he said. "A few days in the sun didn't hurt you any. Roz all brown and beautiful?"

"She got a burn the first day and after that she kept out of the sun. Me, I never burn. I just lie there and soak it up like a storage battery or something. We had a great time, but what a shock to come home to the house and find some yo-yos turned the place inside out."

"They make much of a score?"

I shrugged. "They didn't get much cash because I never keep cash around the house. I generally have a couple of hundred dollars down at the bottom of my tobacco humidor and it's still there. Let's see. They took Roz's jewelry, except for what she had with her, and how much jewelry do you take to the lake? The insurance floater covers her jewelry up to ten thousand dollars, and I'd guess what she lost was probably worth two or three times that. So in that sense we took a beating, but on the other hand I didn't pay anywhere near fair market value for her stuff, so it's not that bad."

"Still, those were pieces she was crazy about. They get those ruby earrings?"

"Yeah, they went."

"That's a hell of a thing."

"She's not happy about it, I'll say that much. What else? Her full-length mink's in storage so they didn't get that, but she had some other furs in the closet that I don't know why she didn't put in storage, and of course they're gone now. They left the TV-stereo unit. You know the set, it's a big console unit, and for once I'm glad I bought it that way instead of picking up separate components, because evidently they decided it would be too much of a hassle to cart it out. But they took a couple of radios and a typewriter and little odds and ends like that."

"Hardly worth the trouble, it sounds like

to me. What can you get for a secondhand radio?"

"Not much, I wouldn't think. Isn't that our turn coming up?"

"Uh-huh. So the jewelry was the main thing, right?"

I nodded. "They took a lot of stuff. They took one of my sport jackets, can you imagine that? I guess the son of a bitch saw something he liked and it was the right size for him."

"That's amazing. Which jacket?"

"The Black Watch plaid. The damn thing's three years old and I was frankly a little sick of it, but I'm positive it was hanging in the closet when we left, so I guess some penny-ante burglar doesn't care if he's wearing the latest styles or not."

"Amazing. You call the police?"

"I had no choice, Pete. I'll tell you something, the worst part of all this isn't what you lose when they rob you. It's the ordeal you wind up putting yourself through. We walked in there tired out from all that driving and the place looked like a cyclone hit it, and I called the fellow who takes care of my insurance and he told me I had to report the burglary to the police. He said nothing would be recovered but unless the incident's officially reported the company won't honor a claim. So we had these two plainclothes bulls over for half the afternoon, and Roz was shaky anyway and the cops knew they had to go through the motions but also knew it was a waste of time, and they're asking me like do I have the serial number from the typewriter, and who keeps track of that crap?"

"Nobody."

"Of course not. Even if you wrote it down you'd never remember where you put it."

"Or the crook would steal the notebook along with the typewriter."

"Exactly. So they're asking me this garbage because it's their job, and in spite of myself I'm feeling guilty that I didn't know the serial number, and they're asking about the bill of sale for this thing or that thing, and who's got copies of things like that? Watch out, there's a kid on a bicycle."

"I see him, Eddie. You're jumpy as hell, you know that?"

"I'm sorry."

"I know not to run over kids on bicycles and I knew it was our turn coming up. It's not as if I never drove a truck before."

I put a hand on his arm. "Sorry," I said. "I *am* jumpy as hell and I'm sorry. Those cops, I finally told them enough was enough, and I poured drinks all around and everybody relaxed. They said off the record I could forget about seeing any of the stuff again, which I already knew, and I let them finish their drinks and got them the hell out of there. And I took Roz upstairs and got a handful of Valium into her."

"Not a whole handful, I hope."

"Maybe two pills."

"That's better."

"And I had one more drink for myself and then I put the plug in the jug because I didn't want to get loopy, not going out tonight. I almost called you and canceled out and opened the bottle again, but I figured that would be stupid."

"You sure?" He looked at me. "I could turn the car around, you know. There's other nights."

"Keep driving."

"You're absolutely sure?"

"Absolutely. But can you imagine guys like that?"

"You mean the cops?"

"No, I don't mean the cops. They're just doing their job. I mean the guys who ripped us off."

He laughed. "Maybe they're just doing their jobs, too, Eddie."

"That's some job, robbing people's homes. Can you imagine doing that?"

"No."

"Roz kept saying how she's always felt so safe and secure where we are, a good neighborhood and all, and how can she feel that way now? Well, that's nonsense, she'll get used to it again, but I know what she means."

"It's such an invasion of privacy."

"That's exactly what it is. People in her living space, you know what I mean? People in her house, getting dirt on her carpets, going through her things, sticking their noses into her private life. An invasion of privacy, that's exactly what it is. And for what, will you tell me that?"

"For ten cents on the dollar, and that's if they're lucky."

"If they get that much it's a lot. If they net two grand out of everything they took off us it's a hell of a lot, and in the process they gave us a bad day and put us to a lot of trouble and I don't know what it's going to cost to replace everything and clean up the mess they made. Going into people's houses like that, and that's nothing — suppose we were home?"

"Well, they probably were careful to make sure you weren't."

114

"Yeah, but if they're sloppy enough to rob us in the first place, how careful do they figure to be?"

We kicked it around some more. By the time we got to the gate I was feeling a whole lot calmer. I guess it helped to talk about it, and Pete was always easy to talk to.

He pulled the truck to a stop and I got out and opened the padlock and unfastened the chain, then swung the gate open. After the truck was through I closed the gate and locked it again. Then I climbed back into the truck and Pete cut across the lot to the warehouse.

"No trouble with the key, Eddie?"

"None."

"Good. What'd they do at your place, kick the door in?"

"Forced the lock with a crowbar, something like that."

"Slobs, it sounds like."

"Yeah, that's what they were. Slobs."

He maneuvered the truck, parking it with its back doors up against the loading dock. I climbed down and opened them, and while I was standing there the automatic door on the loading dock swung up. I had a bad second or two then, as if there'd be men with guns up on the dock, but of course it was empty. A second or two later the night watchman appeared through a door a dozen yards to our left. He gave us a wave, then took a drink of something from a brown paper bag.

Pete got out of the truck and we went over to the old man. "Thought I'd run the door open for you," he said. "Have a little something?"

He offered the paper bag to us. We declined without asking what it was and he took another little sip for himself. "You boys'll treat me right," he said. "Won't you, now?"

"No worries, Pops."

"You didn't have no trouble with that key, did you?"

"On the gate? No, it was a perfect fit."

"Now when you go out you'll break the chain so they won't know you had no key, right?"

"Takes too much time, Pops. Nobody's gonna suspect you and if they do they can't prove anything."

"They're gonna ask me questions," he whined.

"That's how you'll be earning your money. And they'll ask you questions whatever we do with the lock."

He wasn't crazy about it, but another sip

from his bottle eased his mind some. "Guess you know what you're doing," he said. "Now be sure and tie me tight but not *too* tight, if you know what I mean. And I don't know about tape on my mouth."

"Well, that's up to you, Pops."

He decided on the tape after all. Pete got a roll of it from the truck, along with a coil of clothesline, and the three of us went inside. While Pete tied the old fellow up I got started stacking the color TV's in the truck. I made sure I arranged them compactly because I wanted to fit in as many as the truck would hold. It's not going to be a cinch, replacing all the jewelry Roz lost.

You Could Call It Blackmail

He was in the garden when the phone rang. It rang several times before he remembered that Marjorie had taken Lisa to her piano lesson. He walked unhurriedly back to the house, expecting the caller to hang up before he reached the telephone, but it was still ringing when he got to it.

"David? This is Ellie."

"What's the matter?"

"Why?"

"Your voice. Is something wrong?"

"Everything's fine. No, everything's *not* fine."

"Ellie?"

"I'd like to see you. Could we meet for lunch?"

"Yes, of course. Just let me think. Today is what? Monday. I'm supposed to come into the city the day after tomorrow to have lunch with someone at Simon and Schuster. I hope I remember her name before I see her. I'm sure I could get out of it."

"No, don't do that. It doesn't have to be lunch. If we could meet for a drink?"

"Sure. Not that it would be any problem to cancel lunch. Let me think. There's an Italian place called the Grand Ticino on Thompson off Bleecker. It's always quiet during the day. I must be the only person who goes there, and *I* don't get there more than once or twice a year."

"How do you spell it?"

He spelled it. "Two o'clock Wednesday? I'll call what's-her-name and move lunch back to noon."

"Two is fine. I hope you remember her name."

"Penny Tobias. I just did."

The luncheon with Penny Tobias did not go well. Its unstated purpose was clear to both parties in advance; Simon & Schuster was interested in enticing David Barr away from his present publishers, while he in turn was not entirely adverse to being enticed. Things would have gone well enough if he hadn't had Ellie Kilberg on his mind. But ever since her call he had been writing any number of mental drafts of the conversation they would have, and he couldn't stop doing this while Penelope Tobias stuffed fettucine into herself and rattled on about the glories of the S & S spring list. He wasn't genuinely unpleasant, but he was certainly inattentive and was positive it showed.

A few minutes after one she broke a long silence by signaling abruptly for the check. "I certainly don't want to keep you," she said.

"Penny, I'm sorry as hell."

"Oh? Whatever for?"

"My manners. I have to meet an old friend in a little while and I guess it's bothering me more than I thought it would."

"You mean it's not me? Here I was all set to switch to a new brand of mouthwash."

He was twenty minutes early for his meeting with Ellie. The waiter, an elderly man with stooped shoulders, astonished him by greeting him by name.

"Mr. Barr, we never see you no more."

"I live up in Connecticut now."

"All alone, Mr. Barr?"

"A lady's meeting me for cocktails, but I'm very early and I don't think I can hold out until she gets here. I think an extra dry martini with a twist."

He made the drink last. At five minutes of two the only other customers settled

120

their bill and left, and perhaps a minute later Ellie appeared. He got to his feet while the waiter bustled about seating her. Her eyes had the brittle sparkle of an amphetamine high.

She said, "If that's a martini I think I want one."

He ordered drinks for both of them. Until the waiter brought them she asked questions about Marjorie and Lisa and his work. Then she raised her glass, looked at it for a moment and drained it in three quick swallows.

"I should have told him to wait," he said. " 'Keep the meter running and I'll be ready in a minute.' I don't think I ever saw you drink like that."

"Probably not."

"Want another?"

"No. I wanted that one a lot, but it's all I want for the time being." She opened her purse and found a pack of cigarettes. It was empty, and she crumpled it fiercely and put it down beside the ashtray.

"There's a machine in front," he said. "I'll get them for you."

He returned with a pack of Parliaments and opened them for her, then held a match. Her hand closed on his wrist as she got the cigarette lit. She let go, inhaled, blew out smoke, looked at him and away and at him again.

"Okay," she said.

He didn't say anything.

"I thought of writing Dear Abby, but she would just refer me to my priest, minister or rabbi. And I don't *have* a priest, minister or rabbi. You were the only person I could think of."

"Must be my clerical image."

"It's that you're a friend of mine and a friend of Bert's. More than that. He and I have a lot of friends in common, but you were his friend before I married him, and you and I —"

"Were very good friends once upon a time."

"I think I *will* have another drink. This is turning out to be harder than I thought." When the drinks came she took a small sip and placed her glass on the tablecloth. She helped herself to a second cigarette and let him light it for her.

She said, "For the past two days I've been trying to figure out how to start this conversation. I'm no closer now than I was at the beginning. I love Bert very much. We have a good marriage."

"I've always thought so."

"Have you?"

"Yes. I don't think I know two people who like each other's company as much. You both certainly give that impression."

"It's not a pose. It's very real." She lowered her eyes, worried the rim of the ashtray with the tip of her cigarette. "We have a problem. Or *I* have a problem. That's obvious, I didn't drag you here to discuss how perfectly happy I am."

"No."

"How well do you know Bert?"

"Well, that's a tough question. I've known him for, what, twenty years? We were in college together. He was a sophomore when I was a freshman, although I'm a month older. So I guess I've known him *longer* than anyone else I'm really friendly with now."

"But."

"Right: but. But he's the most guarded man I ever met, so in a sense I don't know him very well at all. Ellie, about two months ago I met a guy in a bar in Weston. He'd just got off the train and he was going to have one quick one before he went home to his wife, and the two of us wound up drinking and talking until close to midnight. I never saw him before and I'll never see him again. I don't remember his name. If he even told me his name. But I knew

123

that sonofabitch more intimately than I ever got to know Bert Kilberg."

"He keeps himself very much to himself."

"Yes."

"David? This is what I want to ask you. How would he react if I had an affair?"

"You mean if he found out about it."

"Well, yes."

"Because I don't know why he'd have to know. Are you seeing somebody?"

"Oh, no."

"But you're thinking about it."

"I seem to feel the need."

He nodded. "Most people do," he said. "Sooner or later."

She excused herself to go to the ladies' room, first asking him to order another round of drinks. When she returned they were already on the table. "Scotch and water," he said. "I decided to switch to something less toxic and I thought you might be inclined to keep me company."

"Meaning don't let the lady get smashed. For which I'll surely thank you later. This is a nice place, although I don't see how they can afford to stay open. How come you never brought me here?"

"I only bring married ladies here."

"Is that the truth? It's a good answer,

anyway. David, I think I need an affair. But I hate keeping secrets from him. I know I'd have the urge to tell him."

"Well, then, let me just tell you something." He leaned forward. "Every time you get that urge, you just step on it full force. You squelch it. If you absolutely can't help yourself, write it out on a sheet of paper and burn it and flush the ashes down the toilet. Because all you can accomplish by telling him is to create purposeless headaches for two people and possibly three. Or four, if the guy you pick is married. And he should be."

"Why do you say that?"

"Because, my dear, cheating is safer when there are two of you doing it. You've both got the same thing to lose. And it's more comfortable, it puts you both on common ground." He laughed shortly. "In other words, when you want to have an affair go pick out a married man, and there's something Dear Abby'll never tell you."

"Wherever would I find one?"

"Oh, that wouldn't be a problem. Married men are looking for it a lot more earnestly than single ones. With your looks you wouldn't have any trouble." Lightly he said, "You could always pick an old flame. For nostalgia, if nothing else."

"You're a very sweet man, David."

There was an awkward moment which they both attempted to cover by reaching for their drinks. Then she said, "He's not married."

"Who's not?"

"The man I'm sleeping with."

"Oh. Then this should-I-or-shouldn't-I wasn't as hypothetical as it sounded."

She shook her head. "I wasn't going to tell you but it doesn't make much sense not to. It's been going on for a little over a month. He's eight years younger than I am, he's not married, and the two of us have nothing whatsoever in common. His only strong point is that he makes me feel excited and exciting."

"Uh-huh."

"But I don't love him. I'm in bed next to him afterward and look at him and wish it was Bert next to me."

"Where did you find him? I'm assuming it's no one I know."

"It's not. I met him at Berlitz. He's my instructor."

"Berlitz? Oh, you're taking Spanish or something. I think Marjorie mentioned it."

"German. He was born in Germany and he looks like the really vicious blond captain in all the war movies. And I'm the girl who wouldn't buy a Volkswagen. Oh, hell. For the past month I haven't been able to figure out whether I'm wildly happy or wildly miserable. I don't know why I dragged you here, David, but I guess I just had to talk to someone. And you were elected."

They continued talking through another round of drinks. Then he put her in a cab, returned to the bar for one last drink and took a cab of his own to Grand Central and caught the 4:17. "It was one of those endless lunches," he told Marjorie, "and I don't think it accomplished a thing. I behaved like a Dale Carnegie dropout."

He called his agent, catching her just before she left the office. He said, "Mary, I think we can forget all about Mr. Simon and Mr. Schuster." He gave her a brief version of the lunch, omitting mention of the reasons for his inattentiveness.

"Well, I always knew you were a bad judge of your own work, Dave. I thought it just applied to fiction, but evidently it's the same in other areas. Penny Tobias thinks you're sensational."

"You're kidding."

"She called me around one-thirty. She said now she knows why your books are so perceptive, you're the most sensitive person she ever met and she really hopes we can work something out because she personally would be so proud to publish you."

"Well, I'll be damned."

"I'm going to dine out on this story, Dave."

"Change one thing when you do, huh? Penny called you at *four*-thirty, right after she got back from lunch."

"Oh, dear," said Mary Fradin. "Davey was a bad boy."

Something was bothering him, and it was several days before he managed to figure out what it was. Then he waited until Marjorie was out of the house and dialed the Kilberg apartment. When Ellie answered he said, "This is David, but if you're not alone I'll be a wrong number."

"I'm alone. What is it?"

"Well, a couple of things. First of all, it's occurred to me that you might be having second thoughts about telling me as much as you did, and I hope you won't. Nothing we talked about will go any further."

"Oh, I know that."

"The other thing is silly but I'm going to mention it anyway because it's been bothering me. It occurs to me that this kraut might get to be a problem. This is probably not going to happen, and you can chalk it up to an overactive imagination, but just promise me one thing. If it looks as though he's going to cause you any trouble at all I want you to call me. Don't go to Bert and don't try to handle things yourself. Just call me."

"What kind of trouble?"

"Any kind."

"You're very sweet, but nothing like that is going to happen."

"I know it isn't. Now say you promise."

"It's silly. *All right.* I promise."

During the next two months David Barr saw Bert Kilberg twice on business matters and spoke to him perhaps a half dozen times over the telephone. He had wondered how this new knowledge of his friend would affect their relationship, and he was pleased to discover that it made no difference.

One Saturday evening he and Marjorie drove into New York to have dinner and see a show with Bert and Ellie. The secret he and Ellie shared did not seem to have changed the dynamics of the relationship among the four of them. He felt somewhat

129

closer to Ellie for it, but he didn't think any of that showed on the surface.

Bert did not know that he and Ellie had been lovers years before she married Bert. It was possible that Marjorie had inferred as much, but if so she had kept her thoughts to herself.

Then one afternoon the telephone rang while he was working in his study. A little later Marjorie told him it had been Ellie. "I'm supposed to give you her fondest regards," she said. "She said it twice, as a matter of fact, so I suppose she really means it. It's funny."

"What is?"

"She called for my Stroganoff recipe, and I'm positive I gave it to her when they were here in December."

Within the hour he invented a pretext to drive into town. He called her from the drugstore.

He said, "Was that a signal? Or have I been reading too many spy novels?"

"I'm just keeping a promise."

"That's what I was afraid of. How bad is it?"

"Oh, it's pretty bad, David. I guess my judgment leaves something to be desired. From now on I'll ask you to pick my lovers for me."

"There's a title that goes with the duty and I'm not crazy about it. But tell me what he's pulled."

"Well, he's a bastard. He got very possessive for a starter. A lot of romantic nonsense, and I swear I did nothing to encourage it. He wanted me to leave Bert and run off with him. The fool. As if I would."

"And?"

"And then he turned on me. He started calling me at home, which I'd told him several times he was absolutely never to do. Then he, uh, began asking for small loans. Ten dollars, twenty dollars. Then he said he needed five hundred dollars, and of course I told him no, and I also told him I didn't think we should see each other anymore."

"Well, you were right about that."

"And now he's trying to blackmail me. I don't know if you'd call it blackmail from a legal point of view because he hasn't exactly made any threats. But just this morning he called and said that if I wouldn't lend him some money, then perhaps Bert would give him a loan. Needless to say he and Bert have never met, so my interpretation is that it's blackmail."

"I think you could call it blackmail. That was this morning?"

"Yes. I don't remember what I told him. But he called back less than an hour later with a whole song and dance about how he loves me and we should run off together. I'm scared of what he might do next. I think I would have called you even if you hadn't said what you did, because I wouldn't know who else to call and I just can't handle this one myself. But how did you know this would happen?"

"It was just a hunch. Let me think a minute. What's this bastard's name?"

"Klaus Eberhard."

"And his address?" She gave it to him and he wrote it down. "All right. Now this is important. Did you ever say anything to him about me? Anything at all?"

"No, I'm positive I never did. I never talked to him about anything, really. We just —"

"You just studied bedroom Deutsch, right. Call him up right now and tell him you'll meet him at his place tomorrow afternoon at three. Can you do that?"

"I never want to see him again, David."

"You'll never have to. I'll keep the appointment for you."

"I don't want you paying him."

"Don't worry about it. Just make the call. I'm in a phone booth, I'll give you my number and you can call me back and tell me the appointment's set."

He got to New York shortly after noon the next day. He stopped at a restaurant near Grand Central but when he looked at the menu he realized he was too edgy to eat anything. He had a drink but decided not to have a second one.

In a shop on Madison Avenue he bought a black hat with a very short brim. In a drugstore a few blocks further along Madison he bought two flashlight batteries and put one in either pocket of his suit jacket. Then he walked for a while, writing and rewriting scenes in his mind.

At half past two he got out of a cab at the corner of Eighty-eighth and York and walked to the address Ellie had given him. He rang a variety of bells until some obliging tenant buzzed him through the front door. He walked up two flights of stairs and knocked on Klaus Eberhard's door. It was opened by a man about thirty with pale blond hair and an open, engaging face. He was at least four inches taller than David Barr and weighed about the same. He wore an Italian knit sport shirt and tailored denim slacks, and he looked more like a ski instructor than an S.S. captain.

"Eberhard?"

"Yes, I am Eberhard." His English was just barely accented. "How may I help you?"

"Klaus Eberhard?"

"But yes."

He put his hands in his pockets and closed his fingers around the flashlight batteries. "You'd better close the door," he said, stepping around Eberhard and into the apartment. "I have a message from Mrs. Kilberg and we don't want the neighbors tuning in."

Eberhard closed the door and put the chain bolt on. As he was turning around again, Barr hit him on the side of the jaw with all his strength. The German fell back against the door and Barr waded in after him, striking him repeatedly in the face and chest. The weight of the batteries increased the effect of the blows immeasurably. He could hear ribs give way as he battered them, and when he landed a punch to Eberhard's nose there was an immediate geyser of blood.

He stepped back at last and Eberhard slid to the floor. Barr stood over him. He pitched his voice low and put the rasp of the New York streets into it. He said, "Now listen good, you son of a bitch. You are gonna stay away from Mrs. Kilberg. You are never gonna call her or see her or nothing. You spot her on the street, you better get your ass out of the way in a big hurry, because next time I kill you. This time I just send you to the hospital, but next time I kill you."

Eberhard couldn't get any words out. His lips moved but no sound was forthcoming.

"You get the message?" He drew back his foot. "Answer me."

"Do not hurt me."

"You understand what I been tellin' you?"

"I understand. Chust don't hurt me."

"I got paid to break your arm. I'll make it a clean break."

The German was beyond resistance. He lay there, his head propped oddly against the door, while Barr placed a foot on his upper arm. Then he gripped the younger man's wrist and pulled up against the elbow joint until he heard a snapping sound. Klaus Eberhard gave a short grunt and passed out.

On the street Barr walked two blocks until he came to a trashcan. He deposited the two flashlight batteries and the hat and walked over to First Avenue to find a bar. He had two double scotches, tossing them off one after the other, then ordered a tall scotch and water. He drank about half of it before going to the men's room.

He was not sick to his stomach. He'd expected nausea, only hoping to control it until he was finished with Eberhard, but all he felt now was an unfamiliar sense of exhilaration and a bit of pain in his hands. The knuckles of his right hand were badly skinned. He washed his hands and decided he could explain the damage as having been caused by a fall.

He returned to the bar and finished his drink. Then he went to the telephone and dialed her number.

He said, "You can forget that son of a bitch. You won't hear from him again."

"What happened?"

"I'll probably tell you sometime. But not now. Just forget he ever existed. He'll stay clear of you, and I wouldn't be surprised if he leaves town."

"I hope you didn't give him any money."

"Put your mind at rest."

There was a pause. "I don't know what to say."

"You don't have to say anything."

"I suppose 'Thank you' would be a good place to start, but it seems inadequate. However —"

"Don't say anything." He breathed in and out. The feeling of exhilaration was still present. "Ellie? I'll be in the city again on Tuesday. I'd like you to meet me for lunch."

"Something you don't want to say on the phone?"

"Just a social lunch," he said.

She was silent for a moment. Then she said, "All right. It's such a complicated world, isn't it? Where shall I meet you?"

"How about the same place as last time? The Grand Ticino?"

"Of course. That's where you take married women, isn't it?"

"Is noon a good time for you?"

"Such a complicated world. Yes, noon is fine."

"Noon Tuesday at the Grand Ticino," he said. "I'll see you then."

He had another drink and took a cab to the train station. He had some time to kill before his train left. He bought a magazine and sat in the main waiting room until his train was ready for boarding.

On the train, half an hour out of New York, he found himself wondering whether he had unconsciously planned the end of it as well. It seemed to him that he had not known he was going to make a lunch date with her, and yet it also seemed to him that he must have known. Had he designed the whole episode with Eberhard with just that end in mind?

He thought it over and decided it didn't really matter.

When he got back home Marjorie asked him how the meeting had gone. "Went very well," he said. "If they do make the movie they want me for the screenplay. That's a big if, of course. I have to go in Tuesday for a conference with the director, and then we sit around and wait for the studio to say yes or no. But this afternoon was productive. I know I made a real impression on Eberhard."

"That's wonderful."

"Yes, you'd have been proud of me," said David Barr.

Change of Life

In a sense, what happened to Royce Arnstetter wasn't the most unusual thing in the world. What happened to him was that he got to be thirty-eight years old. That's something that happens to most people and it isn't usually such a much, just a little way station on the road of life, a milepost precisely halfway between thirty-two and forty-four, say.

Not the most significant milestone in the world for most of us either. Since the good Lord saw fit to equip the vast majority of us with ten fingers, we're apt to attach more significance to those birthdays that end with a nought. Oh, there are a few other biggies — eighteen, twenty-one, sixty-five — but usually it's hitting thirty or forty or fifty that makes a man stop and take stock of his life.

For Royce Arnstetter it was old number thirty-eight. The night before he'd gone to bed around ten o'clock — he just about always went to bed around ten o'clock —

and his wife Essie said, "Well, when you wake up you'll be thirty-eight, Royce."

"Sure will," he said.

Whereupon she turned out the light and went back to the living room to watch a rerun of *Hee Haw* and Royce rolled over and went to sleep. Fell right off to sleep too. He never did have any trouble doing that.

Then just about exactly eight hours later he opened his eyes and he was thirty-eight years old. He got out of bed quietly, careful not to wake Essie, and he went into the bathroom and studied his face as a prelude to shaving it.

"Be double damned," he said. "Thirty-eight years old and my life's half over and I never yet did a single thing."

While it is given to relatively few men to know in advance the precise dates of their death, a perhaps surprising number of them think they know. Some work it out actuarially with slide rules. Some dream their obituaries and note the date on the newspaper. Others draw their conclusions by means of palmistry or phrenology or astrology or numerology or some such. (Royce's birthday, that we've been talking about, fell on the fourth of March that year, same as it did every year. That made him a Pisces, and he had Taurus rising, Moon in Leo, Venus in Capricorn, Mars in Taurus, and just a shade over three hundred dollars in the First National Bank of Schuyler County. He knew about the bank account but not about the astrology business. I'm just putting it in case you care. He had lines on the palms of his hands and bumps on the top of his head, but he'd never taken any particular note of them, so I don't see why you and I have to.)

It's hard to say why Royce had decided he'd live to be seventy-six years old. The ages of his four grandparents at death added up to two hundred and ninety-seven, and if you divide that by four (which I just took the trouble to do for you) you come up with seventy-four and a quarter change. Royce's pa was still hale and hearty at sixty-three, and his ma had died some years back at fifty-one during an electric storm when a lightning-struck old silver maple fell on her car while she was in it.

Royce was an only child.

Point is, you can juggle numbers until you're blue in the face and get about everything but seventy-six in connection with Royce Arnstetter. Maybe he dreamed the number, or maybe he saw *The Music Man* and counted trombones, or maybe he was hung up on the Declaration of Independence.

Point is, it hardly matters why Royce had this idea in his head. But he had it, and he'd had it for as many years as he could remember. If you could divide seventy-six by three he might have had a bad morning some years earlier, and if he'd picked seventy-five or seventy-seven he might have skipped right on by the problem entirely, but he picked seventy-six and even Royce knew that half of seventy-six was thirty-eight, which was what he was.

He had what the French, who have a way with words, call an *idée fixe.* If you went and called it a fixed idea you wouldn't go far wrong. And you know what they say about the power of a fixed idea whose time has come.

Or maybe you don't, but it doesn't matter much. Let's get on back to Royce, still staring at himself in the mirror. What he did was fairly usual. He lathered up and started shaving.

But this time, when he had shaved precisely half of his face, one side of his neck and one cheek and one half of his chin and one half of his mustache, he plumb stopped and washed off the rest of the lather.

"Half done," he said, "and half to go."

He looked pretty silly, if you want to know.

Now I almost said earlier that the only thing noteworthy about the number thirty-eight, unless you happen to be Royce Arnstetter, is that it's the caliber of a gun. That would have had a nice ironical sound to it, at least the first time I ran it on by you, but the thing is it would be a fairly pointless observation. Only time Royce ever handled a pistol in his whole life was when he put in his six months in the National Guard so as not to go into the army, and what they had there was a forty-five automatic, and he never did fire it.

As far as owning guns, Royce had a pretty nice rimfire .22 rifle. It was a pretty fair piece of steel in its day and Royce's pa used to keep it around as a varmint gun. That was before Royce married Essie Handridge and took a place on the edge of town, and Royce used to sit up in his bedroom with the rifle and plink away at woodchucks and rabbits when they made a pass at his ma's snap beans and lettuce and such. He didn't often hit anything. It was his pa's gun, really, and it was only in Royce's keeping because his Pa had taken to drinking some after Royce's ma got crushed by the silver maple. "Shot out a whole raft of windows last Friday and don't even recall it," Royce's pa said. "Now why don't you just hold onto this here for me? I got enough to worry about as it is."

Royce kept the gun in his closet. He didn't even keep any bullets for it, because what did he need with them?

The other gun was a Worthington twelve-gauge, which is a shotgun of a more or less all-purpose nature. Royce's was double-barrel, side by side, and there was nothing automatic about it. After you fired off both shells you had to stop and open the gun and take out the old shells and slap in a couple of fresh ones. Once or twice a year Royce would go out the first day of small-game season and try to get himself a rabbit or a couple pheasant. Sometimes he did and sometimes not. And every now and then he'd try for a deer, but he never did get one of them. Deer have been thin in this part of the state since a few years after the war.

So basically Royce wasn't much for guns. What he really preferred was fishing, which was something he was tolerably good at. His pa was always a good fisherman and it was about the only thing the two of them enjoyed doing together. Royce wasn't enough of a nut to tie his own flies, which his pa had done now and then, but he could cast and he knew what bait to use for what fish and all the usual garbage fishermen have to know if they expect to do themselves any good. He knew all that stuff, Royce did, and he took double-good care of his fishing tackle and owned nothing but quality gear. Some of it was bought second-hand but it was all quality merchandise and he kept it in the best kind of shape.

But good as he was with a fishing rod and poor as he might be with a gun, it didn't make no nevermind, because how in blue hell are you going to walk into a bank and hold it up with a fly rod?

Be serious, will you now?

Well, Royce was there at twenty minutes past nine, which was eleven minutes after the bank opened, which in turn was nine minutes after it was supposed to open. It's not only the First National Bank of Schuyler County, it's the only bank, national or otherwise, in the county. So if Buford Washburn's a handful of minutes late opening up, nobody's about to take his business across the street, because across the street's nothing but Eddie Joe Tyler's sporting goods store. (Royce bought most of his fishing tackle from Eddie Joe, except for the Greenbriar reel he bought when they auctioned off George McEwan's leavings. His pa bought the Worthington shotgun years ago in Clay County off a man who advertised it in the Clay County *Weekly Republican*. I don't know what-all that has to do with anything, but the shotgun's important because Royce had it on his shoulder when he walked on into the bank.)

There was only the one teller behind the counter, but then there was only Royce to give her any business. Buford Washburn was at his desk along the side, and he got to his feet when he saw Royce. "Well, say there, Royce," he said.

"Say, Mr. Washburn," said Royce.

Buford sat back down again. He didn't stand more than he had to. He was maybe six, seven years older than Royce, but if he lived to be seventy-six it would be a miracle, being as his blood pressure was high as July corn and his belt measured fifty-two inches even if you soaked it in brine. Plus he drank. Never before dinner, but that leaves you a whole lot of hours if you're a night person.

The teller was Ruth Van Dine. Her ma wanted her to get braces when she was twelve, thirteen, but Ruth said she didn't care to. I'd have to call that a big mistake on her part. "Say there, Royce," she said. "What can I do for you?"

Now Royce shoved his savings passbook across the top of the counter. Don't ask me why he brought the blame thing. I couldn't tell you.

"Deposit?"

"Withdrawal."

"How much?"

Every dang old cent you got in this here bank was what he was going to say. But what came out of his mouth was, "Every dang old cent."

"Three hundred twelve dollars and forty-five cents? Plus I guess you got some extra interest coming which I'll figure out for you."

"Well —"

"Better make out a slip, Royce. Just on behind you?"

He turned to look for the withdrawal slips and there was Buford Washburn, also standing. "They off at the sawmill today, Royce? I didn't hear anything."

"No, I guess they're workin', Mr. Washburn. I guess I took the day."

"Can't blame you, beautiful day like this. What'd you do, go and get a little hunting in?"

"Not in March, Mr. Washburn."

"I don't guess nothing's in season this time of year."

"Not a thing. I was just gone take this here across to Eddie Joe. Needs a little gunsmithin'."

"Well, they say Eddie Joe knows his stuff."

"I guess he does, Mr. Washburn."

"Now this about drawing out all your money," Buford said. He fancied himself smoother than a bald tire at getting from small talk to business, Buford did. "I guess you got what they call an emergency."

"Somethin' like."

"Well now, maybe you want to do what most folks do, and that's leave a few dollars in to keep the account open. Just for convenience. Say ten dollars? Or just draw a round amount, say you draw your three hundred dollars. Or —" And he went through a whole routine about how Royce could take his old self a passbook loan and keep the account together and keep earning interest and all the rest of it, which I'm not going to spell out here for you.

Upshot of it was Royce wound up drawing three hundred dollars. Ruth Van Dine gave it to him in tens and twenties because he just stood there stiffer than new rope when she asked him how did he want it. Three times she asked him, and she's a girl no one ever had to tell to speak up, and each time it was like talking to a wall, so she counted out ten tens and ten twenties and gave it to him, along with his passbook. He thanked her and walked out with the passbook and money in one hand and the other holding the twelve gauge Worthington, which was still propped up on his shoulder.

Before he got back in his panel truck he said, "Half my life, Lord, half my dang life."

Then he got in the truck.

When he got back to his house he found Essie in the kitchen soaking the labels off some empty jam jars. She turned and saw him, then shut off the faucet and turned to look at him again. She said, "Why, Royce honey, what are you doing here? Did you forget somethin'?"

"I didn't forget nothin'," he said. What

he forgot was to hold up the bank like he'd set out to do, but he didn't mention that.

"You didn't get laid off," she said mournfully. (I didn't put in a question mark there because her voice didn't turn up at the end. She said it sort of like it would be O.K. if Royce did get laid off from the sawmill, being that the both of them could always go out in the backyard and eat dirt. She was always a comfort, Essie was.)

"Didn't go *to* work," Royce said. Today's my dang birthday," Royce said.

" 'Course it is! Now I never wished you a happy birthday but you left 'fore I was out of bed. Well, happy birthday and many more. Thirty-nine years, land sakes."

"Thirty-*eight!*"

"What did I say? Why, I said thirty-*nine.* Would you believe that. I know it's thirty-eight, 'course I know that. Why are you carrying that gun, I guess there's rats in the garbage again."

"Half my life," Royce said.

"Is there?"

"Is there what?"

"Rats in the garbage again?"

"Now how in blue hell would I know is there rats in the garbage?"

"But you have that *gun,* Royce."

150

He discovered the gun, took it off his shoulder, and held it out in both hands, looking at it like it was the prettiest thing since a new calf.

"That's your shotgun," Essie said.

"Well, I guess I know that. Half my dang life."

"What about half your life?"

"My life's half gone," he said, "and what did I ever do with it, would you tell me that? Far as I ever been from home is Franklin County and never stayed there overnight, just went and come back. Half my life and I never left the dang old state."

"I was thinkin' we might run out to Silver Dollar City this summer," Essie said. "It's like an old frontier city come to life or so they say. That's across the state line, come to think on it."

"Never been anyplace, never done any dang thing. Never had no woman but you."

"Well now."

"I'm gone to Paris," Royce said.

"What did you say?"

"I'm gone to Paris is what I said. I'm gone rob Buford Washburn's bank and I'm not even gone call him Mr. Washburn this time. Gone to Paris France, gone buy a

151

Cadillac big as a train, gone do every dang thing I never did. Half my life, Essie."

Well, she frowned. You blame her? "Royce," she said, "you better lie down."

"Paris France."

"What I'll do," she said, "I'll just call on over at Dr. LeBeau's. You lie down and put the fan on and I'll just finish with these here jars and then call the doctor. You know something? Just two more cases and we'll run out of your ma's plum preserves. Two cases of twenty-four jars to the case is forty-eight jars and we'll be out. Now I never thought we'd be out of them plums she put up but we'll be plumb out, won't we. Hear me talk, plumb out of plums, I did that without even thinking."

Essie wasn't normally quite this scatter-brained. Almost, but not quite. Thing is, she was concerned about Royce, being as he wasn't acting himself.

"Problem is getting in a rut," Royce said. He was talking to his own self now, not to Essie. "Problem is you leave your-self openings and you come back down because it's the easy thing to do. Like in the bank."

"Royce, ain't you goin' to lay down?"

"Fillin' out a dang slip," Royce said.

"Royce? You know somethin'? You did

152

the funniest thing this mornin', honey. You know what you did? You went and you only shaved the half of your face. You shaved the one half and you didn't shave the other half."

(Now this is something that both Ruth Van Dine and Buford Washburn had already observed, and truth to tell they had both called it to Royce's attention — in a friendly way, of course. I'd have mentioned it but I figured if I kept sliding in the same little piece of conversation over and over it'd be about as interesting for you as watching paint dry. But I had to mention when Essie said it out of respect, see, because it was the last words that woman ever got to speak, because right after she said it Royce stuck the shotgun right in her face and fired off one of the barrels. Don't ask me which one.)

"Now the only way to go is forward," Royce said. "Fix things so you got no bolt hole and you got to do what you got to do." He went to the cupboard, got a shotgun shell, broke open the gun, dug out the empty casing, popped in the new shell, and closed the gun up again.

On the way out of the door he looked at Essie and said, "You weren't so bad, I don't guess."

★ ★ ★

Well, Royce drove on back to the bank and parked directly in front of it, even though there's a sign says plainly not to, and he stepped on into that bank with the twelve-gauge clenched in his hand. It wasn't over his shoulder this time. He had his right hand wrapped around the barrel at the center of gravity or close to it. (It's not the worst way to carry a gun, though you'll never see it advocated during a gun safety drive.)

He was asked later if he felt remorse at that time about Essie. It was the sort of dumb question they ask you, and it was especially dumb in light of the fact that Royce probably didn't know what the hell remorse meant, but in plain truth he didn't. What he felt was in motion.

And in that sense he felt pretty fine. Because he'd been standing plumb still for thirty-eight years and never even knew it, and now he was in motion, and it hardly mattered where exactly he was going.

"I want every dang cent in this bank!" he sang out, and Buford Washburn just about popped a blood vessel in his right eye, and Ruth Van Dine stared, and old Miz Cristendahl who had made a trip to town

154

just to get the interest credited to her account just stood there and closed her eyes so nothing bad would happen to her. (I guess it worked pretty good. That woman's still alive, and she was seventy-six years old when Calvin Coolidge didn't choose to run. All those Cristendahls live pretty close to forever. Good thing they're not much for breeding or the planet would be armpit deep in Cristendahls.)

"Now you give me every bit of that money," he said to Ruth. And he kept saying it, and she got rattled.

"I *can't*," she said finally, "because anyway it's not mine to give and I got no authority and besides there's another customer ahead of you. What you got to do is you got to speak to Mr. Buford Washburn."

And what Buford said was, "Now, Royce, say, Royce, you want to put down that gun."

"I'm gone to Paris France, Mr. Washburn." You notice he forgot and went and called him Mr. Washburn. Old habits die hard.

"Royce, you still didn't finish your morning shave. What's got into you, boy?"

"I killed my wife, Mr. Washburn."

"Royce, why don't you just have a seat

155

and I'll get you a cold glass of Royal Crown. Take my chair."

So Royce pointed the gun at him. "You better give me that money," he said, "or I could go and blow your dang head off your dumb shoulders."

"Boy, does your pappy have the slightest idea what you're up to?"

"I don't see what my pa's got to do with this."

"Because your pappy, he wouldn't take kindly to you carrying on this way, Royce. Now just sit down in my chair, you hear?"

At this point Royce was getting riled, plus he was feeling the frustration of it. Here he went and burned his britches by shooting Essie and where was he? Still trying to hold up a bank that wouldn't take him seriously. So what he did, he swung the gun around and shot out the plate-glass window. You wouldn't think the world would make that much noise in the course of coming to an end.

"Well, now you went and did it," Buford told him. "You got the slightest idea what a plate-glass window costs? Royce, boy, you went and bought yourself a peck of trouble."

So what Royce did, he shot Ruth Van Dine.

Now that doesn't sound like it makes a whole vast amount of sense, but Royce had his reasons, if you want to go and call them by that name. He couldn't kill Buford, according to his thinking, because Buford was the only one who could authorize giving him the money. And he didn't think to shoot Miz Cristendahl because he didn't notice her. (Maybe because she closed her eyes. Maybe those ostriches know what they're about. I'm not going to say they don't.)

On top of which Ruth was screaming a good bit and it was getting on Royce's nerves.

He wasn't any Dead-Eye Dick, as I may have pointed out before, and although he was standing right close to Ruth he didn't get a very good shot at her. A twelve gauge casts a pretty tight pattern as close as he was to her, with most of the charge going right over her head. There was enough left to do the job, but it was close for a while. Didn't kill her right off, left them plenty of time to rush her to Schuyler County Memorial and pop her into the operating room. It was six hours after that before she died, and there's some say better doctors could have saved her. That's a question I'll stay away from myself. It's said she'd of been a vegetable even if she lived, so maybe it's all for the best.

Well, that was about the size of it. Buford fainted, which was plain sensible on his part, and Miz Cristendahl stood around with her eyes shut and her fingers in her ears, and Royce Arnstetter went behind the counter and opened the cash drawer and started pulling out stacks of money. He got all the money on top of the counter. There wasn't a whole hell of a lot of it. He was looking for a bag to put it in when a couple of citizens rushed in to see what was going on.

He picked up the gun and then just threw it down in disgust because it was full of nothing but two spent shells. And he couldn't have reloaded if he'd thought of it because he never did bring along any extra shells when he left the house. Just the two that were loaded into the gun, and one of those took out the window and the other took out poor Ruth. He just threw the gun down and said a couple bad words and thought what a mess he'd made of everything, letting the first half of his life just dribble out and then screwing up the second half on the very first day of it.

158

He would of pleaded at the trial but he had this young court-appointed lawyer who wanted to do some showboating, and the upshot of it was he wound up drawing ninety-nine-to-life, which sounds backwards to me, as the average life runs out way in front of the ninety-nine mark, especially when you're thirty-eight to start with.

He's in the state prison now over to Millersport. It's not quite as far from his home as Franklin County where he went once, but he didn't get to stay overnight that time. He sure gets to stay overnight now.

Well, there's people to talk to and he's learning things. His pa's been to visit a few times. They don't have much to say to each other but when did they ever? They'll reminisce about times they went fishing. It's not so bad.

He thinks about Essie now and then. I don't know as you'd call it remorse though.

"Be here until the day I die," he said one day. And a fellow inmate sat him down and told him about parole and time off for good behavior and a host of other things, and this fellow worked it out with pencil and paper and told Royce he'd likely be breathing free air in something like thirty-three years.

"Means I'll have five left to myself," Royce said.

The fellow gave him this look.

"I'm fixin' to live until I'm seventy-six," Royce explained. "Thirty-eight now and thirty-three more in here is what? Seventy-one, isn't it? Seventy-six take away seventy-one and you get five, don't you? Five years left when I'm out of here." And he scratched his head and said, "Now what am I gone do with them five years?"

Well, I just guess he'll have to think of something.

Death of
the Mallory Queen

"I am going to be murdered," Mavis
Mallory said, "and I want you to do something about it."

Haig did something, all right. He spun
around in his swivel chair and stared into
the fish tank. There's a whole roomful of
tanks on the top floor, and other aquar-
iums, which he wishes I would call aquaria,
scattered throughout the house.

(Well, not the whole house. The whole
house is a carriage house on West Twen-
tieth Street, and on the top two floors live
Leo Haig and Wong Fat and more tropical
fish than you could shake a jar of tubifex
worms at, but the lower two floors are still
occupied by Madam Juana and her girls.
How do you say *filles de joie* in Spanish,
anyway? Never mind. If all of this sounds a
little like a cut-rate, low-rent version of
Nero Wolfe's establishment on West
Thirty-fifth Street, the similarity is not ac-

cidental. Haig, you see, was a lifelong reader of detective fiction, and a penny-ante breeder of tropical fish until a legacy made him financially independent And he was a special fan of the Wolfe canon, and he thinks that Wolfe really exists, and that if he, Leo Haig, does a good enough job with the cases that come his way, sooner or later he might get invited to dine at the master's table.)

"Mr. Haig —"

"*Huff,*" Haig said.

Except that he didn't exactly *say* huff. He *went* huff. He's been reading books lately by Sondra Ray and Leonard Orr and Phil Laut, books on rebirthing and physical immortality, and the gist of it seems to be that if you do enough deep circular breathing and clear out your limiting deathist thoughts, you can live forever. I don't know how he's doing with his deathist thoughts, but he's been breathing up a storm lately, as if air were going to be rationed any moment and he wants to get the jump on it.

He huffed again and studied the rasboras, which were the fish that were to-and-froing it in the ten-gallon tank behind his desk. Their little gills never stopped working, so I figured they'd live forever, too, unless their deathist thoughts were lurking to do them in. Haig gave another huff and turned around to look at our client.

She was worth looking at. Tall, willowy, richly curved, with a mane of incredible red hair. Last August I went up to Vermont, toward the end of the month, and all the trees were green except here and there you'd see one in the midst of all that green that had been touched by an early frost and turned an absolutely flaming scarlet, and that was the color of Mavis Mallory's hair. Haig's been quoting a lot of lines lately about the rich abundance of the universe we live in, especially when I suggest he's spending too much on fish and equipment, and looking at our client I had to agree with him. We live in an abundant world, all right.

"Murdered," he said.

She nodded.

"By whom?"

"I don't know."

"For what reason?"

"I don't know."

"And you want me to prevent it."

"No."

His eyes widened. "I beg your pardon?"

"How could you prevent it?" She wrinkled her nose at him. "I understand you're a genius, but what defense could you provide against a determined killer? You're not exactly the physical type."

Haig, who has been described as looking like a basketball with an Afro, huffed in reply. "My own efforts are largely in the cerebral sphere," he admitted. "But my associate, Mr. Harrison, is physically resourceful as well, and —" he made a tent of his fingertips "— still, your point is well taken. Neither Mr. Harrison nor I are bodyguards. If you wish a bodyguard, there are larger agencies which —"

But she was shaking her head. "A waste of time," she said. "The whole Secret Service can't protect a president from a lone deranged assassin. If I'm destined to be murdered, I'm willing to accede to my destiny."

"Huff," Haig huffed.

"What I want you to do," she said, "and Mr. Harrison, of course, except that he's so young I feel odd calling him by his last name." She smiled winningly at me. "Unless you object to the familiarity?"

"Call me Chip," I said.

"I'm delighted. And you must call me Mavis."

"Huff."

164

"Who wants to murder you?" I asked.

"Oh, dear," she said. "It sometimes seems to me that everyone does. It's been four years since I took over as publisher of *Mallory's Mystery Magazine* upon my father's death, and you'd be amazed how many enemies you can make in a business like this."

Haig asked if she could name some of them.

"Well, there's Abner Jenks. He'd been editor for years and thought he'd have a freer hand with my father out of the picture. When I reshuffled the corporate structure and created Mavis Publications, Inc., I found out he'd been taking kickbacks from authors and agents in return for buying their stories. I got rid of him and took over the editorial duties myself."

"And what became of Jenks?"

"I pay him fifty cents a manuscript to read slush pile submissions. And he picks up some freelance work for other magazines as well, and he has plenty of time to work on his own historical novel about the Venerable Bede. Actually," she said, "he ought to be grateful to me."

"Indeed," Haig said.

"And there's Darrell Crenna. He's the owner of Mysterious Ink, the mystery bookshop on upper Madison Avenue. He wanted Dorothea Trill, the Englishwoman who writes those marvelous gardening mysteries, to do a signing at his store. In fact he'd advertised the appearance, and I had to remind him that Miss Trill's contract with Mavis Publications forbids her from making any appearances in the States without our authorization."

"Which you refused to give."

"I felt it would cheapen the value of Dorothea's personal appearances to have her make too many of them. After all, Crenna talked an author out of giving a story to *Mallory's* on the same grounds, so you could say he was merely hoist with his own petard. Or strangled by his own clematis vine, like the woman in Dorothea's latest." Her face clouded. "I hope I haven't spoiled the ending for you?"

"I've already read it," Haig said.

"I'm glad of that. Or I should have to add you to the list of persons with a motive for murdering me, shouldn't I? Let me see now. Lotte Benzler belongs on the list. You must know her shop. The Murder Store?"

Haig knew it well, and said so. "And I trust you've supplied Ms. Benzler with an equally strong motive? Kept an author

166

from her door? Refused her permission to reprint a story from *Mallory's* in one of the anthologies she edits?"

"Actually," our client said, "I fear I did something rather more dramatic than that. You know Bart Halloran?"

"The creator of Rocky Sledge, who's so hard-boiled he makes Mike Hammer seem poached? I've read him, of course, but I don't know him."

"Poor Lotte came to know him very well," Mavis Mallory purred, "and then I met dear Bart, and then it was I who came to know him very well." She sighed. "I don't think Lotte has ever forgiven me. All's fair in love and publishing, but some people don't seem to realize it."

"So there are three people with a motive for murdering you."

"Oh, I'm sure there are more than three. Let's not forget Bart, shall we? He was able to shrug it off when I dropped him, but he took it harder when his latest got a bad review in *Mallory's*. But I thought *Kiss my Gat* was a bad book, and why should I say otherwise?" She sighed again. "Poor Bart," she said. "I understand his sales are slipping. Still, he's still a name, isn't he? And he'll be there Friday night."

"Indeed?" Haig raised his eyebrows.

He's been practicing in front of the mirror, trying to raise just one eyebrow, but so far he hasn't got the knack of it. "And just where will Mr. Halloran be Friday night?"

"Where they'll all be," Mavis Mallory said. "At Town Hall, for the panel discussion and reception to celebrate the twenty-fifth anniversary of *Mallory's Mystery Magazine.* Do you know, I believe everyone with a motive to murder me will be gathered together in one room?" She shivered happily. "What more could a mystery fan ask for?"

"Don't attend," Haig said.

"Don't be ridiculous," she told him. "I'm Mavis Mallory of Mavis Publications, I *am Mallory's* — in fact I've been called the Mallory Queen. I'll be chairing the panel discussion and hosting the celebration. How could I possibly fail to be present?"

"Then get bodyguards."

"They'd put such a damper on the festivities. And I already told you they'd be powerless against a determined killer."

"Miss Mallory —"

"And please don't tell me to wear a bulletproof vest. They haven't yet designed one that flatters the full-figured woman."

I swallowed, reminded again that we live in an abundant universe. "You'll be killed," Haig said flatly.

"Yes," said our client, "I rather suspect I shall. I'm paying you a five thousand dollar retainer now, in cash, because you might have a problem cashing a check if I were killed before it cleared. And I've added a codicil to my will calling for payment to you of an additional twenty thousand dollars upon your solving the circumstances of my death. And I do trust you and Chip will attend the reception Friday night? Even if I'm not killed, it should be an interesting evening."

"I have read of a tribe of Africans," Haig said dreamily, "who know for certain that gunshot wounds are fatal. When one of their number is wounded by gunfire, he falls immediately to the ground and lies still, waiting for death. He does this even if he's only been nicked in the finger, and, by the following morning, death will have inevitably claimed him."

"That's interesting," I said. "Has it got anything to do with the Mallory Queen?"

"It has everything to do with her. The woman —" he huffed again, and I don't think it had much to do with circular breathing "— the damnable woman is convinced she will be murdered. It would profoundly disappoint her to be proved wrong. She *wants* to be murdered, Chip, and her thoughts are creative, even as yours and mine. In all likelihood she will die on Friday night. She would have it no other way."

"If she stayed home," I said. "If she hired bodyguards —"

"She will do neither. But it would not matter if she did. The woman is entirely under the influence of her own death urge. Her death urge is stronger than her life urge. How could she live in such circumstances?"

"If that's how you feel, why did you take her money?"

"Because all abundance is a gift from the universe," he said loftily. "Further, she engaged us not to protect her but to avenge her, to solve her murder. I am perfectly willing to undertake to do that." *Huff.* "You'll attend the reception Friday night, of course."

"To watch our client get the ax?"

"Or the dart from the blowpipe, or the poisoned cocktail, or the bullet, or the bite from the coral snake, or what you will. Perhaps you'll see something that will enable us to solve her murder on the spot and earn the balance of our fee."

"Won't you be there? I thought you'd planned to go."

"I had," he said. "But that was before Miss Mallory transformed the occasion from pleasure to business. Nero Wolfe never leaves his house on business, and I think the practice a sound one. You will attend in my stead, Chip. You will be my eyes and my legs. *Huff.*"

I was still saying things like *Yes, but* when he swept out of the room and left for an appointment with his rebirther. Once a week he goes all the way up to Washington Heights, where a woman named Lori Schneiderman gets sixty dollars for letting him stretch out on her floor and watching him breathe. It seems to me that for that kind of money he could do his huffing in a bed at the Plaza Hotel, but what do I know?

He'd left a page full of scribbling on his desk and I cleared it off to keep any further clients from spotting it. *I, Leo, am safe and immortal right now,* he'd written five times. *You, Leo, are safe and immortal right now,* he'd written another five times. *Leo is safe and immortal right now,* he'd written a final five times. This was how he was working through his unconscious death urge and strengthening his life urge. I tell you, a person has to go through a lot of crap if he wants to live forever.

Friday night found me at Town Hall, predictably enough. I wore my suit for the occasion and got there early enough to snag a seat down front, where I could keep a private eye on things.

There were plenty of things to keep an eye on. The audience swarmed with readers and writers of mystery and detective fiction, and if you want an idea of who was in the house, just write out a list of your twenty-five favorite authors and be sure that seventeen or eighteen of them were in the house. I saw some familiar faces, a woman who'd had a long run as the imperiled heroine of a Broadway suspense melodrama, a man who'd played a police detective for three years on network television, and others whom I recognized from films or television but couldn't place out of context.

On stage, our client Mavis Mallory occupied the moderator's chair. She was wearing a strapless and backless floor-length black dress, and in combination with her creamy skin and fiery hair, its effect was dramatic. If I could have changed one thing it would have been the color of the dress. I suppose Haig would have said it was the color of her unconscious death urge.

Her panelists were arranged in a semicircle around her. I recognized some but not others, but before I could extend my knowledge through subtle investigative technique, the entire panel was introduced. The members included Darrell Crenna of Mysterious Ink and Lotte Benzler of The Murder Store. The two sat on either side of our client, and I just hoped she'd be safe from the daggers they were looking at each other.

Rocky Sledge's creator, dressed in his standard outfit of chinos and a tee shirt with the sleeve rolled to contain a pack of unfiltered Camels, was introduced as Bartholomew Halloran. "Make that Bart," he snapped. *If you know what's good for you,* he might have added.

Halloran was sitting at Mavis Mallory's left. A tall and very slender woman with elaborately coiffed hair and a lorgnette sat between him and Darrell Crenna. She turned out to be Dorothea Trill, the Englishwoman who wrote gardening mysteries. I always figured the chief gardening mystery was what to do with all the zucchini. Miss Trill seemed a little looped, but maybe it was the lorgnette.

On our client's other side, next to Lotte Benzler, sat a man named Austin Porterfield. He was a Distinguished Professor of English Literature at New York University, and he'd recently published a rather learned obituary of the mystery story in the *New York Review of Books.* According to him, mystery fiction had drawn its strength over the years from the broad base of its popular appeal. Now other genres had more readers, and thus mystery writers were missing the mark. If they wanted to be artistically important, he advised them, then get busy producing Harlequin romances and books about nurses and stewardesses.

On Mr. Porterfield's other side was Janice Cowan, perhaps the most prominent book editor in the mystery field. For years she had moved from one important publishing house to another, and at each of them she had her own private imprint. "A Jan Cowan Novel of Suspense" was a good guarantee of literary excellence, whoever happened to be Miss Cowan's employer that year.

After the last of the panelists had been

introduced, a thin, weedy man in a dark suit passed quickly among the group with a beverage tray, then scurried off the stage. Mavis Mallory took a sip of her drink, something colorless in a stemmed glass, and leaned toward the microphone. "What Happens Next?" she intoned. "That's the title of our little discussion tonight, and it's a suitable title for a discussion on this occasion. A credo of *Mallory's Mystery Magazine* has always been that our sort of fiction is only effective insofar as the reader cares deeply what happens next, what takes place on the page he or she has yet to read. Tonight, though, we are here to discuss what happens next in mystery and suspense fiction. What trends have reached their peaks, and what trends are swelling just beyond the horizon."

She cleared her throat, took another sip of her drink. "Has the tough private eye passed his prime? Is the lineal descendant of Sam Spade and Philip Marlowe just a tedious outmoded macho sap?" She paused to smile pleasantly at Bart Halloran, who glowered back at her. "Conversely, has the American reader lost interest forever in the mannered English mystery? Are we ready to bid adieu to the body in the library, or —" she paused for an amiable nod at the slightly cockeyed Miss Trill "— the corpse in the formal gardens?

"Is the mystery, if you'll pardon the expression, *dead* as a literary genre? One of our number —" and a cheerless smile for Professor Porterfield "— would have us all turn to writing *Love's Saccharine Savagery* and *Penny Wyse, Stockyard Nurse.* Is the mystery bookshop, a store specializing in our brand of fiction, an idea whose time has come — and gone? And what do book publishers have to say on this subject? One of our number has worked for so many of them; she should be unusually qualified to comment."

Mavis certainly had the full attention of her fellow panelists. Now, to make sure she held the attention of the audience as well, she leaned forward, a particularly arresting move given the nature of the strapless, backless black number she was more or less wearing. Her hands tightened on the microphone.

"Please help me give our panel members full attention," she said, "as we turn the page to find out —" she paused dramatically "— What Happens Next!"

What happened next was that the lights went out. All of them, all at once, with a great crackling noise of electrical failure.

Somebody screamed, and then so did somebody else, and then screaming became kind of popular. A shot rang out. There were more screams, and then another shot, and then everybody was shouting at once, and then some lights came on.

Guess who was dead.

That was Friday night. Tuesday afternoon, Haig was sitting back in his chair on his side of our huge old partners' desk. He didn't have his feet up — I'd broken him of that habit — but I could see he wanted to. Instead he contented himself with taking a pipe apart and putting it back together again. He had tried smoking pipes, thinking it a good mannerism for a detective, but it never took, so now he fiddles with them. It looks pretty dumb but it's better than putting his feet up on the desk.

"I don't suppose you're wondering why I summoned you all here," he said.

They weren't wondering. They all knew, all of the panelists from the other night, plus two old friends of ours, a cop named Gregorio who wears clothes that could never be purchased on a policeman's salary, and another cop named Seidenwall, who wears clothes that could. They knew they'd been gathered together to watch

Leo Haig pull a rabbit out of a hat, and it was going to be a neat trick because it looked as though he didn't even have the hat.

"We're here to clear up the mysterious circumstances of the death of Mavis Mallory. All of you assembled here, except for the two gentlemen of the law, had a motive for her murder. All of you had the opportunity. All of you thus exist under a cloud of suspicion. As a result, you should all be happy to learn that you have nothing to fear from my investigation. Mavis Mallory committed suicide."

"Suicide!" Gregorio exploded. "I've heard you make some ridiculous statements in your time, but that one grabs the gateau. You have the nerve to sit there like a toad on a lily pad and tell me the red-headed dame killed herself?"

"Nerve?" Haig mused. "Is nerve ever required to tell the truth?"

"Truth? You wouldn't recognize the truth if it dove into one of your fish tanks and swam around eating up all the brine shrimp. The Mallory woman got hit by everything short of tactical nuclear weapons. There were two bullets in her from different guns. She had a wavy-bladed knife stuck in her back and a short dagger in her

178

chest, or maybe it was the other way around. The back of her skull was dented by a blow from a blunt instrument. There was enough rat poison in her system to put the Pied Piper out of business, and there were traces of curare, a South American arrow poison, in her martini glass. Did I leave something out?"

"Her heart had stopped beating," Haig said.

"Is that a fact? If you ask me, it had its reasons. And you sit there and call it suicide. That's some suicide."

Haig sat there and breathed, in and out, in and out, in the relaxed, connected breathing rhythm that Lori Schneiderman had taught him. Meanwhile they all watched him, and I in turn watched them. We had them arranged just the way they'd been on the panel, with Detective Vincent Gregorio sitting in the middle where Mavis Mallory had been. Reading left to right, I was looking at Bart Halloran, Dorothea Trill, Darrell Crenna, Gregorio, Lotte Benzler, Austin Porterfield and Janice Cowan. Detective Wallace Seidenwall sat behind the others, sort of off to the side and next to the wall. If this were novel length I'd say what each of them was wearing and who scowled and who looked interested, but Haig says there's not enough plot here for a novel and that you have to be more concise in short stories, so just figure they were all feeling about the way you'd feel if you were sitting around watching a fat little detective practice rhythmic breathing.

"Some suicide," Haig said. "Indeed. Some years ago a reporter went to a remote county in Texas to investigate the death of a man who'd been trying to expose irregularities in election procedures. The coroner had recorded the death as suicide, and the reporter checked the autopsy and discovered that the deceased had been shot six times in the back with a high-powered rifle. He confronted the coroner with this fact and demanded to know how the man had dared call the death suicide.

" 'Yep,' drawled the coroner. 'Worst case of suicide I ever saw in my life.' "

Gregorio just stared at him.

"So it is with Miss Mallory," Haig continued. "Hers is the worst case of suicide in my experience. Miss Mallory was helplessly under the influence of her own unconscious death urge. She came to me, knowing that she was being drawn toward death, and yet she had not the slightest impulse to gain protection. She wished only that I contract to investigate her demise and see to its resolution. She deliberately assembled seven persons who had reason to rejoice in her death, and enacted a little drama in front of an audience. She —"

"Six persons," Gregorio said, gesturing to the three on either side of him. "Unless you're counting her, or unless all of a sudden I got to be a suspect."

Haig rang a little bell on his desk top, and that was Wong Fat's cue to usher in a skinny guy in a dark suit. "Mr. Abner Jenks," Haig announced. "Former editor of *Mallory's Mystery Magazine*, demoted to slush reader and part-time assistant."

"He passed the drinks," Dorothea Trill remembered. "So that's how she got the rat poison."

"I certainly didn't poison her," Jenks whined. "Nor did I shoot her or stab her or hit her over the head or —"

Haig held up a hand. There was a pipe stem in it, but it still silenced everybody. "You all had motives," he said. "None of you intended to act on them. None of you planned to make an attempt on Miss Mallory's life. Yet thought is creative and Mavis Mallory's thoughts were powerful. Some people attract money to them, or

181

love, or fame. Miss Mallory attracted violent death."

"You're making a big deal out of nothing," Gregorio said. "You're saying she wanted to die, and that's fine, but it's still a crime to give her a hand with it, and that's what every single one of them did. What's that movie, something about the Orient Express and they all stab the guy? That's what we got here, and I think what I gotta do is hook 'em all on a conspiracy charge."

"That would be the act of a witling," Haig said. "First of all, there was no conspiracy. Perhaps more important, there was no murder."

"Just a suicide."

"Precisely," said Haig. *Huff.* "In a real sense, all death is suicide. As long as a man's life urge is stronger than his death urge, he is immortal and invulnerable. Once the balance shifts, he has an unbreakable appointment in Samarra. But Miss Mallory's death is suicide in a much stricter sense of the word. No one else tried to kill her, and no one else succeeded. She unquestionably created her own death."

"And shot herself?" Gregorio demanded. "And stuck knives in herself, and bopped herself over the head? And —"

"No," Haig said. *Huff.* "I could tell you that she drew the bullets and knives to herself by the force of her thoughts, but I would be wasting my —" *huff!* "— breath. The point is metaphysical, and in the present context immaterial. The bullets were not aimed at her, nor did they kill her. Neither did the stabbings, the blow to the head, the poison."

"Then what did?"

"The stopping of her heart."

"Well, that's what kills everyone," Gregorio said, as if explaining something to a child. "That's how you know someone's dead. The heart stops."

Haig sighed heavily, and I don't know if it was circular breathing or resignation. Then he started telling them how it happened.

"Miss Mallory's death urge created a powerful impulse toward violence," he said. "All seven of you, the six panelists and Mr. Jenks, had motives for killing the woman. But you are not murderous people, and you had no intention of committing acts of violence. Quite without conscious intent, you found yourselves bringing weapons to the Town Hall event. Perhaps you thought to display them to an audience of mystery fans. Perhaps you felt

183

a need for a self-defense capability. It hardly matters what went through your minds.

"All of you, as I said, had reason to hate Miss Mallory. In addition, each of you had reason to hate one or more of your fellow panel members. Miss Benzler and Mr. Crenna are rival booksellers; their cordial loathing for one another is legendary. Mr. Halloran was romantically involved with the panel's female members, while Mr. Porterfield and Mr. Jenks were briefly, uh, closeted together in friendship. Miss Trill had been very harshly dealt with in some writings of Mr. Porterfield. Miss Cowan had bought books by Mr. Halloran and Miss Trill, then left the books stranded when she moved on to another employer. I could go on, but what's the point? Each and every one of you may be said to have had a sound desire to murder each and every one of your fellows, but in the ordinary course of things nothing would have come of any of these desires. We all commit dozens of mental murders a day, yet few of us ever dream of acting on any of them."

"I'm sure there's a point to this," Austin Porterfield said.

"Indeed there is, sir, and I am fast approaching it. Miss Mallory leaned forward, grasping her microphone, pausing for full dramatic value, and the lights went out. And it was then that knives and guns and blunt instruments and poison came into play."

The office lights dimmed as Wong Fat operated a wall switch. There was a sharp intake of breath, although the room didn't get all that dark, and there was a balancing *huff* from Haig. "The room went dark," he said. "That was Miss Mallory's doing. She chose the moment, not just unconsciously, but with knowing purpose. She wanted to make a dramatic point, and she succeeded beyond her wildest dreams.

"As soon as those lights went out, everyone's murderous impulses, already stirred up by Mavis Mallory's death urge, were immeasurably augmented. Mr. Crenna drew a Malayan kris and moved to stab it into the heart of his competitor, Miss Benzler. At the same time, Miss Benzler drew a poniard of her own and circled around to direct it at Mr. Crenna's back. Neither could see. Neither was well oriented. And Mavis Mallory's unconscious death urge drew both blades to her own body, even as it drew the bullet Mr. Porterfield meant for Mr. Jenks, the deadly blow Mr. Halloran meant for Cowan, the bullet Miss Cowan intended for Miss Trill, and the curare Miss Trill had meant to place in Mr. Halloran's glass.

"Curare, incidentally, works only if introduced into the bloodstream; it would have been quite ineffective if ingested. The rat poison Miss Mallory did ingest was warfarin, which would ultimately have caused her death by internal bleeding; it was in the glass when Abner Jenks served it to her."

"Then Jenks tried to kill her," Gregorio said.

Haig shook his head. "Jenks did not put the poison in the glass," he said "Miss Lotte Benzler had placed the poison in the glass before Miss Mallory picked it up."

"Then Miss Benzler —"

"Was not trying to kill Miss Mallory either," Haig said, "because she placed the poison in the glass she intended to take for herself. She had previously ingested a massive dose of Vitamin K, a coagulant which is the standard antidote for warfarin, and intended to survive a phony murder attempt on stage, both to publicize The Murder Store and to discredit her competitor, Mr. Crenna. At the time, of course, she'd had no conscious intention of sticking a poniard into the same Mr. Crenna, the very poniard that wound up in Miss Mallory."

"You're saying they all tried to kill each other," Gregorio said. "And they all killed her instead."

"But they didn't succeed."

"They didn't? How do you figure that? She's dead as a bent doornail."

"She was already dead."

"How?"

"Dead of electrocution," Haig told him. "Mavis Mallory put out all the lights in Town Hall by short-circuiting the microphone. She got more than she bargained for, although in a sense it was precisely what she'd bargained for. In the course of shorting out the building's electrical system, she herself was subjected to an electrical charge that induced immediate and permanent cardiac arrest. The warfarin had not yet had time to begin inducing fatal internal bleeding. The knives and bullets pierced the skin of a woman who was already dead. The bludgeon crushed a dead woman's skull. Miss Mallory killed herself."

Wong Fat brought the lights up. Gregorio blinked at the brightness. "That's a pretty uncertain way to do yourself in," he said. "It's not like she had her foot in a pail of water. You don't necessarily get a shock shorting out a line that way, and the shock's not necessarily a fatal one."

"The woman did not consciously plan her own death," Haig told him. "An official verdict of suicide would be of dubious validity. Accidental death, I suppose, is what the certificate would properly read." He huffed mightily. "Accidental death! As that Texas sheriff would say, it's quite the worst case of accidental death I've ever witnessed."

And that's what it went down as, accidental death. No charges were ever pressed against any of the seven, although it drove Gregorio crazy that they all walked out of there untouched. But what could you get them for? Mutilating a corpse? It would be hard to prove who did what, and it would be even harder to prove that they'd been trying to kill each other. As far as Haig was concerned, they were all acting under the influence of Mavis Mallory's death urge, and were only faintly responsible for their actions.

"The woman was ready to die, Chip," he said, "and die she did. She wanted me to solve her death and I've solved it, I trust to the satisfaction of the lawyers for her estate. And you've got a good case to write up. It won't make a novel, and there's not nearly enough sex in it to satisfy the book-buying public, but I shouldn't wonder that it will make a good short story. Perhaps for *Mallory's Mystery Magazine,* or a publication of equal stature."

He stood up. "I'm going uptown," he announced, "to get rebirthed. I suggest you come along. I think Wolfe must have been a devotee of rebirthing, and Archie as well."

I asked him how he figured that.

"Rebirthing reverses the aging process," he explained. "How else do you suppose the great detectives manage to endure for generations without getting a day older? Archie Goodwin was a brash young man in *Fer-de-lance* in nineteen thirty-four. He was still the same youthful wisenheimer forty years later. I told you once, Chip, that your association with me would make it possible for you to remain eighteen years old forever. Now it seems that I can lead you not only to the immortality of ink and paper but to genuine physical immortality. If you and I work to purge ourselves of the effects of birth trauma, and if we use our breath to cleanse our cells, and if we stamp out deathist thoughts once and forever —"

"Huh," I said. But wouldn't you know it? It came out *huff*.

That Kind of a Day

Traynor got the call at a quarter to nine. The girl on the line was named Linda Haber and she was a secretary — the secretary — at Hofert & Jordan. The boss had been shot, she kept saying. It took Traynor close to five minutes to find out who she was and where she was and to tell her to sit down and stay put. She was still babbling hysterically when he hung up on her and pulled Phil Grey away from a cup of coffee. He said, "Homicide, downtown and west. Let's go."

Hofert & Jordan had two and a half rooms of office space in a squat red-brick building on Woodlawn near Marsh. There was a *No Smoking* sign in the elevator. Grey smoked anyway. Traynor kept his hands in his pockets and waited for the car to get to the fourth floor. The doors opened and a white-faced girl rushed up and asked them if they were the police. Grey said they were. The girl looked grateful.

"Right this way," she said. "Oh, it's so awful!"

They entered an anteroom, with two offices leading from it. One door was marked *David Hofert*, another marked *James Jordan.* They went through the door marked *James Jordan.* Linda Haber was trembling. Grey took her by an arm and eased her toward a chair. Traynor studied the scene.

There was an old oak desk with papers strewn over it; some papers had spilled down onto the floor. There was a gun on the floor a little to the left of the desk, and somewhat farther to that side of the desk there was a man lying face down in a pool of partially dried blood, some of which had spattered onto the papers.

Traynor said, "Mr. Jordan?"

"Mr. Hofert," the Haber girl said. "Is he —" She didn't finish the question. Her face paled and then she fainted.

Some lab people came and took pictures, noted measurements and made chalk marks. They had Hofert's body out of the building in less than half an hour. Grey and Traynor worked as a team, crisp and smooth and efficient. Traynor questioned the secretary when she came to, then had the medical examiner give her a sedative and commissioned a patrolman to drive her home. Grey routed the night elevator operator out of bed and asked him some questions. Traynor called the man who did the legal work for Hofert & Jordan. Grey got a prelim report from the M.E., pending autopsy results. Traynor bought two cups of coffee from a machine in the lobby and brought them upstairs. The coffee tasted of cardboard, from the containers.

"Almost too easy," Traynor said. "Too simple."

Grey nodded.

"At six forty-five last night the Haber kid went home. Jordan and Hofert were both here. Jordan stayed until eight. From six at night until eight in the morning nobody can get in or out of the building without signing the register, and the stairs are locked off at the second-floor landing. You have to sign and you have to use the elevator. Jordan signed out at eight. Hofert never signed out; he was dead."

"What was the time of death?"

"That fit, too. A rough estimate is twelve to fourteen hours. One bullet was in the chest a little below the heart. It took him a little while to die. Say five minutes, not much more than that. Enough time to lose a lot of blood."

"So if he got shot between seven and eight —"

"That's about it. No robbery motive. He has a full wallet on him. No suicide. He was standing up when he got shot, standing and facing the desk, Jordan's desk. The Haber girl couldn't have killed him. She left better than an hour before Jordan did and the sheet bears her out on that."

"Motive?"

Traynor put his coffee on the desk. "Maybe they hated each other," he said. "A little two-man operation jobbing office supplies. The lawyer says they didn't make much and they didn't lose much either. Partners for six years. Jordan's forty-four, Hofert was two years older. The secretary said they argued a lot."

"Everybody argues."

"They argued more. Especially yesterday, according to the secretary. There's a money motive, too. Partnership insurance."

Grey looked puzzled.

"Twin policies paid for out of partnership funds. Each partner is insured, with the face amount payable to the survivor if one of them dies."

"Why?"

"That's what I asked the lawyer. Look,

194

suppose you and I are in business together. Then suppose you die —"

"Thanks."

"— and your wife inherits your share. She can't take a hand in the running of the business. After I pay myself a salary there's not much left in the way of profits for her. What she wants is the cash and what I want is full control of the business. Lots of friction."

"Maybe I'd better live," Grey said.

Traynor ignored him. "The insurance smooths things out. If you die, the insurance company pays me whatever the policy is. Then I have to use the money to buy your share of the business from your widow. She has the cash she needs, and I get the whole business without any cost to me. That way everybody's happy."

"Except me."

"Hofert and Jordan had partnership insurance," Traynor said. "Two policies, each with a face amount of a hundred grand. That's motive and means and opportunity, so pat it's hard to believe. I don't know what we're waiting around here for."

They didn't wait long. Half an hour later they picked up James Jordan at his home on Pattison. They asked him how come he hadn't gone to his office. He said he'd worked late the night before and wasn't feeling too well. They asked him why he had killed his partner. He stared at them and told them he didn't understand what they were talking about. They took him downtown and booked him for murder.

Hofert's widow lived in a ranch house just across the city line. The two kids were in school when Traynor and Grey got there. Mrs. Hofert was worried when she saw them. They told her as gently as you can tell a wife that someone has murdered her husband. A doctor came from down the block to give her a hypo, and an hour later she said she was ready to talk to them. She wasn't, really, but they didn't want to wait. It was a neat case, the kind you wrap up fast.

"That poor, poor man," she said. "He worked so hard. He worked and he worried and he wanted so very much to get ahead. He put his blood into that business. And now he's gone and nothing's left."

Grey started to light a cigarette, then changed his mind. Mrs. Hofert was crying quietly. Nobody said anything for a few minutes.

"I hardly ever saw him," she said. "Isn't

that something? I hardly ever got to see him and now he's gone. So much work. And it wasn't for himself, nothing was ever for himself. He wanted money for us. For me, for the boys. As if we needed it. All we ever needed was him and now he's gone —"

Later, calmer, she said, "And he didn't leave us a thing. He was a gambler, Dave was. Oh, not cards or dice — not that kind of a gambler — stocks, the stock market. He made a decent living but that wasn't enough because he wanted more, he wanted a lot of money, and he tried to make it fast. He wanted to take risks in the business, to borrow money and expand. He had dreams. He always complained that Jim wouldn't let him build the business, that Jim was too conservative. So he took chances in the market, and at first he did all right, I think. He told me he did, and then everything fell in for him and. . . . Oh, I don't understand anything!"

On the way downtown, Grey said, "Try it this way. Hofert went into Jordan's office last night. They'd been arguing off and on all day. He wanted to draw more money out of the company, or to borrow and expand, or anything. He was in terrible shape financially. The house was mortgaged to the roof. He'd already cashed in his personal insurance policies. He was in trouble, desperate. They argued again. Maybe he even threw a punch. The office was a mess, they could have been fighting a little. Then Jordan took out a gun and shot him. Right?"

"That's the only way it plays."

"Let's talk to Jordan again," Grey said.

They double-teamed Jordan and kept questions looping in at him until he had admitted almost everything. He admitted ownership of the gun, said he had bought it two years ago and had kept it in his desk ever since. He admitted quarreling with Hofert that afternoon and said that Hofert kept provoking arguments. He confirmed the secretary's statement about the time of her departure and the fact that he and Hofert had stayed alone in the office.

He denied killing Hofert.

"Why? Why would I do it?"

"You were fighting with him. Maybe he swung at you —"

"Dave? You're crazy. Why should he hit me?"

"Maybe he hated you. Maybe you hated each other. You shot him, panicked and left. You couldn't face his corpse in the morning and you stayed home in bed until we came here for you."

"But I —"

"You stood to gain complete control of the business with him dead. All the profits instead of half, and no partner to get in your hair."

"Profits!" Jordan was shouting now. "I have enough! I have plenty!" He caught his breath, slowed down. "I'm a bachelor, I live alone, I save my money. Check my bank account. What do I want with blood money?"

"Hofert was dead weight. He was in hock up to his ears and he was giving you a bad time. You didn't plan on killing him, Jordan. You did it on the spur of the moment. He provoked it. And —"

"I did not kill David Hofert!"

"You admit it's your gun."

"Yes, damn it, it is my gun. I never fired it in my life. I never pointed it at anything. It was in my desk, in case I ever needed it —"

"And last night you needed it."

"No."

"Last night —"

"Last night I finished my work and went home," Jordan said. "I went home, I was tired, I had a headache. Dave stayed in the office. I told him I might not be in the next morning. 'Take it easy,' he said. That was the last thing he said to me. 'Take it easy.' "

Traynor and Grey looked at each other.

"He was alive when I left him."

"Then who killed him, Jordan? Who lured him into *your* office and took *your* gun and shot him in the chest and —"

They kept up the questions, kept hammering away like a properly efficient team. They got nowhere. Jordan never contradicted himself and never made very much sense. They kicked his story apart and he stayed with it anyway. After fifteen more minutes of getting nowhere they took him back to his cell and locked him away. Traynor stopped to stare at him, at the small round face peering out through the bars of the cage. Jordan looked trapped.

Two hours later, Traynor pushed a pile of papers to one side of his desk, eased his chair back and stood up. Grey asked him where he was going. "Out," Traynor told him.

"He said that Jim Jordan was trying to ruin him," Mrs. Hofert said. "I always felt . . . well, Dave felt persecuted sometimes. He had so many big plans that came to nothing. He thought the world was ganging up on him. I never believed that Jim would actually —"

"We think it happened during an argument," Traynor told her. "Jordan got excited, didn't know exactly what he was doing. If he had planned to murder your husband he would have picked a brighter way to do it. But in the heat of an argument things happen in a hurry."

"The heat of an argument." She sat for a long time looking at nothing at all. Then she said, "I believe everything has a pattern, Mr. Traynor. Do you believe that?'

Traynor didn't answer.

"Dave's life — and his death, trying, struggling, working so very hard and getting every bad break there was. Getting bad breaks *because* he tried so hard, because he wasn't prudent about money. And then having everything build to a climax with everything going wrong at once. And the tragic ending, dying at what he could only have thought of as the worst possible moment. You see, all he wanted to do was provide for me and for the boys. He was . . . he was the kind of man who would have thought it a triumph to die well insured." More long silence. "And not even that. A year ago, six months ago, all his policies were paid up. Then, as things went wrong, he cashed the policies to get money to recoup his losses, and lost that, too. And then the final irony of dying without anything to leave us but a legacy of debts. Do you see the pattern, Mr. Traynor?"

"I think so," Traynor said.

He got very busy then. He went to the lawyer he had spoken to earlier, went alone without Grey. He asked the lawyer some questions, went to an insurance man and asked more questions. He called the Haber girl, and with her he went over the few hours prior to Hofert's death. He got the autopsy results, the lab photos, the lab report. He went to the Hofert & Jordan office and stood in the room where Hofert had died, visualizing everything, running it through in his mind.

It was pushing six o'clock. He picked up a phone, called headquarters and got through to Grey. "Don't leave yet," he said. "I'll be right over. Stay put."

"You got something?"

"Yes," he said.

They were in a small cubbyhole office off the main room. Grey sat at a desk. Traynor stood up and did a lot of pacing.

202

"There were no fingerprints on the gun," he said.

"So? Jordan wiped it."

"Why?"

"Why? If you shot somebody, would you leave prints on the gun?"

Traynor walked over to the door, turned, came halfway back. "If I was going to wipe prints off a gun I would also do something about setting up an alibi," he said. "The way we've got it figured, Jordan killed strictly on impulse and reacted like a scared rabbit. He went for his gun, shot Hofert, ran out of the building and went home and stayed there shaking. He didn't sponge up blood, he didn't try to lug Hofert out of his office, didn't do a thing to disguise the killing. He left the gun right there, didn't try any of the tricks a panicky killer might try. But he wiped the prints off the gun."

"He must have been half out of his mind."

"It still doesn't add. There's another way, though, that does."

"Go on."

"Suppose you're Hofert. Now —"

"Why do we always have to suppose I'm the dead one?"

"Shut up," Traynor said. "Suppose you're

David Hofert. You're deep in debt and you can't see your way clear. You look at yourself in the mirror and figure you're a failure. You want money for your wife, security for your kids. But you haven't got a penny, your insurance policies have lapsed, and your whole world is caving in on you. You're frantic."

"I don't —"

"Wait. You've always been a little paranoid. Now you think the whole world is after you and your partner is purposely trying to make things rough for you. You'd like to go and jump off a bridge, but that wouldn't get you anywhere. If you died in an accident, at least your wife and kids would get the hundred grand, the insurance dough which Jordan would turn over to them for your share of the business. Suicide voids that policy. If you kill yourself, they wind up with nothing."

Grey was nodding slowly now.

"But if your partner kills you —"

"What happens then?"

"It's a cute deal," Traynor said. "I went over it twice, with the lawyer and with the agent who wrote the policies. Now, each man is insured for a hundred grand, with that amount payable to the other or the other's heirs. If Jordan kills Hofert, he

204

can't collect. You can't profit legally through the commission of a felony. But the insurance company still has to pay off. If the policy's paid up, and if it's been in force over two years, the company has to make it good. They can't hand the dough to Jordan if he's the killer, but they have to pay somebody."

"Who? I don't understand you."

"The dead man's estate. Hofert's estate. It can't go to Jordan because he's the murderer, and it can't go to Jordan's heirs because he never has legal title to it to pass on. And the company can't keep it, so it can only go to Hofert's wife and kids."

Grey hesitated, then nodded.

"That's the only way Hofert's family ever gets a dime. They get that hundred thousand as insurance on Hofert's life, and they collect another hundred thousand when Jordan goes to the chair for murder, and they have at least half the business as well. All Hofert has to do is find a way to kill himself and make it look like murder, and he sends all that dough to them and has the satisfaction of sticking Jordan with a murder rap. We get the other kind all the time, the murders that are faked to look like suicides. This one went the opposite way."

"How did he do it?"

"The easiest way in the world," Traynor said. "He covered all bets, gave Jordan motive and means and opportunity. He argued with him all day in front of the secretary. He fixed it so that he and Jordan were alone in the office. When Jordan left, he went into Jordan's office and got Jordan's gun. He messed up the place to stage a struggle. He wrapped the gun in a tissue or something to keep his prints off it. He stood in front of the desk, off to the side, and he angled the shot so that it would look as though he'd been shot by somebody behind the desk. He shot himself in a spot that would be sure to kill him but that would leave him a minute or two of life to drop the gun in a convenient spot. That may have been accidental; maybe he aimed for the heart and missed. We'll never know."

"What does the lab say?"

Traynor shrugged. "Maybe and maybe no, as far as they're concerned. It could have been that way — that's as much as they can say, and that's enough. The paraffin test didn't show that Hofert had fired a gun, but it wouldn't, not if he had a tissue or a handkerchief around his hand. There were tissues on the floor, and a lot of papers that he could have used. The bullet trajectory fits well enough. It's something you don't think of right off the bat. The way Hofert had it planned, we weren't supposed to think of it at all. And it almost worked. It almost had Jordan nailed."

"Now what?"

Traynor looked at him. "Now we tell Jordan to relax," he said. "And after the inquest calls it suicide, we let him go — very simple."

"No," Grey said. "I don't believe it."

"Why not?"

"Because it's crazy. You don't kill yourself to stick somebody for murder. It's too damned iffy, anyway. Why did Jordan stay home that morning?"

"He was feeling sick."

"Sure. He didn't come in, he didn't even call his office. You can make a suicide theory out of it. You can also read it as a very clear-cut murder, and that's the way I'd read it. You want to let Jordan off and take a couple hundred thousand away from Hofert's wife. Is that right?"

"Yes." Traynor looked at the floor. "And you want to see Jordan in the chair, for this one."

"That's the way it reads to me."

"Well, I won't go along with that, Phil."

"And I won't buy suicide. You fought this one because it was too simple, and now you've got us stuck with two answers, one easy and one tough, and I like the easy one and you like the tough one. I hope to hell Jordan confesses and makes it easy for us."

"He won't," Traynor said. "He's innocent."

"How sure are you?"

"Positive."

"That's how sure I am he's guilty. What do we do if he doesn't confess, if he sticks to his story and the lab can't cut it any finer for us? What do we do? Toss a coin?"

No one said anything for a few minutes. Traynor looked at his watch. Grey lit a cigarette.

Traynor said, "I don't buy murder."

"I don't buy suicide."

"He won't confess, Phil. And we'll never know. If Jordan goes on trial he'll get off because I'll hand my angle to his lawyer. He'll beat it. But we'll never know, not really. You'll always think he's guilty and I'll always think he isn't, and we'll never know."

"Maybe we ought to toss that coin."

"If we did," Traynor said, "it would stand on end. It's been that kind of a day."

Leo Youngdahl, R.I.P.

Dear Larry,

I'm not sure if there's a story in this or not.

It happened about a year ago, at a time when I was living in New Hope, Pennsylvania, with a man named Evans Wheeler. New Hope is a small town with a reputation as an artists' colony. There is a theater there. At the time Evans was its assistant manager. I was doing some promotional work for the theater, which is how we originally met, and I was also briefly managing a spectacularly unsuccessful art gallery.

One afternoon in the late summer I returned to the apartment we shared. Evans was reading a magazine and drinking a beer. "There's a letter for you on the table," he said. "From your mother."

He must have assumed this from the postmark. The envelope was addressed in my mother's hand, but he wouldn't have recognized it as we never wrote each other. The city where she lives, and where I was born, is only an inexpensive telephone call away from New Hope. (In other respects, of course, it is much further removed.) My mother and I would speak once or twice a week over the phone.

I remember taking my time opening the envelope. There was a single sheet of blank typing paper inside, folded to enclose a small newspaper clipping. This was an obituary notice, and I read it through twice without having the vaguest idea why it had been sent to me. I even turned it over but the reverse held nothing but a portion of a department store ad. I turned the clipping for a third look and the name, "Youngdahl, Leo," suddenly registered, and I gave a shrill yelp of laughter that ended as abruptly as it had begun.

Evans said, "What's so funny?"

"Leo Youngdahl died."

"I didn't even know he was sick."

I started to laugh again. I really couldn't help it.

"All right, give. Who the hell is Leo Youngdahl? And why is his death so hysterical?"

"It's not really funny. And I don't know

exactly who he is. Was. He was a man, he lived in Bethel. As far as I know, I only met him once. That was six years ago at my father's funeral."

"Oh, that explains it."

"Pardon?"

"I never felt more like a straight man in my life. 'You say you met him at your father's funeral, Gracie?' "

"There's really nothing to it," I said. "It's a sort of a family joke. It would take forever to explain and it wouldn't be funny to anyone else."

"Try me."

"It really wouldn't be funny."

"Oh, for Christ's sake," he said. "You're really too much, you know that?"

"I just meant —"

"I think I'll get out of the house for a while."

"Hey, you're really steamed."

"Not exactly that."

"Come on, sit down. I'll get you another beer. Or would you rather have some Scotch, because I think I will."

"All right."

I made him a drink and got him back in his chair. Then I said, "I honestly don't think this is something you want to hear, but God knows it's nothing to start a fight over. It was just an incident, or rather a couple of incidents. It must have been ten years ago. I was home from school for I think it was Christmas —"

"You said six years ago, and at your father's funeral."

"I was starting at the beginning."

"That's supposed to be the best place."

"Yes, so I've been told. Are you sure you really want to hear this?"

"I'm positive I want to hear it. I won't interrupt."

"Well, it was nine or ten years ago, and it was definitely Christmas vacation. We were all over at Uncle Ed and Aunt Min's house. The whole family, on my mother's side, that is. A couple sets of aunts and uncles and the various children, and my grandmother. It wasn't Christmas dinner but a family dinner during that particular week."

"I get the picture."

"Well, as usual there were three or four separate conversations going on, and occasionally one of them would get prominent and the others would merge with it, the way conversations seem to go at family dinners."

"I've been to family dinners."

"And I don't know who brought it up,

or in what connection, but at some point or other the name Leo Youngdahl was mentioned."

"And everybody broke up."

"No, everybody did not break up, damn it. Suddenly I'm the straight man and I'm beginning to see why you objected to the role. If you don't want to hear this —"

"I'm sorry. The name Leo Youngdahl came up."

"And my father said, 'Wait a minute, I think he's dead.'"

"But he wasn't?"

"My father said he was dead, and somebody else said they were sure he was alive, and in no time at all this was the main subject of conversation at the table. As you can see, nobody knew Mr. Youngdahl terribly well, not enough to say with real certainty whether he was alive or dead. It seems ridiculous now, but there was quite a debate on the subject, and then my cousin Jeremy stood up and said there was obviously only one way to settle it. I believe you met Jeremy."

"The family faggot? No, I never met him, although you keep thinking I did. I've heard enough about him, but no, I never met him."

"Well, he's gay, but that hardly enters

into it. When this happened he was in high school, and if he was gay then nobody knew it at the time. I don't think Jeremy knew it at the time."

"I'm sure he had fun finding out."

"He didn't have any gay mannerisms then. Not that he does now, in the sense of being effeminate, but he can come on a little nellie now and then. I suppose that's a learned attitude, wouldn't you think?"

"I'm sure I wouldn't know, sweetie."

"What he did have, even as a kid, was a very arch sense of humor. There's a Dutch expression, *kochloffel,* which means cooking spoon, in the sense of someone who's always stirring things up. Jeremy was a *kochloffel.* I forget who it was who used to call him that."

"I'm not sure it matters."

"I'm sure it doesn't. Anyway, Jeremy the *kochloffel* went over to the phone and got out the phone book and proceeded to look up Leo Youngdahl in the listings, and announced that he was listed. Of course the faction who said he was dead, including my father, started to say that a listing didn't prove anything, that he could have died since the book came out, or that his wife might have kept the listing active under his name, which was evidently common practice. But Jeremy didn't even wait out the objections, he just started dialing, and when someone answered he said, 'Is Leo Youngdahl there?' And whoever it was said that he was indeed there, and asked who was calling, and Jeremy said, 'Oh, it doesn't matter, I was just checking, and please give Leo my best wishes.' Then he hung up, and everybody laughed and made various speculations as to the reaction that exchange must have caused at the Youngdahl household, and there the matter stood, because the subject was settled and Leo Youngdahl was alive and well."

Evans looked at me and asked if that was the whole story, and how my father's funeral entered into it.

I said, "No, it's not the whole story. I'm going to have another drink. Do you want one?"

He didn't. I made myself one and came back into the room. "My father's funeral," I said. "I don't want to go into all of it now, but it was a very bad time for me. I'm sure it usually is. In this case there were complicating factors, including the fact that I was away from home when he died. It happened suddenly and I felt guilty about not being there. What happened was he had a heart attack and died about fifteen hours later, and I was in New York and was spending the night with a man and they couldn't reach me by phone and —"

"Look, why don't you sit down."

"No, I'd rather stand. Let's just say I was guilty and let it go at that. *Feeling* guilty. I wish you would stop it with those wise Freudian nods."

"Oh, for God's sake."

"I'm sorry. Where was I? Another thing, it was my first real experience with death. Both of my grandfathers had died when I was too young to understand what was going on. This was the first death I related to personally as an adult.

"The point of this is that we were all at the funeral parlor the day before the funeral — actually it was the night before — and there was this endless stream of people paying condolence calls. My mother and brother and I had to sit there forever while half the town came up to take our hands and tell us how sorry they were and what a wonderful man my father was. I didn't recognize more than half of them. Bethel's not that large, but my father was a rather prominent man —"

"So you've told me."

"You're a son of a bitch. Have I told you that?"

"Hey!"

"Oh, I'm sorry. But just let me get this over with. Finally one of these strangers took my mother's hand and said, 'Edna, I'm terribly sorry,' or whatever the hell he said, and then he turned his head toward me — I was sitting next to her between her and Gordon — and said, 'I don't think you know me, my name is Leo Youngdahl,' and I cracked up completely."

"You cried? Yes, I can see that, hearing the name and all —"

"No, no, no! You're missing the whole point. I cracked up, I *laughed!*"

"Oh."

"It was such incredible comic relief. The only thing on earth the name Leo Youngdahl meant to me was Jeremy phoning to find out if he was alive or dead, and now meeting him for the first time and at my father's funeral. I have never laughed so uncontrollably in my life."

"What did he do?"

"That's just it. *He never knew I was laughing.* Nobody ever knew, because my mother did the most positively bril-

217

liant thing anybody ever did in their lives. *She* knew I was laughing, and she knew why, but without the slightest hesitation she put her arm around me and drew me down and said, 'Don't cry, baby, don't cry, it's all right,' and I finally got hold of myself enough to turn off the laughter and turn it into the falsest tears I've ever shed, and by the time I picked my face up Leo Youngdahl was gone and I was able to handle myself. I went downstairs and washed my face and settled myself down, and after that I was all right."

I lit a cigarette, and Evans said something or other, but I wasn't done yet. That might have been the end of the story. But I sometimes have difficulty determining where to end a story.

"Later that night the parade ended and we went home. Mother and Gordon and I had coffee, and neither of us mentioned the incident in front of Gordon. I don't know why. I told him the next day and he couldn't get over how it had happened right next to him and he had missed it, and we both went on and on about how incredibly poised she had been. I don't know how you develop that kind of social grace under pressure.

"After Gordon went to bed, I thanked her for covering for me and we talked about the whole thing and laughed about it. Then she said, 'You know, that's just the kind of thing your Dad would have loved. He would have loved it.' And then her face changed and she said, 'And I can never tell him about it, oh God, I can never tell him anything again,' and *she* cried. We both cried, and just remembering it —"

"Come here, baby."

"No. The last time I talked to him was three days before he died. Over the phone, and we quarreled. I don't remember what about. Oh, I *do* remember. It doesn't matter."

"Of course not."

"We quarreled, and then they tried to reach me to tell me he was dying, and they couldn't and then he was dead and there were all those things I couldn't tell him. And now Leo Youngdahl is dead. I can't even remember what he looked like."

"Come on, let's get out of here. Let's go over to Sully's and I'll buy you a drink."

"No, you go."

"I'll stay with you."

"No, *you* go. I want a little time alone. I'm a mess. I'll meet you over there in a little while. You said Sully's?"

"Sure."

And so that's the story, if indeed it is a story. I thought about sending a contribution to the American Cancer Society in Leo Youngdahl's memory. I never did. I often conceive gestures of that sort but rarely carry them out.

There's nothing more to it, except to say that within two weeks of that conversation Evans Wheeler packed his things and moved out. There is no earthly way to attribute his departure to that particular conversation. Nor is there any earthly way I can be convinced that the two events are unrelated.

I still have Leo Youngdahl's obituary notice around somewhere. At least I think I do. I certainly don't remember ever throwing it away.

As always,
Jill

The Books
Always Balance

The first envelope arrived on a Tuesday. This marked it as slightly atypical from the start, as Myron Hettinger received very little mail at his office on Tuesdays. Letters mailed on Fridays arrived Monday morning, and letters mailed on Monday, unless dispatched rather early in the day, did not arrive until Wednesday, or at the earliest on Tuesday afternoon. This envelope, though, arrived Tuesday morning. John Palmer brought it into Myron Hettinger's office a few minutes past ten, along with the other mail. Like the other envelopes, it was unopened. Only Myron Hettinger opened Myron Hettinger's mail.

The rest of the mail, by and large, consisted of advertisements and solicitations of one sort or another. Myron Hettinger opened them in turn, studied them very briefly, tore them once in half and threw them into the wastebasket. When he came to this particular envelope, however, he paused momentarily.

He studied it. It bore his address. The address had been typed in a rather ordinary typeface. It bore, too, a Sunday evening postmark. It bore a four-cent stamp commemorating the one hundred fiftieth anniversary of the founding of a land grant college in the Midwest. It did not bear a return address or any other hint as to who had sent it or what might be contained therein.

Myron Hettinger opened the envelope. There was no letter inside. There was instead a photograph of two partially clad persons. One of them was a man who looked to be in his early fifties, balding, perhaps fifteen pounds overweight, with a narrow nose and rather thin lips. The man was with a woman who looked to be in her middle twenties, blonde, small-boned, smiling, and extraordinarily attractive. The man was Myron Hettinger, and the woman was Sheila Bix.

For somewhere between fifteen and thirty seconds, Myron Hettinger looked at the picture. Then he placed it upon the top of his desk and walked to the door of his office, which he locked. Then he returned to his desk, sat down in his straight-backed chair, and made sure that the envelope contained nothing but the photograph. After assuring himself of this, he tore the photograph twice in half, did as much with the envelope, placed the various scraps of paper and film in his ashtray, and set them aflame.

A less stable man might have ripped photo and envelope into an inestimable number of shreds, scattered the shreds to four or more winds, and crouched in mute terror behind his heavy desk. Myron Hettinger was stable. The photograph was not a threat but merely the promise of a threat, a portent of probable fumenace. Fear could wait until the threat itself came to the fore.

A more whimsical man might have pasted the photograph in his scrapbook, or might have saved it as a memory piece. Myron Hettinger was not whimsical; he had no scrapbook and kept no memorabilia.

The fire in the ashtray had a foul odor. After it ceased to burn, Myron Hettinger turned on the air conditioner.

The second envelope arrived two days later in Thursday morning's mail. Myron Hettinger had been expecting it, with neither bright anticipation nor with any real fear. He found it among a heavy stack of letters. The envelope was the same as the first. The address was the same, the typeface appeared to be the same, and the stamp, too, was identical with the stamp on the first envelope. The postmark was different, which was not surprising.

This envelope contained no photograph. Instead it contained an ordinary sheet of cheap stationery on which someone had typed the following message:

> Get one thousand dollars in ten and twenty dollar bills. Put them in a package and put the package in a locker in the Times Square station of the IRT. Put the key in an envelope and leave it at the desk of the Slocum Hotel addressed to Mr. Jordan. Do all this today or a photo will be sent to your wife. Do not go to the police. Do not hire a detective. Do not do anything stupid.

The final three sentences of the unsigned letter were quite unnecessary. Myron Hettinger had no intention of going to the police, or of engaging the services of a detective. Nor did he intend to do anything stupid.

224

After letter and envelope had been burned, after the air conditioner had cleared the small room of its odor, Myron Hettinger stood at his window, looking out at East Forty-third Street and thinking. The letter bothered him considerably more than the photograph had bothered him. It was a threat. It might conceivably intrude upon the balanced perfection of his life. This he couldn't tolerate.

Until the letter had arrived, Myron Hettinger's life had indeed been perfect. His work was perfect, to begin with. He was a certified public accountant, self-employed, and he earned a considerable amount of money every year by helping various persons and firms pay somewhat less in the way of taxes than they might have paid without his services. His marriage, too, was perfect. His wife, Eleanor, was two years his junior, kept his home as he wanted it kept, cooked perfect meals, kept him company when he wished her company, let him alone when he wished to be alone, kept her slightly prominent nose out of his private affairs and was the beneficiary of a trust fund which paid her in the neighborhood of twenty-five thousand dollars per year.

Finally, to complete this picture of perfection, Myron Hettinger had a perfect mistress. This woman, of course, was the woman pictured in the unpleasant photograph. Her name was Sheila Bix. She provided comfort, both physical and emotional, she was the essence of discretion, and her demands were minimal — rent for her apartment, a small sum for incidentals, and an occasional bonus for clothing.

A perfect career, a perfect wife, a perfect mistress. This blackmailer, this *Mr. Jordan,* now threatened all three components of Myron Hettinger's perfect life. If the damnable photograph got into Mrs. Hettinger's hands, she would divorce him. He was very certain of this. If the divorce were scandalous, as it well might be, his business would suffer. And if all of this happened, it was quite likely that, for one reason or another, he would wind up losing Sheila Bix as well.

Myron Hettinger closed his eyes and drummed his fingers upon his desk top. He did not want to hurt his business, did not want to lose wife or mistress. His business satisfied him, as did Eleanor and Sheila. He did not *love* either Eleanor or Sheila, not any more than he *loved* his business. Love, after all, is an imperfect emotion. So is hate. Myron Hettinger did not hate this

Mr. Jordan, much as he would have enjoyed seeing the man dead.

But what could he do?

There was, of course, one thing and only one thing that he could do. At noon he left his office, went to his bank, withdrew one thousand dollars in tens and twenties, packed them neatly in a cigar box, and deposited the box in a locker in the Times Square station of the IRT. He tucked the locker key into an envelope, addressed the envelope to the annoying Mr. Jordan, left the envelope at the desk of the Slocum Hotel, and returned to his office without eating lunch. Later in the day, perhaps because of Mr. Jordan or perhaps because of the missed meal, Myron Hettinger had a rather severe case of heartburn. He took bicarbonate of soda.

The third envelope arrived a week to the day after the second. Thereafter, for four weeks, Myron Hettinger received a similar envelope every Thursday morning. The letters within varied only slightly. Each letter asked for a thousand dollars. Each letter directed that he go through the rather complicated business of putting money in locker and leaving locker key at hotel desk. The letters differed each from the other only as to the designated hotel.

Three times Myron Hettinger followed the instructions to the letter. Three times he went to his bank, then to the subway station, then to the appointed hotel, and finally back to his office. Each time he missed lunch, and each time, probably as a direct result, he had heartburn. Each time he remedied it with bicarbonate of soda.

Things were becoming routine.

Routine in and of itself was not unpleasant. Myron Hettinger preferred order. He even devoted a specific page of his personal books to his account with the intrusive Mr. Jordan, listing each thousand-dollar payment the day it was paid. There were two reasons for this. First of all, Myron Hettinger never let an expenditure go unrecorded. His books were always in order and they always balanced. And secondly, there was somewhere in the back of his mind the faint hope that these payments to Mr. Jordan could at least be deducted from his income taxes.

Aside from his Thursday ventures, Myron Hettinger's life stayed pretty much as it had been. He did his work properly, spent two evenings a week with Sheila Bix, and spent five evenings a week with his wife.

He did not mention the blackmail to his wife, of course. Not even an idiot could have done this. Nor did he mention it to Sheila Bix. It was Myron Hettinger's firm conviction that personal matters were best discussed with no one. He knew, and Mr. Jordan knew, and that already was too much. He had no intention of enlarging this circle of knowledgeable persons if he could possibly avoid it.

When the sixth of these letters arrived — the seventh envelope in all from Mr. Jordan — Myron Hettinger locked his office door, burned the letter, and sat at his desk in deep thought. He did not move from his chair for almost a full hour. He did not fidget with desk-top gadgets. He did not doodle.

He thought.

This routine, he realized, could not possibly continue. While he might conceivably resign himself to suffering once a week from heartburn, he could not resign himself to the needless expenditure of one thousand dollars per week. One thousand dollars was not a tremendous amount of money to Myron Hettinger. Fifty-two thousand dollars was, and one did not need the mind of a certified public accountant to determine that weekly payments of one thousand dollars would run into precisely such a sum yearly. The payments, then, had to stop.

This could be accomplished in one of two ways. The blackmailer could be allowed to send his wretched photograph to Myron Hettinger's perfect wife, or he could be caused to stop his blackmailing. The first possibility seemed dreadful in its implications, as it had seemed before. The second seemed impossible.

He could, of course, appeal to his blackmailer's nobler instincts by including a plaintive letter with his payments. Yet this seemed potentially useless. Having no nobler instincts of his own, Myron Hettinger was understandably unwilling to attribute such instincts to the faceless Mr. Jordan.

What else?

Well, he could always kill Mr. Jordan.

This seemed to be the only solution, the only way to check this impossible outflow of cash. It also seemed rather difficult to bring off. It is hard to kill a man without knowing who he is, and Myron Hettinger had no way of finding out more about the impertinent Mr. Jordan. He could not lurk at the appointed hotel; Mr. Jordan, knowing him, could simply wait him out before putting in an appearance. Nor could he lurk near the subway locker, for the same reason.

And how on earth could you kill a man without either knowing him or meeting him?

Myron Hettinger's mind leaped back to an earlier thought, the thought of appealing to the man's nobler instincts through a letter. Then daylight dawned. He smiled the smile of a man who had solved a difficult problem through the application of sure and perfect reasoning.

That day, Myron Hettinger left his office at noon. He did not go to his bank, however. Instead he went to several places, among them a chemical supply house, a five-and-dime and several drugstores. He was careful not to buy more than one item at any one place. We need not concern ourselves with the precise nature of his purchases. He was buying the ingredients for a bomb, and there is no point in telling the general public how to make bombs.

He made his bomb in the stall of a public lavatory, using as its container the same sort of cigar box in which he normally placed one thousand dollars in ten and twenty dollar bills. The principle of the bomb was simplicity itself. The working ingredient was nitroglycerine, a happily volatile substance which would explode upon the least provocation. A series of devices so arranged things that, were the cover of the cigar box to be lifted, enough hell would be raised to raise additional hell in the form of an explosion. If the box were not opened, but were dropped or banged, a similar explosion would occur. This last provision existed in the event that Mr. Jordan might suspect a bomb at the last moment and might drop the thing and run off. It also existed because Myron Hettinger could not avoid it. If you drop nitroglycerine, it explodes.

Once the bomb was made, Myron Hettinger did just what he always did. He went to the Times Square IRT station and deposited the bomb very gently in a locker. He took the key, inserted it in an envelope on which he had inscribed Mr. Jordan's name, and left the envelope at the desk of the Blackmore Hotel. Then he returned to his office. He was twenty minutes late this time.

He had difficulty keeping his mind on his work that afternoon. He managed to list the various expenses he had incurred in making the bomb on the sheet devoted to payments made to Mr. Jordan, and he smiled at the thought that he would be able to mark the account closed by morning. But he had trouble doing much else that day. Instead he sat and thought about the beauty of his solution.

The bomb would not fail. There was enough nitroglycerine in the cigar box to atomize not only Mr. Jordan but virtually anything within twenty yards of him, so the blackmailer could hardly hope to escape. There was the possibility — indeed, one might say the probability — that a great many persons other than Mr. Jordan might die. If the man was fool enough to open his parcel in the subway station, or if he was clumsy enough to drop it there, the carnage would be dreadful. If he took it home with him and opened it in the privacy of his own room or apartment, considerably less death and destruction seemed likely to occur.

But Myron Hettinger could not have cared less about how many persons Mr. Jordan carried with him to his grave. Men or women or children, he was sure he could remain totally unconcerned about their untimely deaths. If Mr. Jordan died, Myron Hettinger would survive. It was that simple.

At five o'clock, a great deal of work undone, Myron Hettinger got to his feet. He left his office and stood for a moment on the sidewalk, breathing stuffy air and considering his situation. He did not want to go home now, he decided. He had done something magnificent, he had solved an unsolvable problem, and he felt a need to celebrate.

An evening with Eleanor, while certainly comfortable, did not impress him as much of a celebration. An evening with Sheila Bix seemed far more along the lines of what he wanted. Yet he hated to break established routine. On Mondays and on Fridays he went to Sheila Bix's apartment. All other nights he went directly home.

Still, he had already broken one routine that day, the unhappy routine of payment. And why not do in another routine, if just for one night?

He called his wife from a pay phone. "I'll be staying in town for several hours," he said. "I didn't have a chance to call you earlier."

"You usually come home on Thursdays," she said.

"I know. Something's come up."

His wife did not question him, nor did she ask just what it was that had come up. She was the perfect wife. She told him that

234

she loved him, which was quite probably true, and he told her that he loved her, which was most assuredly false. Then he replaced the receiver and stepped to the curb to hail a taxi. He told the driver to take him to an apartment building on West Seventy-third Street just a few doors from Central Park.

The building was an unassuming one, a remodeled brownstone with four apartments to the floor. Sheila's apartment, on the third floor, rented for only one hundred twenty dollars per month, a very modest rental for what the tabloids persist in referring to as a love nest. This economy pleased him, but then it was what one would expect from the perfect mistress.

There was no elevator. Myron Hettinger climbed two flights of stairs and stood slightly but not terribly out of breath in front of Sheila Bix's door. He knocked on the door and waited. The door was not answered. He rang the bell, something he rarely did. The door was still not answered.

Had this happened on a Monday or on a Friday, Myron Hettinger might have been understandably piqued. It had never happened on a Monday or on a Friday. Now, though, he was not annoyed. Since Sheila

Bix had no way of knowing that he was coming, he could hardly expect her to be present.

He had a key, of course. When a man has the perfect mistress, or even an imperfect one, he owns a key to the apartment for which he pays the rent. He used this key, opened the door and closed it behind him. He found a bottle of scotch and poured himself the drink which Sheila Bix poured for him every Monday and every Friday. He sat in a comfortable chair and sipped the drink, waiting for the arrival of Sheila Bix and dwelling both on the pleasant time he would have after she arrived and on the deep satisfaction to be derived from the death of the unfortunate Mr. Jordan.

It was twenty minutes to six when Myron Hettinger entered the comfortable, if inexpensive apartment, and poured himself a drink. It was twenty minutes after six when he heard footsteps on the stairs and then heard a key being fitted into a lock. He opened his mouth to let out a hello, then stopped. He would say nothing, he decided. And she would be surprised.

This happened.

The door opened. Sheila Bix, a blonde vision of loveliness, tripped merrily into the room with shining eyes and the lightest of feet. Her arms were extended somewhat oddly. This was understandable, for she was balancing a parcel upon her pretty head much in the manner of an apprentice model balancing a book as part of a lesson in poise.

It took precisely as long for Myron Hettinger to recognize the box upon her head as it took for Sheila Bix to recognize Myron Hettinger. Both reacted nicely. Myron Hettinger put two and two together with speed that made him a credit to his profession. Sheila Bix performed a similar feat, although she came up with a somewhat less perfect answer.

Myron Hettinger did several things. He tried to get out of the room. He tried to make the box stay where it was, poised precariously upon that pretty and treacherous head. And, finally, he made a desperate lunge to catch the box before it reached the floor, once Sheila Bix had done the inevitable, recoiling in horror and spilling the box from head through air.

His lunge was a good one. He left his chair in a single motion. His hands reached out, groping for the falling cigar box.

There was a very loud noise, but Myron Hettinger only heard the beginnings of it.

Hot Eyes, Cold Eyes

Some days were easy. She would go to work and return home without once feeling the invasion of men's eyes. She might take her lunch and eat it in the park. She might stop on the way home at the library for a book, at the deli for a barbequed chicken, at the cleaner's, at the drugstore. On those days she could move coolly and crisply through space and time, untouched by the stares of men.

Doubtless they looked at her on those days, as on the more difficult days. She was the sort men looked at, and she had learned that early on — when her legs first began to lengthen and take shape, when her breasts began to bud. Later, as the legs grew longer and the breasts fuller, and as her face lost its youthful plumpness and was sculpted by time into beauty, the stares increased. She was attractive, she was beautiful, she was — curious phrase — easy on the eyes. So men looked at her, and on the easy days she didn't seem to notice, didn't let their rude stares penetrate the invisible shield that guarded her.

But this was not one of those days.

It started in the morning. She was waiting for the bus when she first felt the heat of a man's eyes upon her. At first she willed herself to ignore the feeling, wished the bus would come and whisk her away from it, but the bus did not come and she could not ignore what she felt and, inevitably, she turned from the street to look at the source of the feeling.

There was a man leaning against a red brick building not twenty yards from her. He was perhaps thirty-five, unshaven, and his clothes looked as though he'd slept in them. When she turned to glance at him his lips curled lightly, and his eyes, red-rimmed and glassy, moved first to her face, then drifted insolently the length of her body. She could feel their heat; it leaped from the eyes to her breasts and loins like an electric charge bridging a gap.

He placed his hand deliberately upon his crotch and rubbed himself. His smile widened.

She turned from him, drew a breath, let it out, wished the bus would come. Even now, with her back to him, she could feel the embrace of his eyes. They were like hot hands upon her buttocks and the backs of her thighs.

The bus came, neither early nor late, and she mounted the steps and dropped her fare in the box. The usual driver, a middle-aged fatherly type, gave her his usual smile and wished her the usual good morning. His eyes were an innocent watery blue behind thick-lensed spectacles.

Was it only her imagination that his eyes swept her body all the while? But she could feel them on her breasts, could feel too her own nipples hardening in response to their palpable touch.

She walked the length of the aisle to the first available seat. Male eyes tracked her every step of the way.

The day went on like that. This did not surprise her, although she had hoped it would be otherwise, had prayed during the bus ride that eyes would cease to bother her when she left the bus. She had learned, though, that once a day began in this fashion its pattern was set, unchangeable.

Was it something she did? Did she invite their hungry stares? She certainly didn't do anything with the intention of provoking male lust. Her dress was conservative enough, her makeup subtle and unremarkable. Did she swing her hips when she walked? Did she wet her lips and pout like a sullen sexpot? She was positive she did nothing of the sort, and it often seemed to her that she could cloak herself in a nun's habit and the results would be the same. Men's eyes would lift the black skirts and strip away the veil.

At the office building where she worked, the elevator starter glanced at her legs, then favored her with a knowing, wet-lipped smile. One of the office boys, a rabbity youth with unfortunate skin, stared at her breasts, then flushed scarlet when she caught him at it. Two older men gazed at her from the water cooler. One leaned over to murmur something to the other. They both chuckled and went on looking at her.

She went to her desk and tried to concentrate on her work. It was difficult, because intermittently she felt eyes brushing her body, moving across her like searchlight beams scanning the yard in a prison movie. There were moments when she wanted to scream, moments when she wanted to spin around in her chair and hurl something. But she remained in control of herself and did none of these things. She had survived days of this sort often enough in the past. She would survive this one as well.

The weather was good, but today she spent her lunch hour at her desk rather than risk the park. Several times during the afternoon the sensation of being watched was unbearable and she retreated to the ladies room. She endured the final hours a minute at a time, and finally it was five o'clock and she straightened her desk and left.

The descent on the elevator was unbearable. She bore it. The bus ride home, the walk from the bus stop to her apartment building, were unendurable. She endured them.

In her apartment, with the door locked and bolted, she stripped off her clothes and hurled them into a corner of the room as if they were unclean, as if the day had irrevocably soiled them. She stayed a long while under the shower, washed her hair, blow-dried it, then returned to her bedroom and stood nude before the full-length mirror on the closet door. She studied herself at some length, and intermittently her hands would move to cup a breast or trace the swell of a thigh, not to arouse but to assess, to chart the dimensions of her physical self.

And now? A meal alone? A few hours with a book? A lazy night in front of the television set?

She closed her eyes, and at once she felt other eyes upon her, felt them as she had been feeling them all day. She knew that she was alone, that now no one was watching her, but this knowledge did nothing to dispel the feeling.

She sighed.

She would not, could not, stay home tonight.

When she left the building, stepping out into the cool of dusk, her appearance was very different. Her tawny hair, which she'd worn pinned up earlier, hung free. Her makeup was overdone, with an excess of mascara and a deep blush of rouge in the hollows of her cheeks. During the day she'd worn no scent beyond a touch of Jean Naté applied after her morning shower; now she'd dashed on an abundance of the perfume she wore only on nights like this one, a strident scent redolent of musk. Her dress was close-fitting and revealing, the skirt slit oriental-fashion high on one thigh, the neckline low to display her decolletage. She strode purposefully on her high-heeled shoes, her buttocks swaying as she walked.

She looked sluttish and she knew it, and gloried in the knowledge. She'd checked the mirror carefully before leaving the apartment and she had liked what she saw. Now, walking down the street with her handbag bouncing against her swinging hip, she could feel the heat building up within her flesh. She could also feel the eyes of the men she passed, men who sat on stoops or loitered in doorways, men walking with purpose who stopped for a glance in her direction. But there was a difference. Now she relished those glances. She fed on the heat in those eyes, and the fire within herself burned hotter in response.

A car slowed. The driver leaned across the seat, called to her. She missed the words but felt the touch of his eyes. A pulse throbbed insistently throughout her entire body now. She was frightened — of her own feelings, of the real dangers she faced — but at the same time she was alive, gloriously alive, as she had not been in far too long. Before she had walked through the day. Now the blood was singing in her veins.

She passed several bars before finding the cocktail lounge she wanted. The interior was dimly lit, the floor soft with carpeting. An overactive air conditioner had lowered the temperature to an almost uncomfortable level. She walked bravely into the room. There were several empty tables along the wall but she passed them by, walking her swivel-hipped walk to the bar and taking a stool at the far end.

The cold air was stimulating against her warm skin. The bartender gave her a minute, then ambled over and leaned against the bar in front of her. He looked at once knowing and disinterested, his heavy lids shading his dark brown eyes and giving them a sleepy look.

"Stinger," she said.

While he was building the drink she drew her handbag into her lap and groped within it for her billfold. She found a ten and set it on top of the bar, then fumbled reflexively within her bag for another moment, checking its contents. The bartender placed the drink on the bar in front of her, took her money, returned with her change. She looked at her drink, then at her reflection in the back bar mirror.

Men were watching her.

She could tell, she could always tell. Their gazes fell on her and warmed the skin where they touched her. Odd, she thought, how the same sensation that had been so disturbing and unpleasant all day long was so desirable and exciting now.

She raised her glass, sipped her drink. The combined flavor of cognac and creme de menthe was at once warm and cold upon her lips and tongue. She swallowed, sipped again.

"That a stinger?"

He was at her elbow and she flicked her eyes in his direction while continuing to face forward. A small man, stockily built, balding, tanned, with a dusting of freckles across his high forehead. He wore a navy blue Quiana shirt open at the throat, and his dark chest hair was beginning to go gray.

"Drink up," he suggested. "Let me buy you another."

She turned now, looked levelly at him. He had small eyes. Their whites showed a tracery of blue veins at their outer corners. The irises were a very dark brown, an unreadable color, and the black pupils, hugely dilated in the bar's dim interior, covered most of the irises.

"I haven't seen you here," he said, hoisting himself onto the seat beside her. "I usually drop in around this time, have a couple, see my friends. Not new in the neighborhood, are you?"

Calculating eyes, she thought. Curiously passionless eyes, for all their cool intensity. Worst of all, they were small eyes, almost beady eyes.

"I don't want company," she said.

"Hey, how do you know you don't like me if you don't give me a chance?" He was grinning, but there was no humor in it. "You don't even know my name, lady. How can you despise a total stranger?"

"Please leave me alone."

"What are you, Greta Garbo?" He got up from his stool, took a half step away from her, gave her a glare and a curled lip. "You want to drink alone," he said, "why don't you just buy a bottle and take it home with you? You can take it to bed and suck on it, honey."

He had ruined the bar for her. She scooped up her change, left her drink unfinished. Two blocks down and one block over she found a second cocktail lounge virtually indistinguishable from the first one. Perhaps the lighting was a little softer, the background music the slightest bit lower in pitch. Again she passed up the row of tables and seated herself at the bar. Again she ordered a stinger and let it rest on the bar top for a moment before taking the first exquisite sip.

Again she felt male eyes upon her. And again they gave her the same hot-cold sensation as the combination of brandy and creme de menthe.

This time when a man approached her she sensed his presence for a long moment before he spoke. She studied him out of the corner of her eye. He was tall and lean, she noted, and there was a self-contained air about him, a sense of considerable self-assurance. She wanted to turn, to look directly into his eyes, but instead she raised her glass to her lips and waited for him to make a move.

"You're a few minutes late," he said.

She turned, looked at him. There was a weathered, raw-boned look to him that matched the western-style clothes he wore — the faded chambray shirt, the skin-tight denim jeans. Without glancing down she knew he'd be wearing boots and that they would be good ones.

"I'm late?"

He nodded. "I've been waiting for you for close to an hour. Of course it wasn't until you walked in that I knew it was you I was waiting for, but one look was all it took. My name's Harley."

She made up a name. He seemed satisfied with it, using it when he asked her if he could buy her a drink.

"I'm not done with this one yet," she said.

"Then why don't you just finish it and come for a walk in the moonlight?"

"Where would we walk?"

"My apartment's just a block and a half from here."

"You don't waste time."

"I told you I waited close to an hour for you. I figure the rest of the evening's too precious to waste."

She had been unwilling to look directly into his eyes but she did so now and she was not disappointed. His eyes were large and well-spaced, blue in color, a light blue of a shade that often struck her as cold and forbidding. But his eyes were anything but cold. On the contrary, they burned with passionate intensity.

She knew, looking into them, that he was a dangerous man. He was strong, he was direct and he was dangerous. She could tell all this in a few seconds, merely by meeting his relentless gaze.

Well, that was fine. Danger, after all, was an inextricable part of it.

She pushed her glass aside, scooped up her change. "I don't really want the rest of this," she said.

"I didn't think you did. I think I know what you really want."

"I think you probably do."

He took her arm, tucked it under his own. They left the lounge, and on the way out she could feel other eyes on her, envious eyes. She drew closer to him and swung her hips so that her buttocks bumped into his lean flank. Her purse slapped against her other hip. Then they were out the door and heading down the street.

She felt excitement mixed with fear, an emotional combination not unlike her stinger. The fear, like the danger, was part of it.

His apartment consisted of two sparsely furnished rooms three flights up from street level. They walked wordlessly to the bedroom and undressed. She laid her clothes across a wooden chair, set her handbag on the floor at the side of the platform bed. She got onto the bed and he joined her and they embraced. He smelled faintly of leather and tobacco and male perspiration, and even with her eyes shut she could see his blue eyes burning in the darkness.

She wasn't surprised when his hands gripped her shoulders and eased her downward on the bed. She had been expecting this and welcomed it. She swung her head, letting her long hair brush across his flat abdomen, and then she moved to accept him. He tangled his fingers in her hair, hurting her in a not unpleasant way. She inhaled his musk as her mouth embraced him, and in her own fashion she matched his strength with strength of her own, teasing, taunting, heightening his passion and then cooling it down just short of culmination. His breathing grew ragged and muscles worked in his legs and abdomen.

At length he let go of her hair. She moved upward on the bed to join him and he rolled her over onto her back and covered her, his mouth seeking hers, his flesh burying itself in her flesh. She locked her thighs around his hips. He pounded at her loins, hammering her, hurting her with the brute force of his masculinity.

How strong he was, and how insistent. Once again she thought what a dangerous man he was, and what a dangerous game she was playing. The thought served only to spur her own passion on, to build her fire higher and hotter.

She felt her body preparing itself for orgasm, felt the urge growing to abandon herself, to lose control utterly. But a portion of herself remained remote, aloof, and she let her arm hang over the side of the bed and reached for her purse, groped within it.

And found the knife.

Now she could relax, now she could give up, now she could surrender to what she felt. She opened her eyes, stared upward. His own eyes were closed as he thrust furiously at her. *Open your eyes,* she urged him silently. *Open them, open them, look at me* —

And it seemed that his eyes did open to meet hers, even as they climaxed together, even as she centered the knife over his back and plunged it unerringly into his heart.

Afterward, in her own apartment, she put his eyes in the box with the others.

With a Smile for the Ending

I had one degree from Trinity, and one was enough, and I'd had enough of Dublin, too. It is a fine city, a perfect city, but there are only certain persons that can live there. An artist will love the town, a priest will bless it, and a clerk will live in it as well as elsewhere. But I had too little of faith and of talent and too much of a hunger for the world to be priest or artist or pen warden. I might have become a drunkard, for Dublin's a right city for a drinking man, but I've no more talent for drinking than for deception — yet another lesson I learned at Trinity, and equally a bargain. (Tell your story, Joseph Cameron Bane would say. Clear your throat and get on with it.)

I had family in Boston. They welcomed me cautiously and pointed me toward New York. A small but pretentious publishing house hired me; they leaned toward foreign editors and needed someone to balance off their flock of Englishmen. Four months was enough, of the job and of the city. A good place for a young man on the way up, but no town at all for a pilgrim.

He advertised for a companion. I answered his ad and half a dozen others, and when he replied I saw his name and took the job at once. I had lived with his books for years: *The Wind at Morning*, *Cabot's House*, *Ruthpen Hallburton*, *Lips That Could Kiss*, others, others. I had loved his words when I was a boy in Ennis, knowing no more than to read what reached me, and I loved them still at Trinity where one was supposed to care only for more fashionable authors. He had written a great many books over a great many years, all of them set in the same small American town. Ten years ago he'd stopped writing and never said why. When I read his name at the bottom of the letter I realized, though it had never occurred to me before, that I had somehow assumed him dead for some years.

We traded letters. I went to his home for an interview, rode the train there and watched the scenery change until I was in the country he had written about. I walked from the railway station carrying both suitcases, having gambled he'd want me to stay. His housekeeper met me at the door.

I stepped inside, feeling as though I'd dreamed the room, the house. The woman took me to him, and I saw that he was older than I'd supposed him, and next saw that he was not. He appeared older because he was dying. "You're Riordan," he said. "How'd you come up? Train?"

"Yes, sir."

"Pete run you up?" I looked blank, I'm sure. He said that Pete was the town's cab driver, and I explained that I'd walked.

"Oh? Could have taken a taxi."

"I like to walk."

"Mmmmm," he said. He offered me a drink. I refused, but he had one. "Why do you want to waste time watching a man die?" he demanded. "Not morbid curiosity, I'm sure. Want me to teach you how to be a writer?"

"No, sir."

"Want to do my biography? I'm dull and out of fashion, but some fool might want to read about me."

"No, I'm not a writer."

"Then why are you here, boy?"

He asked this reasonably, and I thought about the question before I answered it. "I like your books," I said finally.

"You think they're good? Worthwhile? Literature?"

"I just like them."

"What's your favorite?"

"I've never kept score," I answered.

He laughed, happy with the answer, and I was hired.

There was very little to do that could be called work. Now and then there would be a task too heavy for Mrs. Dettweiler, and I'd do that for her. There were occasional errands to run, letters to answer. When the weather turned colder he'd have me make up the fire for him in the living room. When he had a place to go, I'd drive him; this happened less often as time passed, as the disease grew in him.

And so, in terms of the time allotted to various tasks, my job was much as its title implied. I was his companion. I listened when he spoke, talked when he wanted conversation, and was silent when silence was indicated. There would be a time, his doctor told me, when I would have more to do, unless Mr. Bane would permit a nurse. I knew he would not, any more than he'd allow himself to die anywhere but in his home. There would be morphine shots for me to give him, because sooner or later the oral drug would become ineffective. In time he would be confined, first to his home and then to his room and at last to his bed, all a gradual preparation for the ultimate confinement.

"And maybe you ought to watch his drinking," the doctor told me. "He's been hitting it pretty heavy."

This last I tried once and no more. I said something foolish, that he'd had enough, that he ought to take it with a little water; I don't remember the words, only the stupidity of them, viewed in retrospect.

"I did not hire a damned warden," he said. "You wouldn't have thought of this yourself, Tim. Was this Harold Keeton's idea?"

"Well, yes."

"Harold Keeton is an excellent doctor," he said. "But only a doctor, and not a minister. He knows that doctors are supposed to tell their patients to cut down on smoking and drinking, and he plays his part. There is no reason for me to limit my drinking, Tim. There is nothing wrong with my liver or with my kidneys. The only thing wrong with me, Tim, is that I have cancer.

"I have cancer, and I'm dying of it. I intend to die as well as I possibly can. I intend to think and feel and act as I please, and go out with a smile for the ending. I intend, among other things, to drink what

I want when I want it. I do not intend to get drunk, nor do I intend to be entirely sober if I can avoid it. Do you understand?"

"Yes, Mr. Bane."

"Good. Get the chessboard."

For a change, I won a game.

The morning after Rachel Avery was found dead in her bathtub I came downstairs to find him at the breakfast table. He had not slept well, and this showed in his eyes and at the corners of his mouth.

"We'll go into town today," he said.

"It snowed during the night, and you're tired. If you catch cold, and you probably will, you'll be stuck in bed for weeks." This sort of argument he would accept. "Why do you want to go to town, sir?"

"To hear what people say."

"Oh? What do you mean?"

"Because Rachel's husband killed her, Tim. Rachel should never have married Dean Avery. He's a man with the soul of an adding machine, but Rachel was poetry and music. He put her in his house and wanted to own her, but it was never in her to be true, to him or to another. She flew freely and sang magnificently, and he killed her.

"I want to learn just how he did it, and decide what to do about it. Perhaps you'll go to town without me. You notice things well enough. You sense more than I'd guessed you might, as though you know the people."

"You wrote them well."

This amused him. "Never mind," he said. "Make a nuisance of yourself if you have to, but see what you can learn. I have to find out how to manage all of this properly. I know a great deal, but not quite enough."

Before I left I asked him how he could be so sure. He said, "I know the town and the people. I knew Rachel Avery and Dean Avery. I knew her mother very well, and I knew his parents. I knew they should not have married, and that things would go wrong for them, and I am entirely certain that she was killed and that he killed her. Can you understand that?"

"I don't think so," I replied. But I took the car into town, bought a few paperbound books at the drugstore, had an unnecessary haircut at the barber's, went from here to there and back again, and then drove home to tell him what I had learned.

"There was a coroner's inquest this

morning," I said. "Death by drowning induced as a result of electrical shock, accidental in origin. The funeral is tomorrow."

"Go on, Tim."

"Dean Avery was in Harmony Falls yesterday when they finally reached him and told him what had happened. He was completely torn up, they said. He drove to Harmony Falls the day before yesterday and stayed overnight."

"And he was with people all the while?"

"No one said."

"They wouldn't have checked," he said. "No need, not when it's so obviously an accident. You'll go to the funeral tomorrow."

"Why?"

"Because I can't go myself."

"And I'm to study him and study everyone else? Should I take notes?"

He laughed, then chopped off the laughter sharply. "I don't think you'd have to. I didn't mean that you would go in my place solely to observe, Tim, though that's part of it. But I would want to be there because I feel I ought to be there, so you'll be my deputy."

I had no answer to this. He asked me to build up the fire, and I did. I heard the newspaper boy and went for the paper.

The town having no newspaper of its own, the paper he took was from the nearest city, and of course there was nothing in it on Rachel Avery. Usually he read it carefully. Now he skimmed it as if hunting something, then set it aside.

"I didn't think you knew her that well," I said.

"I did and I didn't. There are things I do not understand, Tim; people to whom I've barely spoken, yet whom I seem to know intimately. Knowledge has so many levels."

"You never really stopped writing about Beveridge." This was his fictional name for the town. "You just stopped putting it on paper."

He looked up, surprised, considering the thought with his head cocked like a wren's. "That's far more true than you could possibly know," he said.

He ate a good dinner and seemed to enjoy it. Over coffee I started aimless conversations but he let them die out. Then I said, "Mr. Bane, why can't it be an accident? The radio fell into the tub and shocked her and she drowned."

I thought at first he hadn't heard, or was pretending as much; this last is a special privilege of the old and the ill. Then he said, "Of course, you have to have facts.

What should my intuition mean to you? And it would mean less, I suppose, if I assured you that Rachel Avery could not possibly be the type to play the radio while bathing?"

My face must have showed how much I thought of that. "Very well," he said. "We shall have facts. The water in the tub was running when the body was found. It was running, then, both before and after the radio fell into the tub, which means that Rachel Avery had the radio turned on while the tub was running, which is plainly senseless. She wouldn't be able to hear it well, would she? Also, she was adjusting the dial and knocked it into the tub with her.

"She would not have played the radio at all during her bath — this I simply *know*. She would not have attempted to turn on the radio until her bath was drawn, because no one would. And she would not have tried tuning the set while the water was running because that is sheerly pointless. Now doesn't that begin to make a slight bit of sense to you, Tim?"

They put her into the ground on a cold gray afternoon. I was part of a large crowd at the funeral parlor and a smaller one at the cemetery. There was a minister instead of a priest, and the service was not the one with which I was familiar, yet after a moment all of it ceased to be foreign to me. And then I knew. It was Emily Talstead's funeral from *Cabot's House*, except that Emily's death had justice to it, and even a measure of mercy, and this gray afternoon held neither.

In that funeral parlor I was the deputy of Joseph Cameron Bane. I viewed Rachel's small body and thought that all caskets should be closed, no matter how precise the mortician's art. We should not force ourselves to look upon our dead. I gave small words of comfort to Dean Avery and avoided his eyes while I did so. I sat in a wooden chair while the minister spoke of horrible tragedy and the unknowable wisdom of the Lord, and I was filled with a sense of loss that was complete in itself.

I shared someone's car to the cemetery. At graveside, with a wind blowing that chilled the edge of thought, I let the gloom slip free as a body into an envelope of earth, and I did what I'd come to do; I looked into the face of Dean Avery.

He was a tall man, thick in the shoulders, broad in the forehead, his hair swept straight back without a part, forming upon his head like a crown. I watched his eyes when he did not know that anyone watched him, and I watched the curl of his lip and the way he placed his feet and what he did with his hands. Before long I knew he mourned her not at all, and soon after that I knew the old man was right. He had killed her as sure as the wind blew.

They would have given me a ride back to his house, but I slipped away when the service ended, and spent time walking around, back and forth. By the time I was back at her grave, it had already been filled in. I wondered at the men who do such work, if they feel a thing at all. I turned from her grave and walked back through the town to Bane's house.

I found him in the kitchen with coffee and toast. I sat with him and told him about it, quickly, and he made me go back over all of it in detail so that he could feel he had been there himself. We sat in silence awhile, and then went to the living room. I built up the fire and we sat before it.

"You know now," he said. I nodded, for I did; I'd seen for myself, and knew it and felt it. "Knowing is most of it," he said. "Computers can never replace us, you know. They need facts, information.

What's the term? Data. They need data. But sometimes men can make connections across gaps, without data. You see?"

"Yes."

"So we know." He drank, put down his glass. "But now we have to have our data. First the conclusion, and then backward to the proof."

My eyes asked the question.

"Because it all must round itself out," he said, answering the question without my giving voice to it. "This man killed and seems to have gotten away with it. This cannot be."

"Should we call the police?"

"Of course not. There's nothing to say to them, and no reason they should listen." He closed his eyes briefly, opened them. "We know what he did. We ought to know how, and why. Tell me the men at the funeral, Tim, as many as you remember."

"I don't remember much before the cemetery. I paid them little attention."

"At the cemetery, then. That's the important question, anyway."

I pictured it again in my mind and named the ones I knew. He listened very carefully. "Now there are others who might have been there," he said, "some of whom you may not know, and some you may not remember. Think, now, and tell me if any of these were there."

He named names, five of them, and it was my turn to listen. Two were strangers to me and I could not say if I'd seen them. One I remembered had been there, two others had not.

"Get a pencil and paper," he told me. "Write these names down. Robert Hardesty, Hal Kasper, Roy Teale, Thurman Goodin. Those will do for now."

The first two had been at the funeral, and at the cemetery. The other two had not.

"I don't understand," I said.

"She had a lover, of course. That was why he killed her. Robert Hardesty and Hal Kasper should not have been at the funeral, or at least not at the cemetery. I don't believe they're close to her family or his. Thurman Goodin and Roy Teale should have been at the funeral, at the least, and probably should have been at the cemetery. Now a dead woman's secret love may do what you would not expect him to do. He may stay away from a funeral he would otherwise be expected to attend, for fear of giving himself away, or he might attend a funeral where his presence would not otherwise be required, out of love or respect or no more than morbid yearning. We have four men, two who should have been present and were not, and two who should not have been present but were. No certainty, and nothing you might call data, but I've a feeling one of those four was Rachel Avery's lover."

"And?"

"Find out which one," he said.

"Why would we want to know that?"

"One must know a great many unimportant things in order to know those few things which are important." He poured himself more bourbon and drank some of it off. "Do you read detective stories? They always work with bits and pieces, like a jigsaw puzzle, find out trivia until it all fits together."

"And what might this fit into?"

"A shape. How, why, when."

I wanted to ask more, but he said he was tired and wanted to lie down. He must have been exhausted. He had me help him upstairs, change clothes, and into bed.

I knew Hal Kasper enough to speak to, so it was his shop I started in that night. He had a cigar store near the railroad terminal and sold magazines, paperbound books, candies and stationery. You could place a bet on a horse there, I'd heard. He was thin, with prominent features — large hollow eyes, a long, slim nose, a large mouth with big gray-white teeth in it. Thirty-five or forty, with a childless wife whom I'd never met, I thought him an odd choice for a lover, but I know enough to realize that women did not follow logic's rules when they committed adultery.

He had been at the funeral. Joseph Cameron Bane had found this a little remarkable. He had no family ties on either side with Rachel or Dean Avery. He was below them socially, and not connected through his business. Nor was he an automatic funeral-goer. There were such in the town, I'd been told, as there are in every town; they go to funerals as they turn on a television set or eavesdrop on a conversation, for entertainment and for lack of better to do. But he was not that sort.

"Hi, Irish," he said. "How's the old man?"

I thumbed a magazine. "Asleep," I said.

"Hitting the sauce pretty good lately?"

"I wouldn't say so, no."

"Well, he's got a right." He came out from behind the counter, walked over to me. "Saw you this afternoon. I didn't know you knew her. Or just getting material for that book of yours?"

Everyone assumed I was going to write a novel set in the town, and that this was what had led me to live with Mr. Bane. This would have made as much sense as visiting Denmark in order to rewrite *Hamlet.* I'd stopped denying it. It seemed useless.

"You knew her?" I asked.

"Oh, sure. You know me, Irish. I know everybody. King Farouk, Princess Grace —" He laughed shortly. "Sure, I knew her, a lot better than you'd guess."

I thought I'd learn something, but as I watched his face I saw his large mouth quiver with the beginnings of a leer, and then watched the light die in his eyes and the smile fade from his lips as he remembered that she was dead, cold and in the ground, and not fit to leer over or lust after. He looked ever so slightly ashamed of himself.

"A long time ago," he said, his voice pitched lower now. "Oh, a couple of years. Before she got married, well, she was a pretty wild kid in those days. Not wild like you might think; I mean, she was free, you understand?" He groped with his hands, long-fingered, lean. "She did what she wanted to do. I happened to be there. I was a guy she wanted to be with. Not for too long, but it was honey-sweet while it lasted. This is one fine way to be talking, isn't it? They say she went quick, though; didn't feel anything, but what a stupid way, what a crazy stupid way."

So it was not Hal Kasper who had loved her; not recently, at least. When I told all this to Joseph Cameron Bane he nodded several times and thought for some moments before he spoke.

"Ever widening circles, Tim," he said. "Throw a stone into a still pool and watch the circles spread. Now don't you see her more clearly? You wouldn't call Kasper a sentimental man, or a particularly sensitive man. He's neither of those things. Yet he felt that sense of loss, and that need to pay his last respects. There's purpose in funerals, you know, purpose and value. I used to think they were barbaric. I know better now. He had to talk about her, and had also to be embarrassed by what he'd said. Interesting."

"Why do we have to know all this?"

"Beginning to bother you, Tim?"

"Some."

" 'Because I am involved with mankind,' " he quoted. "You'll learn more tomorrow, I think. Get the chessboard."

I did learn more the next day. I learned

270

first to forget about Roy Teale. I had not recognized his name, but when I found him I saw that he was a man who had been at the funeral, as he might have been expected to be. I also learned, in the barber shop, that he was carrying on a truly passionate love affair, but with his own wife. He sat in a chair and grinned while two of the men ragged him about it.

I left, knowing what I had come to learn; if I'd stayed much longer I'd have had to get another haircut, and I scarcely needed one. I'd taken the car into town that day. It was colder than usual, and the snow was deep. I got into the car and drove to Thurman Goodin's service station. Mr. Bane usually had me fill the car at the station a few blocks to the north, but I did want to see Goodin. He and Robert Hardesty were the only names left on our list. If neither had been the woman's lover, then we were back where we'd started.

A high school boy worked afternoons and evenings for Goodin, but the boy had not come yet, and Thurman Goodin came out to the pump himself. While the tank filled he came over to the side of the car and rested against the door. His face needed shaving. He leaned his long hard body against the car door and said it had been a long time since he'd put any gas into the car.

"Mr. Bane doesn't get out much any more," I said, "and I mostly walk except when the weather's bad."

"Then I'm glad for the bad weather." He lit a cigarette, and inhaled deeply. "Anyway, this buggy usually tanks up over to Kelsey's place. You had better than half a tankful; you could have made it over there without running dry, you know."

I gave him a blank look, then turned it around by saying, "I'm sorry, I didn't hear you. I was thinking about that woman who was killed."

I almost jumped at the sight of his face. A nerve twitched involuntarily, a thing he could not have controlled, but he might have covered up the other telltale signs. His eyes gave him away, and his hands, and the movements of his mouth.

"You mean Mrs. Avery," he said.

His wife was her cousin, Mr. Bane had told me. So he should have been at her funeral, and now should have been calling her Rachel or Rachel Avery. I wanted to get away from him!

"I was at the funeral," I said.

"Funerals," he said. "I got a business to run. Listen, I'll tell you something. Everybody dies. Fast or slow, old or young, it don't make a bit of difference. That's two twenty-seven for the gas."

He took three dollars and went into the station. He came back with the change and I took it from him. My hand shook slightly. I dropped a dime.

"Everybody gets it sooner or later," he said. "Why knock yourself out about it?"

When I told all this to Joseph Cameron Bane he leaned back in his chair with a sparkle in his eyes and the ghost of a smile on his pale lips. "So it's Thurman Goodin," he said. "I knew his father rather well. But I knew everybody's father, Tim, so that's not too important, is it? Tell me what you know."

"Sir?"

"Project, extend, extrapolate. What do you know about Goodin? What did he tell you? Put more pieces into the puzzle, Tim."

I said, "Well, he was her lover, of course. Not for very long, but for some space of time. It was nothing of long standing, and yet some of the glow had worn off."

"Go on, Tim."

"I'd say he made overtures for form's sake and was surprised when she responded. He was excited at the beginning, and then he began to be frightened of it all. Oh, this is silly, I'm making it all up —"

"You're doing fine, boy."

"He seemed glad she was dead. No, I'm putting it badly. He seemed relieved, and guilty about feeling relieved. Now he's safe. She died accidentally, and no one will ever find him out, and he can savor his memories without shivering in the night."

"Yes." He poured bourbon into his glass, emptying the bottle. Soon he would ask me to bring him another. "I agree," he said, and sipped at his whiskey almost daintily.

"Now what do we do?"

"What do you think we do, Tim?"

I thought about this. I said we might check with persons in Harmony Falls and trace Dean Avery's movements there. Or, knowing her lover's name, knowing so much that no one else knew, we might go to the police. We had no evidence, but the police could turn up evidence better than we, and do more with it once they had it.

He looked into the fire. When he did speak, I thought at first that he was talking entirely to himself and not to me at all. "And splash her name all over the earth," he said, "and raise up obscene court trials and filth in the newspapers, and pit lawyers against one another, and either hang him or jail him or free him. Ruin Thurman Goodin's marriage, and ruin Rachel Avery's memory."

"I don't think I understand."

He spun quickly around. His eyes glittered. "Don't you? Tim, Timothy, don't you truthfully understand?" He hesitated, groped for a phrase, then stopped and looked pointedly at his empty glass. I found a fresh bottle in the cupboard, opened it, handed it to him. He poured a drink but did not drink it.

He said, "My books always sold well, you know. But I had a bad press. The small town papers were always kind, but the real critics . . . I was always being charged with sentimentality. They used words like *cloying* and *sugary* and *unrealistic*." I started to say something but he silenced me with an upraised palm. "Please, don't leap to my defense. I'm making a point now, not lamenting a misspent literary youth. Do you know why I stopped writing? I don't think I've ever told anyone. There's never been a reason to tell. I stopped, oh, not because critics were unkind, not because sales were disappointing. I stopped because I discovered that the critics, bless them, were quite right."

"That's not true!"

"But it is, Tim. I never wrote what you could honestly call sentimental slop, but everything always came out right, every book always had a happy ending. I simply *wanted* it to happen that way, I wanted things to work out as they *ought* to work out. Do you see? Oh, I let my people stay in character, that was easy enough. I was a good plot man and could bring that off well enough, weaving intricate webs that led inexorably to the silver lining in every last one of the blacker clouds. The people stayed true but the books became untrue, do you see? Always the happy ending, always the death of truth."

"In *Cabot's House* you had an unhappy ending."

"Not so. In *Cabot's House* I had death for an ending, but a death is not always an occasion for sorrow. Perhaps you're too young to know that, or to feel it within. You'll learn it soon enough. But to return to the point, I saw that my books were false. Good pictures of this town, of some people who lived either in it or in my mind or in both, but false portraits of life. I wrote a book, then, or tried to; an honest one, with loose threads at the end and — what was that precious line of Salinger's?

yes. With a touch of squalor, with love and squalor. I couldn't finish it. I hated it."

He picked up the glass, set it down again, the whiskey untouched. "Do you see? I'm an old man and a fool. I like things to come out right — neat and clean and sugary, wrapped with a bow and a smile for the ending. No police, no trials, no public washing of soiled underwear. I think we are close enough now. I think we have enough of it." He picked up his glass once more and this time drained it. "Get the chessboard."

I got the board. We played, and he won, and my mind spent more of its time with other pawns than the ones we played with now. The image grew on me. I saw them all, Rachel Avery, Dean Avery, Thurman Goodin, carved of wood and all of a shade, either black or white; weighted with lead, and bottomed with a circlet of felt, green felt, and moved around by our hands upon a mirthless board.

"You're afraid of this," he said once. "Why?"

"Meddling, perhaps. Playing the divinity. I don't know, Mr. Bane. Something that feels wrong, that's all."

"Paddy from the peat bog, you've not lost your sense of the miraculous, have you? Wee folk, and gold at the rainbow's end, and things that go bump in the night, and man a stranger and afraid in someone else's world. Don't move there, Tim, your queen's *en prise,* you'll lose her."

We played three games. Then he straightened up abruptly and said, "I don't have the voice to mimic, I've barely any voice at all, and your brogue's too thick for it. Go up to the third floor, would you, and in the room all the way back, there's a closet with an infernal machine on its shelf — a tape recorder. I bought it with the idea that it might make writing simpler. Didn't work at all; I had to see the words in front of me to make them real. I couldn't sit like a fool talking at a machine. But I had fun with the thing. Get it for me, Tim, please."

It was where he'd said, in a box carpeted with dust. I brought it to him, and we went into the kitchen. There was a telephone there. First he tested the recorder, explaining that the tape was old and might not work properly. He turned it on and said, "Now is the time for all good men to come to the aid of the party. The quick brown fox jumped over the lazy dog." Then he winked at me and said, "Just like a typewriter; it's easiest to resort to formula

when you want to say something meaning-
less, Tim. Most people have trouble talking when they have nothing to say. Though
it rarely stops them, does it? Let's see how
this sounds."

He played it back and asked me if the
voice sounded like his own. I assured him
it did. "No one ever hears his own voice
when he speaks," he said. "I didn't realize I
sounded that old. Odd."

He sent me for bourbon. He drank a bit,
then had me get him the phone book. He
looked up a number, read it to himself a
time or two, then turned his attention
again to the recorder.

"We ought to plug it into the telephone,"
he said.

"What for, sir?"

"You'll see. If you connect them lawfully,
they beep every fifteen seconds, so that the
other party knows what you're about,
which hardly seems sensible. Know anything about these gadgets?"

"Nothing," I replied.

He finished the glass of whiskey. "Now
what if I just hold the little microphone to
the phone like this? Between my ear and
the phone, hmm? Some distortion? Oh,
won't matter, won't matter at all."

He dialed a number. The conversation,

as much as I heard of it, went something like this:

"Hello, Mr. Taylor? No, wait a moment, let me see. Is this four-two-one-five? Oh, good. The Avery residence? Is Mrs. Avery in? I don't. . . . Who'm I talking with, please? . . . Good. When do you expect your wife, Mr. Avery? . . . Oh, my! . . . Yes, I see, I see. Why, I'm terribly sorry to hear that, surely. . . . Tragic. Well, I hate to bother you with this, Mr. Avery. Really, it's nothing. . . . Well, I'm Paul Wellings of Wellings and Doyle Travel Agency. . . . Yes, that's right, but I wish. . . . Certainly. Your wife wanted us to book a trip to Puerto Rico for the two of you and. . . . Oh? A surprise, probably. . . . Yes, of course, I'll cancel everything. This is frightful. Yes, and I'm sorry for disturbing you at this —"

There was a little more, but not very much. He rang off, a bitter smile on his pale face, his eyes quite a bit brighter now than usual. "A touch of macabre poetry," he said. "Let him think she was planning to run off with Goodin. He's a cold one, though. So calm, and making me go on and on, however awkward it all was. And now it's all ready on the tape. But how can I manage this way?"

He picked up a phone and called another number. "Jay? This is Cam. Say, I know it's late, but is your tape recorder handy? Well, I'd wanted to do some dictation and mine's burned out a connection or something. Oh, just some work I'm doing. No, I haven't mentioned it, I know. It's something different. If anything ever comes of it, then I'll have something to tell you. But is it all right if I send Tim around for your infernal machine? Good, and you're a prince, Jay."

So he sent me to pick up a second recorder from Jason Falk. When I brought it to him, he positioned the two machines side by side on the table and nodded. "I hate deception," he said, "yet it seems to have its place in the scheme of things. I'll need half an hour or so alone, Tim. I hate to chase you away, but I have to play with these toys of mine."

I didn't mind. I was glad to be away from him for a few moments, for he was upsetting me more than I wanted to admit. There was something bad in the air that night, and more than my Irish soul was telling me so. Joseph Cameron Bane was playing God. He was manipulating people, toying with them. *Writing* them, and with no books to put them in.

It was too cold for walking. I got into the car and drove around the streets of the town, then out of the town and off on a winding road that went up into the hills beyond the town's edge. The snow was deep but no fresh snow was falling, and the moon was close to full and the sky cluttered with stars. I stopped the car and got out of it and took a long look back at the town below, his town. I thought it would be good right now to be a drinking man and warm myself from a bottle and walk in the night and pause now and then to gaze at the town below.

"You were gone long," he said.

"I got lost. It took time to find my way back."

"Tim, this still bothers you, doesn't it? Of course it does. Listen to me. I am going to put some people into motion, that is all. I am going to let some men talk to one another, and I am going to write their lines for them. Do you understand? Their opening lines. They wouldn't do it themselves. They wouldn't start it. I'll start it, and then they'll help it play itself out."

He was right, of course. Avery could not be allowed to get away with murder, nor should the dead woman's sins be placed on public display for all to stare at. "Now listen to this," he said, bright-eyed again. "I'm proud of myself, frankly."

He dialed a number, then poised his index finger above one of the buttons on the recorder. He was huddled over the table so that the telephone mouthpiece was just a few inches from the recorder's speaker. The phone was answered, and he pressed a button and I heard Dean Avery's voice. "Goodin?"

A pause. Then, "This is Dean Avery. I know all about it, Goodin. You and my wife. You and Rachel. I know all about it. And now she's dead. An accident. Think about it, Goodin. You'll have to think about it."

He replaced the receiver.

"How did you . . ."

He looked at my gaping mouth and laughed aloud at me. "Just careful editing," he said. "Playing from one machine to the next, back and forth, a word here, a phrase there, all interwoven and put together. Even the inflection can be changed by raising or lowering the volume as you bounce from one machine to the other. Isn't it startling? I told you I have fun with this machine. I never got anything written on it, but I had a good time fooling around with it."

"All those phrases — you even had his name."

"It was *good* of you to call. And the tail syllable of some other word, *happen,* I think. The two cropped out and spliced together and tossed back and forth until they fit well enough. I was busy while you were gone, Tim. It wasn't simple to get it all right."

"Now what happens?"

"Goodin calls Avery."

"How do you know?"

"Oh, Tim! I'll call Goodin and tell him how my car's broken down, or that he's won a football pool, or something inane, and do the same thing with his voice. And call Avery for him, and accuse him of the murder. That's all. They'll take it from there. I expect Avery will crack. If I get enough words to play with, I can have Goodin outline the whole murder, how it happened, everything."

His fingers drummed the table top. "Avery might kill himself," he said. "The killers always do in that woman's stories about the little Belgian detective. They excuse themselves and blow their brains out in a gentlemanly manner. There might be a confrontation between the two. I'm not sure."

"Will it wait until morning?"

"I thought I'd call Goodin now."

He was plainly exhausted. It was too late for him to be awake, but the excitement kept him from feeling the fatigue. I hated playing nursemaid. I let him drink too much every day, let him die as he wished, but it was not good for him to wear himself out this way.

"Goodin will be shaken by the call," I told him. "You'll probably have trouble getting him to talk. He may have closed the station for the night."

"I'll call and find out," he said.

He called, the recorder at the ready, and the phone rang and went unanswered. He wanted to wait up and try again, but I made him give it up and wait until the next day. I put him to bed and went downstairs and straightened up the kitchen. There was a half inch of whiskey in a bottle, and I poured it into a glass and drank it, a thing I rarely do. It warmed me and I'd needed warming. I went upstairs and to bed, and still had trouble sleeping.

There were dreams, and bad ones, dreams that woke me and sat me upright with a shapeless wisp of horror falling off like smoke. I slept badly and woke early. I was downstairs while he slept. While I ate toast and drank tea, Mrs. Dettweiler worried aloud about him. "You've got him all worked up," she said. "He shouldn't get like that. A sick man like him, he should rest, he should be calm."

"He wants the excitement. And it's not my doing."

"As sick as he is . . ."

"He's dying, and has a right to do it his own way."

"Some way to talk!"

"It's his way."

"There's a difference."

The radio was playing, tuned to a station in Harmony Falls. Our town had one FM station but the radio did not get FM. Mrs. Dettweiler always played a radio unless Mr. Bane was in the room, in which case he generally told her to turn it off. When she was upstairs in her own room, the television was always on, unless she was praying or sleeping. I listened to it now and thought that he might have used it for his taping and editing and splicing. If you wished to disguise your voice, you might do it that way. If Dean Avery had never heard Thurman Goodin's voice, or not well enough to recognize it, you could work it well enough that way. With all those words and phrases at your disposal . . .

Halfway through the newscast they read an item from our town, read just a brief news story, and I spilled my tea all over the kitchen table. The cup fell to the floor and broke in half.

"Why, for goodness . . ."

I turned off the radio, thought better and reached to pull its plug. He never turned it on, hated it, but it might occur to him to tape from it, and I didn't want that. Not yet.

"Keep that thing off," I said. "Don't let him hear it, and don't tell him anything. If he tries to play the radio, say it's not working."

"I don't . . ."

"Just do as you're told!" I said. She went white and nodded mutely, and I hurried out of the house and drove into town. On the way I noticed that I held the steering wheel so tightly my fingers had gone numb. I couldn't help it. I'd have taken a drink then if there'd been one about. I'd have drunk kerosene, or perfume — anything at all.

I went to the drugstore and to the barbershop, and heard the same story in both places, and walked around a bit to relax, the last with little success. I left the car where I'd parked it and walked back to his house and breathed cold air and gritted my teeth against more than the cold. I did not even realize until much later that it was fairly stupid to leave the car. It seemed quite natural at the time.

He was up by the time I reached the house, wearing robe and slippers, seated at the table with telephone and tape recorder. "Where'd you go?" he wanted to know. "I can't reach Thurman Goodin. Nobody answers his phone."

"Nobody will."

"I've half a mind to try him at home."

"Don't bother."

"No? Why not?" And then, for the first time, he saw my face. His own paled. "Heavens, Tim, what's the matter?"

All the way back, through snow and cold air, I'd looked for a way to tell him — a proper way. There was none. Halfway home I'd thought that perhaps Providence might let him die before I had to tell him, but that could only have happened in one of his novels, not in this world.

So I said, "Dean Avery's dead. It happened last night; he's dead."

"Great God in Heaven!" His face was white, his eyes horribly wide. "How? Suicide?"

"No."

"How?" he asked insistently.

"It was meant to look like suicide. Thurman Goodin killed him. Broke into his house in the middle of the night. He was going to knock him out and poke his head in the oven and put the gas on. He knocked him cold all right, but Avery came to on the way to the oven. There was a row and Thurman Goodin beat him over the head with some tool he'd brought along. I believe it was a tire iron. Beat his brains in, but all the noise woke a few of the neighbors and they grabbed Goodin on his way out the door. Two of them caught him and managed to hold him until the police came, and of course he told them everything."

I expected Bane to interrupt, but he waited without a word. I said, "Rachel Avery wanted him to run away with her. She couldn't stand staying with her husband, she wanted to go to some big city, try the sweet life. He told the police he tried to stop seeing her. She threatened him, that she would tell her husband, that she would tell his wife. So he went to her one afternoon and knocked her unconscious, took off her clothes and put her in the bathtub. She was still alive then. He dropped the radio into the tub to give her

289

a shock, then unplugged it and checked to see if she was dead. She wasn't so he held her head under water until she drowned, and then he plugged the radio into the socket again and left.

"And last night he found out that Avery knew about it, about the murder and the affair and all. So of course he had to kill Avery. He thought he might get away with it if he made it look like suicide, that Avery was depressed over his wife's death and went on to take his own life. I don't think it would have washed. I don't know much about it, but aren't the police more apt to examine a suicide rather carefully? They might see the marks on the head. Perhaps not. I don't really know. They've put Goodin in jail in Harmony Falls, and with two bloody murders like that, he's sure to hang." And then, because I felt even worse about it all than I'd known, "So it all comes out even, after all, the way you wanted it, the loose ends tied up in a bow."

"Good heavens!"

"I'm sorry." And I was, as soon as I'd said the words.

I don't think he heard me. "I am a bad writer and a bad man," he said, and not to me at all, and perhaps not even to himself but to whatever he talked to when the need came. "I thought I created them, I thought I knew them, I thought they all belonged to me."

So I went upstairs and packed my bags and walked all the way to the station. It was a bad time to leave him and a heartless way to do it, but staying would have been worse, even impossible. He was dying, and I couldn't have changed that, nor made the going much easier for him. I walked to the station and took the first train out and ended up here in Los Angeles, working for another foolish little man who likes to hire foreigners, doing the same sort of nothing I'd done in New York, but doing it at least in a warmer climate.

Last month I read he'd died. I thought I might cry but didn't. A week ago I reread one of his books, *Lips That Could Kiss*. I discovered that I did not like it at all, and then I did cry. For Rachel Avery, for Joseph Cameron Bane. For me.

The Most Unusual Snatch

They grabbed Carole Butler a few minutes before midnight just a block and a half from her own front door. It never would have happened if her father had let her take the car. But she was six months shy of eighteen, and the law said you had to be eighteen to drive at night, and her father was a great believer in the law. So she had taken the bus, got off two blocks from her house, and walked half a block before a tall thin man with his hat down over his eyes appeared suddenly and asked her the time.

She was about to tell him to go buy his own watch when an arm came around her from behind and a damp cloth fastened over her mouth and nose. It smelled like a hospital room.

She heard voices, faintly, as if from far away. "Not too long, you don't want to kill her."

"What's the difference? Kill her now or kill her later, she's just as dead."

"You kill her now and she can't make the phone call."

There was more, but she didn't hear it. The chloroform did its work and she sagged, limp, unconscious.

At first, when she came to, groggy and weak and sick to her stomach, she thought she had been taken to a hospital. Then she realized it was just the smell of the chloroform. Her head seemed awash in the stuff. She breathed steadily, in and out, in and out, stayed where she was and didn't open her eyes.

She heard the same two voices she had heard before. One was assuring the other that everything would go right on schedule, that they couldn't miss. "Seventy-five thou," he said several times. "Wait another hour, let him sweat a little. Then call him and tell him it'll cost him seventy-five thou to see his darling daughter again. That's all we tell him, just that we got her, and the price. Then we let him stew in it for another two hours."

"Why drag it out?"

"Because it has to drag until morning anyway. He's not going to have that kind of bread around the house. He'll have to go on the send for it, and that means nine o'clock when the banks open. Give him the whole message right away and he'll have too much time to get nervous and call copper. But space it out just right and we'll have him on the string until morning, and then he can go straight to the bank and get the money ready."

Carole opened her eyes slowly, carefully. The one who was doing most of the talking was the same tall thin man who had asked her the time. He was less than beautiful, she noticed. His nose was lopsided, angling off to the left as though it had been broken and improperly reset. His chin was scarcely there at all. He ought to wear a goatee, she thought. He would still be no thing of beauty, but it might help.

The other one was shorter, heavier, and younger, no more than ten years older than Carole. He had wide shoulders, close-set eyes, and a generally stupid face, but he wasn't altogether bad-looking. Not bad at all she told herself. Between the two of them, they seemed to have kidnapped her. She wanted to laugh out loud.

"Better cool it," the younger one said. "Looks like she's coming out of it."

She picked up her cue, making a great

show of blinking her eyes vacantly and yawning and stretching. Stretching was difficult, as she seemed to be tied to a chair. It was an odd sensation. She had never been tied up before, and she didn't care for it.

"Hey," she said, "where am I?"

She could have answered the question herself. She was, to judge from appearances, in an especially squalid shack. The shack itself was fairly close to a highway, judging from the traffic noises. If she had to guess, she would place the location somewhere below the southern edge of the city, probably a few hundred yards off Highway 130 near the river. There were plenty of empty fishing shacks there, she remembered, and it was a fair bet that this was one of them.

"Now just take it easy, Carole," the thin man said. "You take it easy and nothing's going to happen to you."

"You kidnapped me."

"You just take it easy and —"

She squealed with joy. "This is too much! You've actually kidnapped me. Oh, this is wild! Did you call my old man yet?"

"No."

"Will you let me listen when you do?" She started to giggle. "I'd give anything to

295

see his face when you tell him. He'll split. He'll just fall apart."

They were both staring at her, open-mouthed. The younger man said, "You sound happy about it."

"Happy? Of course I'm happy. This is the most exciting thing that ever happened to me!"

"But your father —"

"I hope you gouge him good," she went on. "He's the cheapest old man on earth. He wouldn't pay a nickel to see a man go over the Falls. How much are you going to ask?"

"Never mind," the thin man said.

"I just hope it's enough. He can afford plenty."

The thin man grinned. "How does seventy-five thousand dollars strike you?"

"Not enough. He can afford more than that," she said. "He's very rich, but you wouldn't know it the way he hangs onto his money."

"Seventy-five thou is pretty rich."

She shook her head. "Not for him. He could afford plenty more."

"It's not what he can afford, it's what he can raise in a hurry. We don't want to drag this out for days. We want it over by morning."

She thought for a minute. "Well, it's your funeral," she said pertly.

The shorter man approached her. "What do you mean by that?"

"Forget it, Ray," his partner said.

"No, I want to find out. What did you mean by that, honey?"

She looked up at them. "Well, I don't want to tell you your business," she said slowly. "I mean, you're the kidnappers. You're the ones who are taking all the chances. I mean, if you get caught they can really give you a hard time, can't they?"

"The chair," the thin man said.

"That's what I thought, so I don't want to tell you how to do all this, but there *was* something that occurred to me."

"Let's hear it."

"Well, first of all, I don't think it's a good idea to wait for morning. You wouldn't know it, of course, but he doesn't have to wait until the banks open. He's a doctor, and I know he gets paid in cash a lot of the time — cash that never goes to the bank, never gets entered in the books. It goes straight into the safe in the basement and stays there."

"Taxes —"

"Something like that. Anyway, I heard him telling somebody that he never has less than a hundred thousand dollars in that safe. So you wouldn't have to wait until the banks open, and you wouldn't have to settle for seventy-five thousand either. You could ask for an even hundred thousand and get it easy."

The two kidnappers looked at her, at each other, then at her again.

"I mean," she said, "I'm only trying to be helpful."

"You must hate him something awful, kid."

"Now you're catching on."

"Doesn't he treat you right?"

"All his money," she said, "and I don't even get my own car. I had to take the bus tonight; otherwise you wouldn't have got me the way you did, so it's his fault I was kidnapped. Why shouldn't he pay a bundle?"

"This is some kid, Howie," the younger man said.

Howie nodded. "You sure about the hundred thousand?"

"He'll probably try to stall, tell us he needs time to raise the dough."

"So tell him you know about the safe."

"Maybe he —"

"And that way he won't call the police," she went on. "Because of not paying taxes on the money and all that. He won't want that to come out into the open, so he'll pay."

"It's like you planned this job yourself, baby," Ray said.

"I almost did."

"Huh?"

"I used to think what a gas it would be if I got kidnapped. What a fit the old man would throw and everything." She giggled. "But I never really thought it would happen. It's too perfect."

"I think I'll make that call now," Howie said. "I'll be back in maybe half an hour. Ray here'll take good care of you, kitten." He nodded and was gone.

She had expected that Howie would make the call and was glad it had turned out that way. Ray seemed to be the easier of the two to get along with. It wasn't just that he was younger and better-looking. He was also, as far as she could tell, more good-natured and a whole lot less intelligent.

"Who would have figured it?" he said now. "I mean, you go and pull a snatch, you don't expect anybody to be so cooperative."

"Have you ever done this before, Ray?"

"No."

"It must be scary."

"Aw, I guess it's easy enough. More

money than a bank job and a whole lot less risk. The only hard part is when the mark — your old man, that is — delivers the money. You have to get the dough without being spotted. Outside of that, it's no sweat at all."

"And afterward?"

"Huh?"

The palms of her hands were moist with sweat. She said, "What happens afterward? Will you let me go, Ray?"

"Oh, sure."

"You won't kill me?"

"Oh, don't be silly," he said.

She knew exactly what he meant. He meant, Let's not talk about it, doll, but of course we'll kill you. What else?

"I'm more fun when I'm alive," she said.

"I'll bet you are."

"You better believe it."

He came closer to her. She straightened her shoulders to emphasize her youthful curves and watched his eyes move over her body.

"That's a pretty sweater," he said. "You look real good in a sweater. I'll bet a guy could have a whole lot of fun with you, baby."

"I'm more fun," she said, "when I'm not tied up. Howie won't be back for a half hour. But I don't guess that would worry you."

"Not a bit."

She sat perfectly still while he untied her. Then she got slowly to her feet. Her legs were cramped and her fingers tingled a little from the limited circulation. Ray took her in his arms and kissed her, then took a black automatic from his pocket and placed it on the table.

"Now don't get any idea about making a grab for the gun," he said. "You'd only get hurt, you know."

Later he insisted on tying her up again.

"But I won't try anything," she protested. "Honest, Ray. You know I wouldn't try anything. I want everything to go off just right."

"Howie wouldn't like it," he said doggedly and that was all there was to it.

"But don't make it too tight," she begged. "It hurts."

He didn't make it too tight.

When Howie came back he was smiling broadly. He closed the door and locked it and lit a cigarette. "Like a charm," he said through a cloud of smoke. "Went like a charm. You're O.K., honey girl."

"What did he say?"

"Got hysterical first of all. Kept telling me not to hurt you, that he'd pay if only we'd release you. He kept saying how much he loved you and all."

She started to laugh. "Oh, beautiful!"

"And you were right about the safe. He started to blubber that he couldn't possibly raise a hundred thousand on short notice. Then I hit him with the safe, said I knew he kept plenty of dough right there in his own basement, and that really got to him. He went all to pieces. I think you could have knocked him over with a lettuce leaf when he heard that."

"And he'll pay up?"

"No trouble at all, and if it's all cash he's been salting away that's the best news yet: no serial numbers copied down, no big bills, no runs of new bills in sequence. That means we don't have to wholesale the kidnap dough to one of the Eastern mobs for forty cents on the dollar. We wind up with a hundred thousand, and we wind up clean."

"And he'll be scared to go to the police afterward," Carole put in. "Did you set up the delivery of the money?"

"No. I said I'd call in an hour. I may cut it to a half hour though. I think we've got him where we want him. This is going so smooth it scares me. I want it over and done with, nice and easy."

She was silent for a moment. Howie wanted it over and done with, undoubtedly wanted no loose ends. Inevitably he was going to think of her, Carole Butler, as an obvious loose end, which meant that he would probably want to tie her off, and the black automatic on the table was just the thing to do the job. She stared at the gun, imagined the sound of it, the impact of the bullet in her flesh. She was terrified, but she made sure none of this showed in her face or in her voice.

Casually she asked, "About the money — how are you going to pick it up?"

"That's the only part that worries me."

"I don't think he'll call the police. Not my old man. Frankly, I don't think he'd have the guts. But if he did, that would be the time when they'd try to catch you, wouldn't it?"

"That's the general idea."

She thought for a moment. "If we were anywhere near the south end of town, I know a perfect spot — but I suppose we're miles from there."

"What's the spot?"

She told him about it — the overpass on Route 130 at the approach to the turnpike.

They could have her father drive onto the pike, toss the money over the side of the overpass when he reached it, and they could be waiting down below to pick it up. Any cops who were with him would be stuck up there on the turnpike and they could get away clean.

"It's not bad," Ray said.

"It's perfect," Howie added. "You thought that up all by yourself?"

"Well, I got the idea from a really super-duper movie —"

"I think it's worth doing it that way." Howie sighed. "I was going to get fancy, have him walk to a garbage can, stick it inside, then cut out. Then we go in and get it out of the can. But suppose the cops had the whole place staked out?" He smiled. "You've got a good head on your shoulders, kitten. It's a shame —"

"What's a shame?"

"That you're not part of the gang, the way your mind works. You'd be real good at it."

That, she knew, was not really what he'd meant. It's a shame we have to kill you anyway, he meant. You're a smart kid, and even a pretty kid, but all the same you're going to get a bullet between the eyes, and it's a shame.

She pictured her father, waiting by the telephone. If he called the police, she knew it would be all over for her, and he might very well call them. But if she could stop him, if she could make sure that he let the delivery of the ransom money go according to plan, then maybe she would have a chance. It wouldn't be the best chance in the world, but anything was better than nothing at all.

When Howie said he was going to make the second phone call she asked him to take her along. "Let me talk to him," she begged. "I want to hear his voice. I want to hear him in a panic. He's always so cool about everything, so smug and superior. I want to see what he sounds like when he gets in a sweat."

"I don't know —"

"I'll convince him that you're desperate and dangerous," she continued. "I'll tell him —" she managed to giggle "— that I know you'll kill me if he doesn't cooperate, but that I'm sure you'll let me go straight home just as soon as the ransom is paid as long as he keeps the police out of it."

"Well, I don't know. It sounds good, but —"

"It's a good idea, Howie," Ray said. "That way he knows we've got her and he knows she's still alive. I think the kid knows what she's talking about."

It took a little talking, but finally Howie was convinced of the wisdom of the move. Ray untied her and the three of them got into Howie's car and drove down the road to a pay phone. Howie made the call and talked for a few minutes, explaining how and where the ransom was to be delivered. Then he gave the phone to Carole.

"Oh, Daddy," she sobbed. "Oh, Daddy, I'm scared! Daddy, do just what they tell you. There are four of them and they're desperate, and I'm scared of them. Please pay them, Daddy. The woman said if the police were brought in she'd cut my throat with a knife. She said she'd cut me and kill me, Daddy, and I'm so scared of them —"

Back in the cabin, as Howie tied her in the chair, he asked, "What was all that gas about four of us? And the bit about the woman?"

"I just thought it sounded dramatic."

"It was dramatic as a nine-alarm fire, but why bother?"

"Well," she said, "the bigger the gang is, the more dangerous it sounds and if he reports it later, let the police go looking for three men and a woman. That way you'll have even less trouble getting away clear.

And of course I'll give them four phony descriptions, just to make it easier for you."

She hoped that would soak in. She could only give the phony descriptions if she were left alive, and she hoped that much penetrated.

It was around three-thirty in the morning when Howie left for the ransom. "I should be about an hour," he said. "If I'm not back in that time, then things are bad. Then we've got trouble."

"What do I do then?" Ray asked.

"You know what to do."

"I mean, how do I get out of here? We've only got the one car, and you'll be in it."

"So beat it on foot, or stay right where you are. You don't have to worry about me cracking. The only way they'll get me is dead, and if I'm dead you won't have to worry about them finding out where we've got her tucked away. Just take care of the chick and get out on foot."

"Nothing's going to go wrong."

"I think you're right. I think this is smooth as silk, but anything to be sure. You got your gun?"

"On the table."

"Ought to keep it on you."

"Well, maybe."

"Remember," Howie said, "you can figure on me getting back in an hour at the outside. Probably be no more than half of that, but an hour is tops. So long."

"Good luck," Carole called after him.

Howie stopped and looked at her. He had a very strange expression on his face. "Yeah," he said finally. "Luck. Sure, thanks."

When Howie was gone, Ray said, "You never should have made the phone call. I mean, I think it was a good idea and all, but that way Howie tied you up, see, and he tied you tight. Me, I would have tied you loose, see, but he doesn't think the same way." He considered things. "In a way," he went on, "Howie is what you might call a funny guy. Everything has to go just right, know what I mean? He doesn't like to leave a thing to chance."

"Could you untie me?"

"Well, I don't know if I should."

"At least make this looser? It's got my fingers numb already. It hurts pretty bad, Ray. Please?"

"Well, I suppose so." He untied her. As soon as she was loose he moved to the table, scooped up the gun, wedged it beneath the waistband of his trousers.

He likes me, she thought. He even wants me to be comfortable and he doesn't particularly want to kill me, but he doesn't trust me. He's too nervous to trust anybody.

"Could I have a cigarette?" she asked.

"Huh? Oh, sure." He gave her one, lit it for her. They smoked together for several minutes in silence. It isn't going to work, she thought, not the way things are going. She had him believing her, but that didn't seem to be enough. Howie was the brains and the boss, and what Howie said went, and Howie would say to kill her. She wondered which one of them would use the gun on her.

"Uh, Carole —"

"What?"

"Oh, nothing. Just forget it."

He wanted her to bring it up, she knew. So she said, "Listen, Ray, let me tell you something. I like you a lot, but to tell you the truth I'm scared of Howie."

"You are?"

"I've been playing it straight with you, and I think you've been straight with me. Ray, you've got the brains to realize you'll be much better off if you let me go." He doesn't, she thought, have any brains at all, but flattery never hurt. "But Howie is different from you and me. He's not — well, normal. I know he wants to kill me."

"Oh, now —"

"I mean it, Ray." She clutched his arm. "If I live, Dad won't report it. He can't afford to. But if you kill me —"

"Yeah, I know."

"Suppose you let me go."

"Afterward?"

She shook her head. "No, now, before Howie comes back. He won't care by then, he'll have the money. You can just let me go, and then the two of you will take the money and get out of town. Nobody will ever know a thing. I'll tell Dad the two of you released me and he'll be so glad to get me back and so scared of the tax men he'll never say a word. You could let me go, Ray, couldn't you? Before Howie gets back?"

He thought it over for a long time, and she could see he wanted to. But he said, "I don't know, Howie would take me apart —"

"Say I grabbed something and hit you, and managed to knock you out. Tell him he tied the ropes wrong and I slipped loose and got you from behind. He'll be mad, maybe, but what will he care? As long as you have the money —"

"He won't believe you hit me."

"Suppose I *did* hit you? Not hard, but enough to leave a mark so you could point to it for proof."

He grinned suddenly. "Sure, Carole, you've been good to me. The first time, when he made that first phone call, you were real good. I'll tell you something, the idea of killing you bothers me. And you're right about Howie. Here, belt me one behind the ear. Make it a good one, but not too hard, O.K.?" And he handed her the gun.

He looked completely astonished when she shot him. He just didn't believe it. She reversed the gun in her hand, curled her index finger around the trigger, and pointed the gun straight at his heart. His eyes bugged out and his mouth dropped open, and he just stared at her, not saying anything at all. She shot him twice in the center of the chest and watched him fall slowly, incredibly, to the floor, dead.

When Howie's car pulled up she was ready. She crouched by the doorway, gun in hand, waiting. The car door flew open and she heard his footsteps on the gravel path. He pulled the door open, calling out jubilantly that it had gone like clockwork, just like clockwork, then he caught sight of Ray's corpse on the floor and did a fantastic double take. When he saw her and the gun, he started to say something, but she emptied the gun into him, four bullets, one after the other, and all of them hit him and they worked; he fell; he died.

She got the bag of money out of his hand before he could bleed on it.

The rest wasn't too difficult. She took the rope with which she'd been tied and rubbed it back and forth on the chair leg until it finally frayed through. Behind the cabin she found a toolshed. She used a shovel, dug a shallow pit, dropped the money into it, filled in the hole. She carried the gun down to the water's edge, wiped it free of fingerprints, and heaved it into the creek.

Finally, when just the right amount of time had passed, she walked out to the highway and kept going until she found a telephone, a highway emergency booth.

"Just stay right where you are," her father said. "Don't call the police. I'll come for you."

"Hurry. Daddy. I'm so scared."

He picked her up. She was shaking, and he held her in his arms and soothed her.

"I was so frightened," she said. "And then when the one man came back with the ransom money, the other man took out a gun and shot him and the third man, and then the man who did the shooting, he and the woman ran away in their other car. I was sure they were going to kill me but the man said not to bother, the gun was empty and it didn't matter now. The woman wanted to kill me with the knife but she didn't. I was sure she would. Oh, Daddy —"

"It's all right now," he said. "Everything's going to be all right."

She showed him the cabin and the two dead men and the rope. "It took me forever to get out of it," she said. "But I saw in the movies how you can work your way out, and I wasn't tied too tight, so I managed to do it."

"You're a brave girl, Carole."

On the way home he said, "I'm not going to call the police, Carole. I don't want to subject you to a lot of horrible questioning. Sooner or later they'll find those two in the cabin, but that has nothing to do with us. They'll just find two dead criminals, and the world's better off without them." He thought for a moment. "Besides," he added, "I'm sure I'd have a hard time explaining where I got that money."

"Did they get very much?"

"Only ten thousand dollars," he said.

"I thought they asked for more."

"Well, after I explained that I didn't have anything like that around the house they listened to reason."

"I see," she said.

You old liar, she thought, it was a hundred thousand dollars, and I know it. And it's mine now. Mine.

"Ten thousand dollars is a lot of money," she said. "I mean, it's a lot for you to lose."

"It doesn't matter."

"If you called the police, maybe they could get it back."

He shuddered visibly, and she held back laughter. "It doesn't matter," he said. "All that matters is that we got you back safe and sound. That's more important than all the money in the world."

"Oh, Daddy," she said, hugging him, "oh, I love you, I love you so much!"

The Ehrengraf Appointment

Martin Ehrengraf was walking jauntily down the courthouse steps when a taller and bulkier man caught up with him. "Glorious day," the man said. "Simply a glorious day."

Ehrengraf nodded. It was indeed a glorious day, the sort of autumn afternoon that made men recall football weekends. Ehrengraf had just been thinking that he'd like a piece of hot apple pie with a slab of sharp cheddar on it. He rarely thought about apple pie and almost never wanted cheese on it, but it was that sort of day.

"I'm Cutliffe," the man said. "Hudson Cutliffe, of Marquardt, Stoner and Cutliffe."

"Ehrengraf," said Ehrengraf.

"Yes, I know. Oh, believe me, I know." Cutliffe gave what he doubtless considered a hearty chuckle. "Imagine running into Martin Ehrengraf himself, standing in line for an IDC appointment just like every-body else."

"Every man is entitled to a proper defense," Ehrengraf said stiffly. "It's a guaranteed right in a free society."

"Yes, to be sure, but —"

"Indigent defendants have attorneys appointed by the court. Our system here calls for attorneys to make themselves available at specified intervals for such appointments, rather than entrust such cases to a public defender."

"I quite understand," Cutliffe said. "Why, I was just appointed to an IDC case myself, some luckless chap who stole a satchel full of meat from a supermarket. Choice cuts, too — lamb chops, filet mignon. You just about have to steal them these days, don't you?"

Ehrengraf, a recent convert to vegetarianism, offered a thin-lipped smile and thought about pie and cheese.

"But Martin Ehrengraf himself," Cutliffe went on. "One no more thinks of you in this context than one imagines a glamorous Hollywood actress going to the bathroom. Martin Ehrengraf, the dapper and debonair lawyer who hardly ever appears in court. The man who only collects a fee if he wins. Is that really true, by the way?

316

You actually take murder cases on a contingency basis?"

"That's correct."

"Extraordinary. I don't see how you can possibly afford to operate that way."

"It's quite simple," Ehrengraf said.

"Oh?"

His smile was fuller than before. "I always win," he said. "It's simplicity itself."

"And yet you rarely appear in court."

"Sometimes one can work more effectively behind the scenes."

"And when your client wins his freedom —"

"I'm paid in full," Ehrengraf said.

"Your fees are high, I understand."

"Exceedingly high."

"And your clients almost always get off."

"They're always innocent," Ehrengraf said. "That does help."

Hudson Cutliffe laughed richly, as if to suggest that the idea of bringing guilt and innocence into a discussion of legal procedures was amusing. "Well, this will be a switch for you," he said at length. "You were assigned the Protter case, weren't you?"

"Mr. Protter is my client, yes."

"Hardly a typical Ehrengraf case, is it? Man gets drunk, beats his wife to death, passes out and sleeps it off, then wakes up and sees what he's done and calls the police. Bit of luck for you, wouldn't you say?"

"Oh?"

"Won't take up too much of your time. You'll plead him guilty to manslaughter, possibly get a reduced sentence on grounds of his previous clean record, and then Protter'll do a year or two in prison while you go about your business."

"You think that's the course I'll pursue, Mr. Cutliffe?"

"It's what anyone would do."

"Almost anyone," said Ehrengraf.

"And there's no reason to make work for yourself, is there?" Cutliffe winked. "These IDC cases — I don't know why they pay us at all, as small as the fees are. A hundred and seventy-five dollars isn't much of an all-inclusive fee for a legal defense, is it? Wouldn't you say your average fee runs a bit higher than that?"

"Quite a bit higher."

"But there are compensations. It's the same hundred and seventy-five dollars whether you plead your client or stand trial, let alone win. A far cry from your usual system, eh, Ehrengraf? You don't have to win to get paid."

"I do," Ehrengraf said.

"How's that?"

"If I lose the case, I'll donate the fee to charity."

"*If* you lose? But you'll plead him to manslaughter, won't you?"

"Certainly not."

"Then what will you do?"

"I'll plead him innocent."

"Innocent?"

"Of course. The man never killed anyone."

"But —" Cutliffe inclined his head, dropped his voice. "You know the man? You have some special information about the case?"

"I've never met him and know only what I've read in the newspapers."

"Then how can you say he's innocent?"

"He's my client."

"So?"

"I do not represent the guilty," Ehrengraf said. "My clients are innocent, Mr. Cutliffe, and Arnold Protter is a client of mine, and I intend to earn my fee as his attorney, however inadequate that fee may be. I did not seek appointment, Mr. Cutliffe, but that appointment is a sacred trust, sir, and I shall justify that trust. Good day, Mr. Cutliffe."

319

"They said they'd get me a lawyer and it wouldn't cost me nothing," Arnold Protter said. "I guess you're it, huh?"

"Indeed," said Ehrengraf. He glanced around the sordid little jail cell, then cast an eye on his new client. Arnold Protter was a thickset round-shouldered man in his late thirties with the ample belly of a beer drinker and the red nose of a whiskey drinker. His pudgy face recalled the Pillsbury Dough Boy. His hands, too, were pudgy, and he held them out in front of his red nose and studied them in wonder.

"These were the hands that did it," he said.

"Nonsense."

"How's that?"

"Perhaps you'd better tell me what happened," Ehrengraf suggested. "The night your wife was killed."

"It's hard to remember," Protter said.

"I'm sure it is."

"What it was, it was an ordinary kind of a night. Me and Gretch had a beer or two during the afternoon, just passing time while we watched television. Then we ordered up a pizza and had a couple more with it, and then we settled in for the evening and started hitting the boilermakers.

You know, a shot and a beer. First thing you know, we're having this argument."

"About what?"

Protter got up, paced, glared again at his hands. He lumbered about, Ehrengraf thought, like a caged bear. His chino pants were ragged at the cuffs and his plaid shirt was a tartan no Highlander would recognize. Ehrengraf, in contrast, sparkled in the drab cell like a diamond on a dustheap. His suit was a herringbone tweed the color of a well-smoked briar pipe, and beneath it he wore a suede doeskin vest over a cream broadcloth shirt with French cuffs and a tab collar. His cufflinks were simple gold hexagons, his tie a wool knit in the same brown as his suit. His shoes were shell cordovan loafers, quite simple and elegant and polished to a high sheen.

"The argument," Ehrengraf prompted.

"Oh, I don't know how it got started," Protter said. "One thing led to another, and pretty soon she's making a federal case over me and this woman who lives one flight down from us."

"What woman?"

"Her name's Agnes Mullane. Gretchen's giving me the business that me and Agnes got something going."

321

"And were you having an affair with Agnes Mullane?"

"Naw, course not. Maybe me and Agnes'd pass the time of day on the staircase, and maybe I had some thoughts on the subject, but nothing ever came of it. But she started in on the subject, Gretch did, and to get a little of my own back I started ragging her about this guy lives one flight up from us."

"And his name is —"

"Gates, Harry Gates."

"You thought your wife was having an affair with Gates?"

Protter shook his head. "Naw, course not. But he's an artist, Gates is, and I was accusing her of posing for him, you know. Naked. No clothes on."

"Nude."

"Yeah."

"And did your wife pose for Mr. Gates?"

"You kidding? You never met Gretchen, did you?"

Ehrengraf shook his head.

"Well, Gretch was all right, and the both of us was used to each other, if you know what I mean, but you wouldn't figure her for somebody who woulda been Miss America if she coulda found her way to Atlantic City. And Gates, what would he need with a model?"

"You said he was an artist."

"*He* says he's an artist," Protter said, "but you couldn't prove it by me. What he paints don't look like nothing. I went up there one time on account of his radio's cooking at full blast, you know, and I want to ask him to put a lid on it, and he's up on top of this stepladder dribbling paint on a canvas that he's got spread out all over the floor. All different colors of paint, and he's just throwing them down at the canvas like a little kid making a mess."

"Then he's an abstract expressionist," Ehrengraf said.

"Naw, he's a painter. I mean, people buy these pictures of his. Not enough to make him rich or he wouldn't be living in the same dump with me and Gretch, but he makes a living at it. Enough to keep him in beer and pizza and all, but what would he need with a model? Only reason he'd want Gretchen up there is to hold the ladder steady."

"An abstract expressionist," said Ehrengraf. "That's very interesting. He lives directly above you, Mr. Protter?"

"Right upstairs, yeah. That's why we could hear his radio clear as a bell."

"Was it playing the night you and your wife drank the boilermakers?"

"We drank boilermakers lots of the time," Protter said, puzzled. "Oh, you mean the night I killed her."

"The night she died."

"Same thing, ain't it?"

"Not at all," said Ehrengraf. "But let it go. Was Mr. Gates playing his radio that night?"

Protter scratched his head. "Hard to remember," he said. "One night's like another, know what I mean? Yeah, the radio was going that night. I remember now. He was playing country music on it. Usually he plays that rock and roll, and that stuff gives me a headache, but this time it was country music. Country music, it sort of soothes my nerves." He frowned. "But I never played it on my own radio."

"Why was that?"

"Gretch hated it. Couldn't stand it, said the singers all sounded like dogs that ate poisoned meat and was dying of it. Gretch didn't like any music much. What she liked was the television, and then we'd have Gates with his rock and roll at top volume, and sometimes you'd hear a little country music coming upstairs from Agnes's radio. She liked country music, but she never played it very loud. With the windows open on a hot day you'd hear it, but otherwise no. Of course what you hear most with the windows open is the Puerto Ricans on the street with their transistor radios."

Protter went on at some length about Puerto Ricans and transistor radios. When he paused for breath, Ehrengraf straightened up and smiled with his lips. "A pleasure," he said. "Mr. Protter, I believe in your innocence."

"Huh?"

"You've been the victim of an elaborate and diabolical frameup, sir. But you're in good hands now. Maintain your silence and put your faith in me. Is there anything you need to make your stay here more comfortable?"

"It's not so bad."

"Well, you won't be here for long. I'll see to that. Perhaps I can arrange for a radio for you. You could listen to country music."

"Be real nice," Protter said. "Soothing is what it is. It soothes my nerves."

An hour after his interview with his client, Ehrengraf was seated on a scarred wooden bench at a similarly distressed oaken table. The restaurant in which he was dining ran to college pennants and German beer steins suspended from the exposed dark wood beams. Ehrengraf was eating hot apple pie topped with sharp cheddar, and at the side of his plate was a small glass of neat Calvados.

The little lawyer was just preparing to take his first sip of the tangy apple brandy when a familiar voice sounded beside him.

"Ehrengraf," Hudson Cutliffe boomed out. "Fancy finding you here. Twice in one day, eh?"

Ehrengraf looked up, smiled. "Excellent pie here," he said.

"Come here all the time," Cutliffe said. "My home away from home. Never seen you here before, I don't think."

"My first time."

"Pie with cheese. If I ate that I'd put on ten pounds." Unbidden, the hefty attorney drew back the bench opposite Ehrengraf and seated himself. When a waiter appeared, Cutliffe ordered a slice of prime rib and a spinach salad.

"Watching my weight," he said. "Protein, that's the ticket. Got to cut down on the nasty old carbs. Well, Ehrengraf, I suppose you've seen your wife-murderer by now, haven't you? Or are you still maintaining he's no murderer at all?"

"Protter's an innocent man."

Cutliffe chuckled. "Commendable attitude, I'm sure, but why don't you save it for the courtroom? The odd juryman may be impressed by that line of country. I'm not, myself. I've always found facts more convincing than attitudes."

"Indeed," said Ehrengraf. "Personally, I've always noticed the shadow as much as the substance. I suspect it's a difference of temperament, Mr. Cutliffe. I don't suppose you're much of a fan of poetry, are you?"

"Poetry? You mean rhymes and verses and all that?"

"More or less."

"Schoolboy stuff, eh? *Boy stood on the burning deck,* that the sort of thing you mean? Had a bellyful of that in school." He smiled suddenly. "Unless you're talking about limericks. I like the odd limerick now and then, I must say. Are you much of a hand for limericks?"

"Not really," said Ehrengraf.

Cutliffe delivered four limericks while Ehrengraf sat with a pained expression on his face. The first concerned a mathematician named Paul, the second a young harlot named Dinah, the third a man from Fort Ord, and the fourth an old woman from Truk.

"It's interesting," Ehrengraf said at length. "On the surface there's no similarity whatsoever between the limerick and abstract expressionist painting. They're not at all alike. And yet they are."

"I don't follow you."

"It's not important," Ehrengraf said. The waiter appeared, setting a plateful of rare beef in front of Cutliffe, who at once reached for his knife and fork. Ehrengraf looked at the meat. "You're going to eat that," he said.

"Of course. What else would I do with it?"

Ehrengraf took another small sip of the Calvados. Holding the glass aloft, he began an apparently aimless dissertation upon the innocence of his client. "If you were a reader of poetry," he found himself saying, "and if you did not systematically dull your sensibilities by consuming the flesh of beasts, Mr. Protter's innocence would be obvious to you."

"You're serious about defending him, then. You're really going to plead him innocent."

"How could I do otherwise?"

328

Cutliffe raised an eyebrow while lowering a fork. "You realize you're letting an idle whim jeopardize a man's liberty, Ehrengraf. Your Mr. Protter will surely receive a stiffer sentence after he's been found guilty by a jury, and —"

"But he won't be found guilty."

"Are you counting on some technicality to get him off the hook? Because I have a friend in the District Attorney's office, you know, and I went round there while you were visiting your client. He tells me the state's case is gilt-edged."

"The state is welcome to the gilt," Ehrengraf said grandly. "Mr. Protter has the innocence."

Cutliffe put down his fork, set his jaw. "Perhaps," he said, "perhaps you simply do not care. Perhaps, having no true financial stake in Arnold Protter's fate, you just don't give a damn what happens to him. Whereas, had you a substantial sum riding on the outcome of the case —"

"Oh, dear," said Ehrengraf. "You're not by any chance proposing a wager?"

Miss Agnes Mullane had had a permanent recently, and her copper-colored hair looked as though she'd stuck her big toe in an electric socket. She had a freckled face,

329

a pug nose and a body that would send whole shifts of construction workers plummeting from their scaffolds. She wore a hostess outfit of a silky green fabric, and her walk, Ehrengraf noted, was decidedly slinky.

"So terrible about the Protters," she said. "They were good neighbors, although I never became terribly close with either of them. She kept to herself, for the most part, but he always had a smile and a cheerful word for me when I would run into him on the stairs. Of course I've always gotten on better with men than with women, Mr. Ehrengraf, though I'm sure I couldn't tell you why."

"Indeed," said Ehrengraf.

"You'll have some more tea, Mr. Ehrengraf?"

"If I may."

She leaned forward, displaying an alluring portion of herself to Ehrengraf as she filled his cup from a Dresden teapot. Then she set the pot down and straightened up with a sigh.

"Poor Mrs. Protter," she said. "Death is so final."

"Given the present state of medical science."

"And poor *Mr.* Protter. Will he have to

spend many years in prison, Mr. Ehrengraf?"

"Not with a proper defense. Tell me, Miss Mullane. Mrs. Protter accused her husband of having an affair with you. I wonder why she should have brought such an accusation."

"I'm sure I don't know."

"Of course you're a very attractive woman —"

"Do you really think so, Mr. Ehrengraf?"

"— and you live by yourself, and tongues will wag."

"I'm a respectable woman, Mr. Ehrengraf."

"I'm sure you are."

"And I would never have an affair with anyone who lived here in this building. Discretion, Mr. Ehrengraf, is very important to me."

"I sensed that, Miss Mullane." The little lawyer got to his feet, walked to the window. The afternoon was warm, and the strains of Latin music drifted up through the open window from the street below.

"Transistor radios," Agnes Mullane said. "They carry them everywhere."

"So they do. When Mrs. Protter made that accusation, Miss Mullane, her husband denied it."

"Why, I should hope so!"

"And he in turn accused her of carrying on with Mr. Gates. Have I said something funny, Miss Mullane?"

Agnes Mullane managed to control her laughter. "Mr. Gates is an artist," she said.

"A painter, I'm told. Would that canvas be one of his?"

"I'm afraid not. He paints abstracts. I prefer representational art myself, as you can see."

"And country music."

"I beg your pardon?"

"Nothing. You're sure Mr. Gates was not having an affair with Mrs. Protter?"

"Positive." Her brow clouded for an instant, then cleared completely. "No," she said, "Harry Gates would never have been involved with her. But what's the point, Mr. Ehrengraf? Are you trying to establish a defense of justifiable homicide? The unwritten law and all that?"

"Not exactly."

"Because I really don't think it would work, do you?"

"No," said Ehrengraf, "I don't suppose it would."

Miss Mullane leaned forward again, not to pour tea but with a similar effect. "It's so noble of you," she said, "donating your time for poor Mr. Protter."

"The court appointed me, Miss Mullane."

"Yes, but surely not all appointed attorneys work so hard on these cases, do they?"

"Perhaps not."

"That's what I thought." She ran her tongue over her lips. "Nobility is an attractive quality in a man," she said thoughtfully. "And I've always admired men who dress well, and who bear themselves elegantly."

Ehrengraf smiled. He was wearing a pale blue cashmere sport jacket over a Wedgwood blue shirt. His tie matched his jacket, with an intricate below-the-knot design in gold thread.

"A lovely jacket," Miss Mullane purred. She reached over, laid a hand on Ehrengraf's sleeve. "Cashmere," she said. "I love the feel of cashmere."

"Thank you."

"And gray flannel slacks. What a fine fabric. Come with me, Mr. Ehrengraf. I'll show you where to hang your things."

In the bedroom Miss Mullane paused to switch on the radio. Loretta Lynn was singing something about having been born a coal miner's daughter.

"My one weakness," Miss Mullane said, "or should I say one of my two weaknesses, along with a weakness for well-dressed men of noble character. I hope you don't mind country music, Mr. Ehrengraf?"

"Not at all," said Ehrengraf. "I find it soothing."

Several days later, when Arnold Protter was released from jail, Ehrengraf was there to meet him. "I want to shake your hand," he told him, extending his own. "You're a free man now, Mr. Protter, I only regret I played no greater part in securing your freedom."

Protter pumped the lawyer's hand enthusiastically. "Hey, listen," he said, "you're ace-high with me, Mr. Ehrengraf. You believed in me when nobody else did, including me myself. I'm just now trying to take all of this in. I'll tell you, I never would have dreamed Agnes Mullane killed my wife."

"It's something neither of us suspected, Mr. Protter."

"It's the craziest thing I ever heard of. Let me see if I got the drift of it straight. My Gretchen was carrying on with Gates after all. I thought it was just a way to get in a dig at her, accusing her of carrying on with him, but actually it was happening all the time."

"So it would seem."

"And that's why she got so steamed when I brought it up." Protter nodded, wrapped up in thought. "Anyway, Gates also had something going with Agnes Mullane. You know something, Mr. Ehrengraf? He musta been nuts. Why would anybody who was getting next to Agnes want to bother with Gretchen?"

"Artists perceive the world differently from the rest of us, Mr. Protter."

"If that's a polite way of saying he was cockeyed, I sure gotta go along with you on that. So here he's getting it on with the both of them, and Agnes finds out and she's jealous. How do you figure she found out?"

"It's always possible Gates told her," Ehrengraf suggested. "Or perhaps she heard you accusing your wife of infidelity. You and Gretchen had both been drinking, and your argument may have been a loud one."

"Could be. A few boilermakers and I tend to raise my voice."

"Most people do. Or perhaps Miss Mullane saw some of Gates's sketches of your wife. I understand there were several

335

found in his apartment. He may have been an abstract expressionist, but he seems to have been capable of realistic sketches of nudes. Of course he's denied they were his work, but he'd be likely to say that, wouldn't he?"

"I guess so," Protter said. "Naked pictures of Gretchen, gee, you never know, do you?"

"You never do," Ehrengraf agreed. "In any event, Miss Mullane had a key to your apartment. One was found among her effects. Perhaps it was Gates's key, perhaps Gretchen had given it to him and Agnes Mullane stole it. She let herself into your apartment, found you and your wife unconscious and pounded your wife on the head with an empty beer bottle. Your wife was alive when Miss Mullane entered your apartment, Mr. Protter, and dead when she left it."

"So I didn't kill her after all."

"Indeed you did not." Ehrengraf smiled for a moment. Then his face turned grave. "Agnes Mullane was not cut out for murder," he said. "At heart she was a gentle soul. I realized that at once when I spoke with her."

"You went and talked to Agnes?"

The little lawyer nodded. "I suspect my

interview with her may have driven her over the edge," he said. "Perhaps she sensed that I was suspicious of her. She wrote out a letter to the police, detailing what she had done. Then she must have gone upstairs to Mr. Gates's apartment, because she managed to secure a twenty-five caliber automatic pistol registered to him. She returned to her own apartment, put the weapon to her chest, and shot herself in the heart."

"She had some chest, too."

Ehrengraf did not comment.

"I'll tell you," Protter said, "the whole thing's a little too complicated for a simple guy like me to take it all in all at once. I can see why it was open and shut as far as the cops were concerned. There's me and the wife drinking, and there's me and the wife fighting, and the next thing you know she's dead and I'm sleeping it off. If it wasn't for you, I'd be doing time for killing her."

"I played a part," Ehrengraf said modestly. "But it's Agnes Mullane's conscience that saved you from prison."

"Poor Agnes."

"A tortured, tormented woman, Mr. Protter."

"I don't know about that," Protter said.

"But she had some body on her, I'll say that for her." He drew a breath. "What about you, Mr. Ehrengraf? You did a real job for me. I wish I could pay you."

"Don't worry about it."

"I guess the court pays you something, huh?"

"There's a set fee of a hundred and seventy-five dollars," Ehrengraf said, "but I don't know that I'm eligible to receive it in this instance because of the disposition of the case. The argument may be raised that I didn't really perform any actions on your behalf, that charges were simply dropped."

"You mean you'll get gypped out of your fee? That's a hell of a note, Mr. Ehrengraf."

"Oh, don't worry about it," said Ehrengraf. "It's not important in the overall scheme of things."

Ehrengraf, his blue pinstripe suit setting off his Caedmon Society striped necktie, sipped daintily at a Calvados. It was Indian Summer this afternoon, far too balmy for hot apple pie with cheddar cheese. He was eating instead a piece of cold apple pie topped with vanilla ice cream, and he'd discovered that Calvados went every bit as nicely with that dish.

Across from him, Hudson Cutliffe sat with a plate of lamb stew. When Cutliffe had ordered the dish, Ehrengraf had refrained from commenting on the barbarity of slaughtering lambs and stewing them. He had decided to ignore the contents of Cutliffe's plate. Whatever he'd ordered, Ehrengraf intended that the man eat crow today.

"You," said Cutliffe, "are the most astonishingly fortunate lawyer who ever passed the bar."

" 'Dame Fortune is a fickle gypsy. And always blind, and often tipsy,' " Ehrengraf quoted. "Winthrop Mackworth Praed, born eighteen-oh-two, died eighteen thirty-nine. But you don't care for poetry, do you? Perhaps you'd prefer the elder Pliny's observation upon the eruption of Vesuvius. He said that Fortune favors the brave."

"A cliché, isn't it?"

"Perhaps it was rather less a cliché when Pliny said it," Ehrengraf said gently. "But that's beside the point. My client was innocent, just as I told you —"

"How on earth could you have known it?"

"I didn't have to know it. I presumed it, Mr. Cutliffe, as I always presume my clients to be innocent, and as in time they are invariably proven to be. And, because you were so incautious as to insist upon a wager —"

"Insist!"

"It was indeed your suggestion," Ehrengraf said. "*I* did not seek *you* out, Mr. Cutliffe. *I* did not seat myself unbidden at *your* table."

"You came to this restaurant," Cutliffe said darkly. "You deliberately baited me, goaded me. You —"

"Oh, come now," Ehrengraf said. "You make me sound like what priests would call an occasion of sin or lawyers an attractive nuisance. I came here for apple pie with cheese, Mr. Cutliffe, and you proposed a wager. Now my client has been released and all charges dropped, and I believe you owe me money."

"It's not as if you got him off. Fate got him off."

Ehrengraf rolled his eyes. "Oh, please, Mr. Cutliffe," he said. "I've had clients take that stance, you know, and they always change their minds in the end. My agreement with them has always been that my fee is due and payable upon their release, whether the case comes to court or not, whether or not I have played any evident part in their salvation. I specified

340

precisely those terms when we arranged our little wager."

"Of course gambling debts are not legally collectible in this state."

"Of course they are not, Mr. Cutliffe. Yours is purely a debt of honor, an attribute which you may or may not be said to possess in accordance with your willingness to write out a check. But I trust you are an honorable man, Mr. Cutliffe."

Their eyes met. After a long moment Cutliffe drew a checkbook from his pocket. "I feel I've been manipulated in some devious fashion," he said, "but at the same time I can't gloss over the fact that I owe you money." He opened the checkbook, uncapped a pen, and filled out the check quickly, signing it with a flourish. Ehrengraf smiled narrowly, placing the check in his own wallet without noting the amount. It was, let it be said, an impressive amount.

"An astonishing case," Cutliffe said, "even if you yourself had the smallest of parts in it. This morning's news was the most remarkable thing of all."

"Oh?"

"I'm referring to Gates's confession, of course."

"Gates's confession?"

"You haven't heard? Oh, this is rich. Harry Gates is in jail. He went to the police and confessed to murdering Gretchen Protter."

"Gates murdered Gretchen Protter?"

"No question about it. It seems he shot her, used the very same small-caliber automatic pistol that the Mullane woman stole and used to kill herself. He was having an affair with both the women, just as Agnes Mullane said in her suicide note. He heard Protter accuse his wife of infidelity and was afraid Agnes Mullane would find out he'd been carrying on with Gretchen Protter. So he went down there looking to clear the air, and he had the gun along for protection, and — are you sure you didn't know about this?"

"Keep talking," Ehrengraf urged.

"Well, he found the two of them out cold. At first he thought Gretchen was dead but he saw she was breathing, and he took a raw potato from the refrigerator and used it as a silencer, and he shot Gretchen in the heart. They never found the bullet during postmortem examination because they weren't looking for it, just assumed massive skull injuries had caused her death. But after he confessed they looked, and there was the bullet right where he

342

said it should be, and Gates is in jail charged with her murder."

"Why on earth did he confess?"

"He was in love with Agnes Mullane," Cutliffe said. "That's why he killed Gretchen. Then Agnes Mullane killed herself, taking the blame for a crime Gates committed, and he cracked wide open. Figures her death was some sort of divine retribution, and he has to clear things by paying the price for the Protter woman's death. The D.A. thinks perhaps he killed them both, faked Agnes Mullane's confession note and then couldn't win the battle with his own conscience. He insists he didn't, of course, just as he insists he didn't draw nude sketches of either of the women, but it seems there's some question now about the validity of Agnes Mullane's suicide note, so it may well turn out that Gates killed her, too. Because if Gates killed Gretchen, why would Agnes have committed suicide?"

"I'm sure there are any number of possible explanations," Ehrengraf said, his fingers worrying the tips of his neatly trimmed mustache. "Any number of explanations. Do you know the epitaph Andrew Marvell wrote for a lady?

To say — she lived a virgin chaste
In this age loose and all unlaced;
Nor was, when vice is so allowed,
Of virtue or ashamed or proud;
That her soul was on Heaven so bent,
No minute but it came and went;
That, ready her last debt to pay,
She summed her life up every day;
Modest as morn, as mid-day bright,
Gentle as evening, cool as night:
— 'Tis true; but all too weakly said;
'Twas more significant, she's dead.

"She's dead, Mr. Cutliffe, and we may leave her to Heaven, as another poet has said. My client was innocent. That's the only truly relevant point. My client was innocent."

"As you somehow knew all along."

"As I knew all along, yes. Yes, indeed, as I knew all along." Ehrengraf's fingers drummed the table top. "Perhaps you could get our waiter's eye," he suggested. "I think I might enjoy another glass of Calvados."

Click!

It was late afternoon by the time Dandridge got back to the lodge. The mountain air was as crisp as the fallen leaves that crunched under his heavy boots. He turned for a last look at the western sky, then hurried up the steps and into the massive building. In his room he paused only long enough to drop his gear onto a chair and hang his bright orange cap on a peg. Then he strode to the lobby and through it to the taproom.

He bellied up to the bar, a big, thick-bodied man. "Afternoon, Eddie," he said to the barman. "The usual poison."

Dandridge's usual poison was sour mash whiskey. The barman poured a generous double into a tumbler and stood, bottle in hand, while Dandridge knocked the drink back in a single swallow. "First of the day," he announced, "and God willing it won't be the last."

Both the Lord and the barman were willing. This time Eddie added ice and a splash of soda. Dandridge accepted the drink, took a small sip of it, nodded his approval and turned to regard the only other man present at the bar, a smaller, less obtrusive man who regarded Dandridge in turn.

"Afternoon," Dandridge said.

"Good afternoon," said the other man. He was smoking a filtered cigarette and drinking a vodka martini. He looked Dandridge over thoroughly, from the rugged face weathered by sun and wind down over the heavy red and black checked jacket and wool pants to the knee-high leather boots. "If I were to guess," the man said, "I'd say you've been out hunting."

Dandridge smiled. "Well, you'd be right," he said. "In a manner of speaking."

" 'In a manner of speaking,' " the smaller man echoed. "I like the phrase. I'd guess further that you had a good day."

"A damn good day. Hard not to on a day like this. When it's this kind of a day, the air just the right temperature and so fresh you know it was just made this morning, and the sun comes through the trees and casts a dappled pattern on the ground, and you've got a spring in your step that makes you positive you're younger than the calendar tells you, well hell, sir, you could never set eyes on bird or beast and you'd still have to call it a good day."

"You speak like a poet."

"Afraid I'm nothing of the sort. I'm in insurance, fire and casualty and the like, and let me tell you there's nothing the least bit poetic about it. But when I get out here the woods and the mountains do their best to make a poet out of me."

The smaller man smiled, raised his glass, took a small sip. "I would guess," he said, "that today wasn't a day in which you failed to — how did you put it? To set eyes on bird or beast."

"No, you'd be right. I had good hunting."

"Then let me congratulate you," the man said. He raised his glass to Dandridge, who raised his in return.

"Dandridge," said Dandridge. "Homer Dandridge."

"Roger Krull," said the other man.

"A pleasure, Mr. Krull."

"My pleasure, Mr. Dandridge."

They drank, and both of their glasses stood empty. Dandridge motioned to the barman, his hand indicating both glasses. "On me," he said. "Mr. Krull, would I be wrong in guessing you're a hunter yourself?"

"In a manner of speaking."

"Oh?"

Krull glanced down into his newly freshened drink. "I've hunted for years," he said. "And I still hunt. I haven't given it up, not by any means. But —"

"It's not the same, is it?"

Krull looked up. "That's absolutely right," he said. "How did you know?"

"Go on," Dandridge urged. "Tell me how it's different."

Krull thought a moment. "I don't know exactly," he said. "Of course the novelty's gone, but hell, the novelty wore off years ago. The thing about any first-time thrill is it's only really present the first time, and eventually it's all gone. But there's something else. The stalking is still exciting, the pursuit, all of that, and there's still that instant of triumph when the prey is in your sights, and then the gun bucks, and then —"

"Yes?"

"Then you stand there, deafened for a moment by the roar of the gun, and you watch your prey gather and fall, and then —" He shrugged heavily. "Then it's a letdown. It even feels like —"

"Yes? Go on, Mr. Krull. Go on, sir."

"Well, I hope you won't take offense,"

Krull said. "It feels like a waste, a waste of life. Here I've taken life away from another creature, but I don't own that life. It's just . . . gone."

Dandridge was silent for a moment. He sipped his drink, made circles on the bar with the glass. He said, "You didn't feel this way in the past, I take it."

"No, not at all. The kill was always thrilling and there were no negative feelings accompanying it. But in the past year, maybe even the past two years, it's all been changing. What used to be a thrill is hollow now." The smaller man reached for his own glass. "I'm sorry I mentioned this," he said. "Sorry as hell. Here you had a good day and I have to bring you down with all this nonsense."

"Not at all, Mr. Krull. Not at all, sir. Eddie, fill these up again, will you? That's a good fellow." Dandridge planted a large hand on the top of the bar. "Don't regret what you've said, Mr. Krull. Be glad of it. I'm glad you spoke up and I'm glad I was here to hear you."

"You are?"

"Absolutely." Dandridge ran a hand through his wiry gray hair. "Mr. Krull — or if I may call you Roger?"

"By all means, Homer."

"Roger, I daresay I've been hunting more years than you have. Believe me, the feelings you've just expressed so eloquently are not foreign to me. I went through precisely what you're going through now. I came very close to giving it up, all of it."

"And then the feelings passed?"

"No," Dandridge said "No, Roger. They did not."

"Then —"

Dandridge smiled hugely. "I'll tell you what I did," he said. "I didn't give it up. I thought of doing that because I grew to hate killing, but the idea of missing the woods and the mountains galled me. Oh, you can go walking in the woods without hunting, but that's not the same thing. The pleasure of the stalk, the pursuit, the matching of human wit and intelligence against the instincts and cunning of game — that's what makes hunting what it is for me, Roger."

"Yes," Krull murmured. "Certainly."

"So what I did," Dandridge said, "was change my style. No more bang-bang."

"I beg your pardon?"

"No more bang-bang," Dandridge said, gesturing. "Now it's click-click instead." And when Krull frowned uncomprehendingly, the big man put his hands in front of his face and mimed the operation of a camera. "Click!" he said.

Light dawned. "Oh," said Krull.

"Exactly."

"Not with a bang but a click."

"Nicely put."

"Photography."

"Let's not say photography," Dandridge demurred. "Let us say hunting with a camera."

"Hunting with a camera."

Dandridge nodded. "So you see now why I said I was a hunter in a manner of speaking. Many people would not call me a hunter. They would say I was a photographer of animals in the wild, while I consider myself a hunter who simply employs a camera instead of a gun."

Krull took his time digesting this. "I understand the distinction," he said.

"I felt that you would."

"The act of taking the picture is equivalent to making the kill. It's how you take the trophy, but you don't go out because you want a picture of an elk any more than a man hunts because he wants to put meat on the table."

"You do understand, Mr. Krull." The glasses, it was noticed, were once more empty. "Eddie!"

351

"My turn this time, Eddie," said Roger Krull. He waited until the drinks were poured and tasted. Then he said, "Do you get the same thrill, Homer?"

"Roger, I get twice the thrill. Another old hunter name of Hemingway said a moral act is one that makes you feel good afterward. Well, if that's the case, then hunting with a gun became immoral for me a couple of years back Hunting with a camera has all the thrills and excitement of gun hunting without the letdown that comes when you realize you've caused pain and death to an innocent creature. If I want meat on the table I'll buy it, Roger. I don't have to kill a deer to prove to myself I'm a man."

"I'll certainly go along with that, Homer."

"Here, let me show you something." Dandridge produced his wallet, drew out a sheaf of color snapshots. "I don't normally do this," he confided. "I could wind up being every bit as much of a bore as those pests who show you pictures of their grandchildren. But I get the feeling you're interested."

"You're damned right I'm interested, Homer."

"Well, now," Dandridge said. "All right,

we'll lead off with something big. This here is a Kodiak bear. I went up to Alaska to get him, hired a guide, tracked the son of a bitch halfway across the state until I got close enough for this one. That's not taken with a telephoto lens, incidentally. I actually got in close and took that one."

"You hire guides and backpack and everything."

"Oh, the whole works, Roger. I'm telling you, it's the same sport right up to the moment of truth. Then I take a picture instead of a life. I take more risks now than I did when I carried a gun through the woods. I never would have stood that close to the bear in order to shoot him. Hell, you can drop them from a quarter of a mile if you want, but I got right in close to take his picture. If he'd have charged —"

They reached for their drinks.

"I'll just show you a few more of these," Dandridge said. "You'll notice some of them aren't game animals, strictly speaking. Of course when you hunt with a camera you're not limited to what the law says is game, and the seasons don't apply. An endangered species doesn't shrink because I take its photograph. I can shoot does, I can photograph in or out of season, anything I want. The fact of the matter is that I prefer to go after trophy animals in season because that makes more of a game out of it, but sometimes it's as much of a challenge to try for a particular songbird that's hard to get up close to. That's a scarlet tanager there, it's a bird that lives in deep woods and spooks easy. Of course I had to use a telephoto lens to get anything worth looking at but it's still considered something of an accomplishment. I got a thrill out of that shot, Roger. Now no one would shoot a little bird like that, nobody would want to, but when you hunt with a camera it's another story entirely, and I don't mind telling you I got a thrill out of that shot."

"I can believe it."

"Now here's a couple of mountain goats, that was quite a trip I had after them, and this antelope, oh, there's a heck of a story goes with this one —"

It was a good hour later when Homer Dandridge returned the photographs to his wallet. "Here I went and talked your ear off," he said apologetically, but Roger Krull insisted quite sincerely that he had been fascinated throughout.

"I wonder," he said. "I just wonder."

"If it would work for you or not?"

Krull nodded. "Of course I had a

camera years ago," he said, "but I never had much interest in it. I couldn't tell you how long it's been since I took a photograph of anything."

"Never had the slightest interest in it myself," Dandridge said. "Until I substituted click for bang, that is."

"No more bang-bang. Click-click instead. I don't know, Homer. I suppose you've got all sorts of elaborate equipment, fancy cameras, all the rest. It'd take me a year and a day to learn how to load one of those things."

"They're easier than you think," Dandridge said. "As a matter of fact, I've got some reasonably fancy gear. Hell, you wouldn't believe the money I used to spend on guns. Or I guess you would if you're a hunter yourself. Well, it's not surprising that I spend money the same way on cameras. I've got a new Japanese model that I'm just getting the hang of, and I've got my eyes on a lens for it that's going to cost me more than a whole camera ought to cost, and the next step's developing my own pictures and I don't suppose that's very far off. Just around the corner, I suspect. In another few months I'll likely have my own darkroom in the basement and be up to my elbows in chemicals."

"That's what I thought. I don't know if I'd want to get into all that."

"But that's the whole thing, Roger. You don't have to. Look, I don't know what your first hunting experience was like, but I remember mine. I was fourteen years old and I was out in a field down near the railroad tracks with an old rimfire twenty-two rifle, and I shot a squirrel out of an oak tree. Just a poor raggedy squirrel that I plinked with a broken-down rifle, and that's as big a hunting thrill as I guess I ever had. Now I'd guess your first experience wasn't a hell of a lot different."

"Not a whole hell of a lot, no."

"Well, when I put down the gun and took up the camera, the camera I took up was a little Instamatic that cost under twenty dollars. And I'll tell you a thing. The picture I took with that little camera was at least as much of a thrill as I get with my Japanese job."

"You can get decent pictures that way?"

"You can get perfect pictures that way," Dandridge said. "If I had any sense I'd still use the Instamatic, but as you go along you want to try getting fancy. And anyway, it hardly matters how good the pictures are. You don't want to sell 'em to *Field and Stream*, do you?"

"Of course not."

"Hell, no. You want to find out if you can go on having the sheer joy and excitement of hunting without having the guilt and sorrow of killing. That's it in a nutshell, right?"

"That's it."

"So pick up a cheap camera and find out."

"By God," said Roger Krull, "that's just what I'll do. There's a drugstore in town that'll have cameras. I'll go there first thing in the morning."

"Do it, Roger."

"Homer, I intend to. Oh, I'm a little dubious about it. I've got to admit as much. But what have I got to lose?"

"That calls for a drink," said Homer Dandridge.

Dandridge was out in the woods early the next morning. His head was clear and his hand steady, as was always the case on hunting trips. In the city he drank moderately, and his rare overindulgences were followed by mind-shattering hangovers. On hunting trips he drank heavily every evening and never had the whisper of a hangover. The fresh air, he thought, probably had something to do with it, and so too did the way the excitement of the chase sent the blood singing in his veins.

He had another good day, shooting several rolls of film, and by the time he returned to the lodge he was ready for that first double shot of sour mash whiskey, and ready too for the good company of Roger Krull. Dandridge was not by nature a proselytizer, and in casual conversations with other hunters he rarely let on that he employed a camera instead of a gun. But Krull had been an obvious candidate for conversion, and now Dandridge was excited at the thought that he had been instrumental in leading another man from bang-bang, as it were, to click-click.

Again he stowed his cap and gear and hurried to the taproom. But this time Krull was not there waiting for him, and Dandridge was disappointed. He drowned his disappointment with a drink, his usual straight double, and then he settled down and sipped a second drink on the rocks with a splash of soda. He had almost finished the drink when Roger Krull made his appearance.

"Well, Roger!" he said. "How did it go?"

"Spent the whole day at it."

"And?"

Roger Krull shrugged. "Hate to say it,"

he said. He took a roll of film from his jacket pocket, weighed it in his hand. "Didn't work for me," he said.

"Oh," Dandridge said.

"I envy you, Homer. I had my doubts last night and I had them this morning, but I went out and got myself a camera and gave it a try. I honestly thought it might be exciting after all. The pursuit and everything, and no death at the end of it."

"And it didn't work."

"No, it didn't. I'll tell you something. I'd like myself better if it had. But for one reason or another it isn't hunting for me without the bang-bang part. Just squeezing the shutter on a camera isn't the same as squeezing a trigger. Some primitive streak, I suppose. I stopped enjoying killing a while ago but it's just not hunting without it."

"Hell," Dandridge said. "I don't know what to say."

And that was true for both of them. They suddenly found themselves with nothing at all to say and the silence was awkward. "Well, I'm damned glad I tried it all the same," Krull said. "I really enjoyed talking with you last night. You're a hell of a guy, Homer."

"You're all right yourself, Roger."

"Take care of yourself, you hear?"

"You, too," Dandridge said. "Say, don't you want this?" He indicated the roll of film, which Krull had left on top of the bar.

"What for?"

"Might get it developed, see how your pictures turned out."

"I don't really care how they turned out, Homer."

"Well —"

"Keep it," Krull said.

Dandridge picked up the film, looked at it for a moment, then dropped it in his pocket. He wondered if Roger Krull had even bothered to purchase a camera at all. Men sometimes came to momentous decisions under the heady influence of alcohol and changed their minds the following morning. Krull might have decided that hunting with a camera made as much sense as taking portrait photographs with a shotgun, and then might have gone through the charade with the film to keep up appearances. Not that Krull had seemed like the sort to go through that kind of nonsense, but people did strange things sometimes.

Psychology was another hobby of Homer Dandridge's.

Well, it was easy enough to find out, he decided. All he had to do was include Krull's film with his own when he sent it off to be developed. It would be interesting to see if there were any pictures on it, and if so it would be even more interesting to see what animals Krull had snapped and how well he had done.

When the pictures came back Homer Dandridge was very confused indeed.

Oh, there were pictures, all right. An even dozen of them, and they had all come out successfully. They did not have the contrast and brightness of the pictures Dandridge took with his expensive Japanese camera, but they were certainly clear enough, and they revealed that Roger Krull had a good intuitive sense of composition.

But they had not been taken in the woods. They had been taken in a city, and their subjects were not animals or birds at all.

They were people. Ten men and two women, captured in various candid poses as they went about their business in a city.

It took Dandridge a moment. Then his jaw fell and a chill raced through him.

God!

He examined the pictures again, thinking that there ought to be something he should do, deciding that there was not. The name Roger Krull was almost certainly an alias. And even if it was not, what could he say? What could he do?

He wasn't even certain in what city the twelve pictures had been taken. And he didn't recognize any of the men or women in them.

Not then. A week later, when they started turning up in the newspaper, then he recognized them.

Passport in Order

Marcia stood up, yawned, and crushed out a cigarette in the round glass ashtray. "It's late," she said. "I should be getting home. How I hate to leave you!"

"You said it was his poker night."

"It is, but he might call me. Sometimes, too, he loses a lot of money in a hurry and comes home early, and in a foul mood, naturally." She sighed, turned to look at him. "I wish it didn't have to be secretive like this — hotel rooms, motels."

"It can't stay this way much longer."

"Why not?"

Bruce Farr ran a hand through his wavy hair, groped for a cigarette and lit it. "Inventory is scheduled in a month," he said. "It won't be ten minutes before they discover I'm into them up to the eyes. They're a big firm, but a quarter of a million dollars worth of jewelry can't be eased out of the vaults without someone noticing it sooner or later."

"Did you take that much?"

He grinned. "That much," he said, "a little at a time. I picked pieces no one would ever look for, but the inventory will show them gone. I made out beautifully on the sale, honey; peddled some of the goods outright and borrowed on the rest. Got a little better than a hundred thousand dollars, safely stowed away."

"All that money, " she said. She pursed her lips as if to whistle. "A hundred thousand —"

"Plus change." His smile spread and she thought how pleased he was with himself. Then he became serious. "Close to half the retail value. It went pretty well, Marcia, but we can't sit on it. We have to get out, out of the country."

"I know, but I'm afraid," Marcia said.

"They won't get us. Once we're out of the country, we don't have a thing to worry about. There are countries where you can buy yourself citizenship for a few thousand U.S. dollars, and beat extradition forever. They can't get us."

She was silent for a moment. When he took her hand and asked her what was wrong, she turned away, then met his eyes. "I'm not that worried about the police. If you say we can get away with it, well, I believe you."

"Then what's scaring you?"

"It's Ray," she said and dropped her eyes. "Ray, my sweet loving husband. He'll find us, darling. I know he will. He'll find us, and he won't care whether we're citizens of Patagonia or Cambodia or wherever we go. He won't try to extradite us. He'll —" her voice broke, "he'll kill us," she finished.

"How can he find us? And what makes you think —"

She was shaking her head. "You don't know him."

"I don't particularly want to. Honey —"

"You don't know him," she repeated. "I do. I wish I didn't, I wish I'd never met him. I'm one of his possessions, I belong to him, and he wouldn't let me get away from him, not in a million years. He knows all kinds of people, terrible people. Criminals, gangsters." She gnawed her lip. "Why do you think I never left him? Why do you think I stay with him? Because I know what would happen if I didn't. He'd find me, one way or another, and he'd kill me, and —"

She broke. His arms went around her and held her, comforted her.

"I'm not giving you up," he said, "and he won't kill us. He won't kill either of us."

"You don't *know* him." Panic rose in her voice. "He's vicious, ruthless. He —"

365

"Suppose we kill him first, Marcia?"

He had to go over it with her a long time before she would even listen to him. They had to leave the country anyway. Neither of them was ready to spend a lifetime, or part of it, in jail. Once they were out they could stay out. So why not burn an extra bridge on the way? If Ray was really a threat to them, why not put him all the way out of the picture?

"Besides," he told her, "I'd like to see him dead. I really would. For months now you've been mine, yet you always have to go home to him."

"I'll have to think about it," she said.

"You wouldn't have to do a thing, baby. I'd take care of everything."

She nodded, got to her feet. "I never thought of — murder," she said. "Is this how murders happen? When ordinary people get caught up over their heads? Is that how it starts?"

"We're not ordinary people, Marcia. We're special. And we're not in over our heads. It'll work."

"I'll think about it," she said. "I'll — I'll think about it."

Marcia called Bruce two days later. She said, "Do you remember what we were talking about? We don't have a month any more."

"What do you mean?"

"Ray surprised me last night. He showed me a pair of airline tickets for Paris. We're set to fly in ten days. Our passports are still in order from last year's trip. I couldn't stand another trip with him, dear. I couldn't live through it."

"Did you think about —"

"Yes, but this is no time to talk about it," she said. "I think I can get away tonight."

"Where and when?"

She named a time and place. When she placed the receiver back in its cradle she was surprised that her hand did not tremble. So easy, she thought. She was deciding a man's fate, planning the end of a man's life, and her hand was as steady as a surgeon's. It astonished her that questions of life and death could be so easily resolved.

She was a few minutes late that night. Bruce was waiting for her in front of a tavern on Randolph Avenue. As she approached, he stepped forward and took her arm.

"We can't talk here," he said. "I don't think we should chance being seen together. We can drive around. My car's across the street."

He took Claibourne Drive out to the east end of town. She lit a cigarette with the dashboard lighter and smoked in silence. He asked her what she had decided.

"I tried not to think about it," she told him. "Then last night he sprang this jaunt on me, this European tour. He's planning on spending three weeks over there. I don't think I could endure it."

"So?"

"Well, I got this wild idea. I thought about what you said, about — about killing him. . . ."

"Yes?"

She drew a breath, let it out slowly. "I think you're right. We have to kill him. I'd never rest if I knew he was after us. I'd wake up terrified in the middle of the night. I know I would. So would you."

He didn't say anything. His eyes were on hers and he clasped her hands.

"I guess I'm a worrier. I'd worry about the police, too. Even if we managed to do what you said, to buy our way out of extradition. The things you read, I don't know. I'd hate to feel like a hunted animal for the rest of my life. I'd rather have the police hunting me than Ray, but even so, I don't think I'd like it."

"So?"

She lit another cigarette. "It's probably silly," she said. "I thought there might be a way to keep them from looking for you, and to get rid of him at the same time. Last night it occurred to me that you're about his build. About six-one, aren't you?"

"Just about."

"That's what I thought. You're younger, and you're much better looking than he is, but you're both about the same height and weight. And I thought — Oh, this is silly!"

"Keep going."

"Oh, this is the kind of crazy thing you see on television. I don't know what kind of a mind I must have to think of it. But I thought that you could leave a note. You'd go to sleep at your house, then get up in the middle of the night and leave a long note explaining how you stole jewelry from your company and lost the money gambling and kept stealing more money and getting in deeper and deeper until there's no way out. And that you're doing the only thing you can do, that you've decided, well, to commit suicide."

"I think I'm beginning to get it."

Her eyes lowered. "It doesn't make any sense, does it?"

"It sure does. You're about as crazy as a fox. Then we kill Ray and make it appear to be me."

She nodded. "I thought of a way we could do it. I can't believe it's really me saying all of this! I thought we could do it that same night. You would come over to the house and I would let you in. We could get Ray in his sleep. Press a pillow over his face or something like that. I don't know. Then we could load him into your car and drive somewhere and. . . ."

"And put him over a cliff." His eyes were filled with frank admiration. "Beautiful, just beautiful."

"Do you really think so?"

"It couldn't be better. They'll have a perfect note, in my handwriting. They'll have my car over a cliff and a burned body in it. And they'll have a good motive for suicide. You're a wonder, honey."

She managed a smile. "Then your company won't be hunting you, will they?"

"Not me or their money. *Gambled every penny away* — that'll throw 'em a curve. I haven't bet more than two bucks on a horse in my life. But your sweetheart of a husband will be gone, and somebody might start wondering where he is. Oh, wait a minute. . . ."

"What?"

"This gets better the more I think about it. He'll take my place in the car and I'll take his on that plane to Europe. We're the same build, his passport is in good order, and the reservations are all made. We'll use those tickets to take the Grand Tour, except that we won't come back. Or if we do, we'll wind up in some other city where nobody knows us, baby. We'll have every bridge burned the minute we cross over. When are you scheduled to take that trip?"

She closed her eyes, thought it through. "A week from Friday," she said. "We fly to New York in the morning, and then on to Paris the next afternoon."

"Perfect. You can expect company Thursday night. Slip downstairs after he goes to bed and let me into the house. I'll have the note written. We'll take care of him and go straight to the airport. We won't even have to come back to the house."

"The money?"

"I'll have it with me. You can do your packing Thursday so we'll have everything ready, passports and all." He shook his head in disbelief. "I always knew you were wonderful, Marcia. I didn't realize you were a genius."

"You really think it will work?"

He kissed her and she clung to him. He kissed her again, then grinned down at her. "I don't see how it can miss," he said.

The days crawled. They couldn't risk seeing each other until Thursday night, but Bruce assured Marcia that it wouldn't be long.

But it *was* long. Although she found herself far calmer than she had dared to expect, Marcia was still anxious, nervous about the way it might go.

Oh, it was long, very long. Bruce called Wednesday afternoon to make final plans. They arranged a signaling system. When Ray was sleeping soundly, she would slip out of bed and go downstairs. She would dial his phone number. He would have the note written, the money stowed in the trunk of his car. As soon as she called he would drive over to her house, and she would be waiting downstairs to let him in.

"Don't worry about what happens then," he said. "I'll take care of the details."

That night and the following day consumed at least a month of subjective time for her. She called him, finally, at twenty minutes of three Friday morning. He answered at once.

"I thought you weren't going to call at all," he said.

"He was up late, but he's asleep now."

"I'll be right over."

She waited downstairs at the front door, heard his car pull to a stop, had the door open for him before he could knock. He stepped quickly inside and closed the door.

"All set," he said. "The note, everything."

"The money?"

"It's in the trunk, in an attaché case, packed to the brim."

"Fine," she said. "It's been fun, darling."

But Bruce never heard the last sentence. Just as her lips framed the words, a form moved behind him and a leather-covered sap arced downward, catching him deftly and decisively behind the right ear. He fell like a stone and never made a sound.

Ray Danahy straightened up. "Out cold," he said. "Neat and sweet. Take a look outside and check the traffic. This is no time for nosy neighbors."

She opened the door, stepped outside. The night was properly dark and silent. She filled her lungs gratefully with fresh air.

Ray said, "Pull his car into the driveway alongside the house. Wait a sec, I think he's got the keys on him." He bent over Farr, dug a set of car keys out of his pocket. "Go ahead," he said.

She brought the car to the side door. Ray appeared in the doorway with Bruce's inert form over one shoulder. He dumped him onto the back seat and walked around the car to get behind the wheel.

"Take our buggy," he told Marcia. "Follow me, but not too close. I'm taking Route Thirty-two north of town. There's a good drop about a mile and a half past the county line."

"Not too good a drop, I hope," she said. "He could be burned beyond recognition."

"No such thing. Dental x-rays — they can't miss. It's a good thing he didn't have the brains to think of that."

"He wasn't very long on brains," she said.

"Isn't," he corrected. "He's not dead yet."

She followed Ray, lagging about a block and a half behind him. At the site he had chosen, she stood by while he took the money from the trunk and checked Farr's pockets to make sure he wasn't carrying anything that might tip anybody off. Ray propped him behind the wheel, put the car in neutral, braced Farr's foot on the gas pedal. Farr was just beginning to stir.

"Goodbye, Brucie," Marcia said. "You don't know what a bore you were."

Ray reached inside and popped the car into gear, then jumped aside. The heavy car hurtled through an ineffective guard rail, hung momentarily in the air, then began the long fast fall. First, there was the noise of the impact. Then there was another loud noise, an explosion, and the vehicle burst into flames.

They drove slowly away, the suitcase full of money between them on the seat of their car. "Scratch one fool," Ray said pleasantly. "We've got two hours to catch our flight to New York, then on to Paris."

"Paris," she sighed. "Not on a shoestring, the way we did it last time. This time we'll do it in style."

She looked down at her hands, her steady hands. How surprisingly calm she was, she thought, and a slow smile spread over her face.

Like a Lamb
to Slaughter

He was a thin young man in a blue pin-stripe suit. His shirt was white with a button-down collar. His glasses had oval lenses in brown tortoiseshell frames. His hair was a dark brown, short but not severely so, neatly combed, parted on the right. I saw him come in and watched him ask a question at the bar. Billie was working afternoons that week. I watched as he nodded at the young man, then swung his sleepy eyes over in my direction. I lowered my own eyes and looked at a cup of coffee laced with bourbon while the fellow walked over to my table.

"Matthew Scudder?" I looked up at him, nodded. "I'm Aaron Creighton. I looked for you at your hotel. The fellow on the desk told me I might find you here."

Here was Armstrong's, a Ninth Avenue saloon around the corner from my Fifty-seventh Street hotel. The lunch crowd was gone except for a couple of stragglers in front whose voices were starting to thicken with alcohol. The streets outside were full of May sunshine. The winter had been cold and deep and long. I couldn't recall a more welcome spring.

"I called you a couple times last week, Mr. Scudder. I guess you didn't get my messages."

I'd gotten two of them and ignored them, not knowing who he was or what he wanted and unwilling to spend a dime for the answer. But I went along with the fiction. "It's a cheap hotel," I said. "They're not always too good about messages."

"I can imagine. Uh. Is there someplace we can talk?"

"How about right here?"

He looked around. I don't suppose he was used to conducting his business in bars but he evidently decided it would be all right to make an exception. He set his briefcase on the floor and seated himself across the table from me. Angela, the new day-shift waitress, hurried over to get his order. He glanced at my cup and said he'd have coffee, too.

"I'm an attorney," he said. My first thought was that he didn't look like a lawyer, but then I realized he probably dealt with civil cases. My experience as a cop had given me a lot of experience with criminal lawyers. The breed ran to several types, none of them his.

I waited for him to tell me why he wanted to hire me. But he crossed me up.

"I'm handling an estate," he said, and paused, and gave what seemed a calculated if well-intentioned smile. "It's my pleasant duty to tell you you've come into a small legacy, Mr. Scudder."

"Someone's left me money?"

"Twelve hundred dollars."

Who could have died? I'd lost touch long since with any of my relatives. My parents went years ago and we'd never been close with the rest of the family.

I said, "Who — ?"

"Mary Alice Redfield."

I repeated the name aloud. It was not entirely unfamiliar but I had no idea who Mary Alice Redfield might be. I looked at Aaron Creighton. I couldn't make out his eyes behind the glasses but there was a smile's ghost on his thin lips, as if my reaction was not unexpected.

"She's dead?"

"Almost three months ago."

"I didn't know her."

"She knew you. You probably knew her,

Mr. Scudder. Perhaps you didn't know her by name." His smile deepened. Angela had brought his coffee. He stirred milk and sugar into it, took a careful sip, nodded his approval. "Miss Redfield was murdered." He said this as if he'd had practice uttering a phrase which did not come naturally to him. "She was killed quite brutally in late February for no apparent reason, another innocent victim of street crime."

"She lived in New York?"

"Oh, yes. In this neighborhood."

"And she was killed around here?"

"On West Fifty-fifth Street between Ninth and Tenth avenues. Her body was found in an alleyway. She'd been stabbed repeatedly and strangled with the scarf she had been wearing."

Late February. Mary Alice Redfield. West Fifty-fifth between Ninth and Tenth. Murder most foul. Stabbed and strangled, a dead woman in an alleyway. I usually kept track of murders, perhaps out of a vestige of professionalism, perhaps because I couldn't cease to be fascinated by man's inhumanity to man. Mary Alice Redfield had willed me twelve hundred dollars. And someone had knifed and strangled her, and —

"Oh, Jesus," I said. "The shopping bag lady."

Aaron Creighton nodded.

New York is full of them. East Side, West Side, each neighborhood has its own supply of bag women. Some of them are alcoholic but most of them have gone mad without any help from drink. They walk the streets, huddle on stoops or in doorways. They find sermons in stones and treasures in trashcans. They talk to themselves, to passersby, to God. Sometimes they mumble. Now and then they shriek.

They carry things around with them, the bag women. The shopping bags supply their generic name and their chief common denominator. Most of them seem to be paranoid, and their madness convinces them that their possessions are very valuable, that their enemies covet them. So their shopping bags are never out of their sight.

There used to be a colony of these ladies who lived in Grand Central Station. They would sit up all night in the waiting room, taking turns waddling off to the lavatory from time to time. They rarely talked to each other but some herd instinct made them comfortable with one another. But they were not comfortable enough to trust their precious bags to one another's safe-keeping, and each sad crazy lady always toted her shopping bags to and from the ladies' room.

Mary Alice Redfield had been a shopping bag lady. I don't know when she set up shop in the neighborhood. I'd been living in the same hotel ever since I resigned from the NYPD and separated from my wife and sons, and that was getting to be quite a few years now. Had Miss Redfield been on the scene that long ago? I couldn't remember her first appearance. Like so many of the neighborhood fixtures, she had been part of the scenery. Had her death not been violent and abrupt I might never have noticed she was gone.

I'd never known her name. But she had evidently known mine, and had felt something for me that prompted her to leave money to me. How had she come to have money to leave?

She'd had a business of sorts. She would sit on a wooden soft drink case, surrounded by three or four shopping bags, and she would sell newspapers. There's an all-night newsstand at the corner of Fifty-seventh and Eighth, and she would buy a few dozen papers there, carry them a block west to the corner of Ninth and set up shop in a doorway. She sold the papers at retail, though I suppose some people tipped her a few cents. I could remember a few occasions when I'd bought a paper and waved away change from a dollar bill. Bread upon the waters, perhaps, if that was what had moved her to leave me the money.

I closed my eyes, brought her image into focus. A thickset woman, stocky rather than fat. Five-three or -four. Dressed usually in shapeless clothing, colorless gray and black garments, layers of clothing that varied with the season. I remembered that she would sometimes wear a hat, an old straw affair with paper and plastic flowers poked into it. And I remembered her eyes, large guileless blue eyes that were many years younger than the rest of her.

Mary Alice Redfield.

"Family money," Aaron Creighton was saying. "She wasn't wealthy but she had come from a family that was comfortably fixed. A bank in Baltimore handled her funds. That's where she was from originally, Baltimore, though she'd lived in New York for as long as anyone can remember.

The bank sent her a check every month. Not very much, a couple of hundred dollars, but she hardly spent anything. She paid her rent —"

"I thought she lived on the street."

"No, she had a furnished room a few doors down the street from where she was killed. She lived in another rooming house on Tenth Avenue before that but moved when the building was sold. That was six or seven years ago and she lived on Fifty-fifth Street from then until her death. Her room cost her eighty dollars a month. She spent a few dollars on food. I don't know what she did with the rest. The only money in her room was a coffee can full of pennies. I've been checking the banks and there's no record of a savings account. I suppose she may have spent it or lost it or given it away. She wasn't very firmly grounded in reality."

"No, I don't suppose she was."

He sipped at his coffee. "She probably belonged in an institution," he said. "At least that's what people would say, but she got along in the outside world, she functioned well enough. I don't know if she kept herself clean and I don't know anything about how her mind worked but I think she must have been happier than she would have been in an institution. Don't you think?"

"Probably."

"Of course she wasn't safe, not as it turned out, but anybody can get killed on the streets of New York." He frowned briefly, caught up in a private thought. Then he said, "She came to our office ten years ago. That was before my time." He told me the name of his firm, a string of Anglo-Saxon surnames. "She wanted to draw a will. The original will was a very simple document leaving everything to her sister. Then over the years she would come in from time to time to add codicils leaving specific sums to various persons. She had made a total of thirty-two bequests by the time she died. One was for twenty dollars — that was to a man named John Johnson whom we haven't been able to locate. The remainder all ranged from five hundred to two thousand dollars." He smiled. "I've been given the task of running down the heirs."

"When did she put me into her will?"

"Two years ago in April."

I tried to think what I might have done for her then, how I might have brushed her life with mine. Nothing.

"Of course the will could be contested,

Mr. Scudder. It would be easy to challenge Miss Redfield's competence and any relative could almost certainly get it set aside. But no one wishes to challenge it. The total amount involved is slightly in excess of a quarter of a million dollars —"

"That much."

"Yes. Miss Redfield received substantially less than the income which her holdings drew over the years, so the principal kept growing during her lifetime. Now the specific bequests she made total thirty-eight thousand dollars, give or take a few hundred, and the residue goes to Miss Redfield's sister. The sister — her name's Mrs. Palmer — is a widow with grown children. She's hospitalized with cancer and heart trouble and I believe diabetic complications and she hasn't long to live. Her children would like to see the estate settled before their mother dies and they have enough local prominence to hurry the will through probate. So I'm authorized to tender checks for the full amount of the specific bequests on the condition that the legatees sign quitclaims acknowledging that this payment discharges in full the estate's indebtedness to them."

There was more legalese of less importance. Then he gave me papers to sign and the whole procedure ended with a check on the table. It was payable to me and in the amount of twelve hundred dollars and no cents.

I told Creighton I'd pay for his coffee.

I had time to buy myself another drink and still get to my bank before the windows closed. I put a little of Mary Alice Redfield's legacy in my savings account, took some in cash, and sent a money order to Anita and my sons. I stopped at my hotel to check for messages. There weren't any. I had a drink at McGovern's and crossed the street to have another at Polly's Cage. It wasn't five o'clock yet but the bar was doing good business already.

It turned into a funny night. I had dinner at the Greek place and read the *Post*, spent a little time at Joey Farrell's on Fifty-eighth Street, then wound up getting to Armstrong's around ten-thirty or thereabouts. I spent part of the evening alone at my usual table and part of it in conversation at the bar. I made a point of stretching my drinks, mixing my bourbon with coffee, making a cup last a while, taking a glass of plain water from time to time.

But that never really works. If you're going to get drunk you'll manage it somehow. The obstacles I placed in my path just kept me up later. By two-thirty I'd done what I had set out to do. I'd made my load and I could go home and sleep it off.

I woke around ten with less of a hangover than I'd earned and no memory of anything after I'd left Armstrong's. I was in my own bed in my own hotel room. And my clothes were hung neatly in the closet, always a good sign on a morning after. So I must have been in fairly good shape. But a certain amount of time was lost to memory, blacked out, gone.

When that first started happening I tended to worry about it. But it's the sort of thing you can get used to.

It was the money, the twelve hundred bucks. I couldn't understand the money. I had done nothing to deserve it. It had been left to me by a poor little rich woman whose name I'd not even known.

It had never occurred to me to refuse the dough. Very early in my career as a cop I'd learned an important precept. When someone put money in your hand you closed your fingers around it and put it in your pocket. I learned that lesson well and never had cause to regret its application. I didn't walk around with my hand out and I never took drug or homicide money but I certainly grabbed all the clean graft that came my way and a certain amount that wouldn't have stood a white glove inspection. If Mary Alice thought I merited twelve hundred dollars, who was I to argue?

Ah, but it didn't quite work that way. Because somehow the money gnawed at me.

After breakfast I went to St. Paul's but there was a service going on, a priest saying Mass, so I didn't stay. I walked down to St. Benedict the Moor's on Fifty-third Street and sat for a few minutes in a pew at the rear. I go to churches to try to think, and I gave it a shot but my mind didn't know where to go.

I slipped six twenties into the poor box. I tithe. It's a habit I got into after I left the department and I still don't know why I do it. God knows. Or maybe He's as mystified as I am. This time, though, there was a certain balance in the act. Mary Alice Redfield had given me twelve hundred dollars for no reason I could comprehend. I was passing on a ten percent commission to the church for no better reason.

I stopped on the way out and lit a couple of candles for various people who weren't alive anymore. One of them was for the bag lady. I didn't see how it could do her any good, but I couldn't imagine how it could harm her, either.

I had read some press coverage of the killing when it happened. I generally keep up with crime stories. Part of me evidently never stopped being a policeman. Now I went down to the Forty-second Street library to refresh my memory.

The *Times* had run a pair of brief back-page items, the first a report of the killing of an unidentified female derelict, the second a follow-up giving her name and age. She'd been forty-seven, I learned. This surprised me, and then I realized that any specific number would have come as a surprise. Bums and bag ladies are ageless. Mary Alice Redfield could have been thirty or sixty or anywhere in between.

The *News* had run a more extended article than the *Times*, enumerating the stab wounds — twenty-six of them — and described the scarf wound about her throat — blue and white, a designer print, but tattered at its edges and evidently somebody's castoff. It was this article that I remembered having read.

But the *Post* had really played the story. It had appeared shortly after the new owner took over the paper and the editors were going all out for human interest, which always translates out as sex and violence. The brutal killing of a woman touches both of those bases, and this had the added kick that she was a character. If they'd ever learned she was an heiress it would have been page three material, but even without that knowledge they did all right by her.

The first story they ran was straight news reporting, albeit embellished with reports on the blood, the clothes she was wearing, the litter in the alley where she was found and all that sort of thing. The next day a reporter pushed the pathos button and tapped out a story featuring capsule interviews with people in the neighborhood. Only a few of them were identified by name and I came away with the feeling that he'd made up some peachy quotes and attributed them to unnamed nonexistent hangers-on. As a sidebar to that story, another reporter speculated on the possibility of a whole string of bag lady murders, a speculation which happily had turned out to be off the mark. The clown had presumably gone around the West Side asking shopping bag ladies if they were afraid of being the killer's next victim.

I hope he faked the piece and let the ladies alone.

And that was about it. When the killer failed to strike again the newspapers hung up on the story. Good news is no news.

I walked back from the library. It was fine weather. The winds had blown all the crap out of the sky and there was nothing but blue overhead. The air actually had some air in it for a change. I walked west on Forty-second Street and north on Broadway, and I started noticing the number of street people, the drunks and the crazies and the unclassifiable derelicts. By the time I got within a few blocks of Fifty-seventh Street I was recognizing a large percentage of them. Each mini-neighborhood has its own human flotsam and jetsam and they're a lot more noticeable come springtime. Winter sends some of them south and others to shelter, and there's a certain percentage who die of exposure, but when the sun warms the pavement it brings most of them out again.

When I stopped for a paper at the corner of Eighth Avenue I got the bag lady into the conversation. The newsie clucked his tongue and shook his head.

"The damnedest thing. Just the damnedest thing."

"Murder never makes much sense."

"The hell with murder. You know what she did? You know Eddie, works for me midnight to eight? Guy with the one droopy eyelid? Now he wasn't the guy used to sell her the stack of papers. Matter of fact that was usually me. She'd come by during the late morning or early afternoon and she'd take fifteen or twenty papers and pay me for 'em, and then she'd sit on her crate down the next corner and she'd sell as many as she could, and then she'd bring 'em back and I'd give her a refund on what she didn't sell."

"What did she pay for them?"

"Full price. And that's what she sold 'em for. The hell, I can't discount on papers. You know the margin we got. I'm not even supposed to take 'em back, but what difference does it make? It gave the poor woman something to do is my theory. She was important, she was a businesswoman. Sits there charging a quarter for something she just paid a quarter for, it's no way to get rich, but you know something? She had money. Lived like a pig but she had money."

"So I understand."

"She left Eddie seven-twenty. You believe that? Seven hundred and twenty dollars, she willed it to him, there was this
lawyer come around two, three weeks ago
with a check. Eddie Halloran. Pay to the
order of. You believe that? She never had
dealings with him. I sold her the papers, I
bought 'em back from her. Not that I'm
complaining, not that I want the woman's
money, but I ask you this: Why Eddie? He
don't know her. He can't believe she
knows his name, Eddie Halloran. Why'd
she leave it to him? He tells this lawyer, he
says maybe she's got some other Eddie
Halloran in mind. It's a common Irish
name and the neighborhood's full of the
Irish. I'm thinking to myself, Eddie,
schmuck, take the money and shut up, but
it's him all right because it says in the will.
Eddie Halloran the newsdealer is what it
says. So that's him, right? But why
Eddie?"

Why me? "Maybe she liked the way he
smiled."

"Yeah, maybe. Or the way he combed his
hair. Listen, it's money in his pocket. I
worried he'd go on a toot, drink it up, but
he says money's no temptation. He says
he's always got the price of a drink in his
jeans and there's a bar on every block but

he can walk right past 'em, so why worry about a few hundred dollars? You know something? That crazy woman, I'll tell you something, I miss her. She'd come, crazy hat on her head, spacy look in her eyes, she'd buy her stack of papers and waddle off all businesslike, then she'd bring the leftovers and cash 'em in, and I'd make a joke about her when she was out of earshot, but I miss her."

"I know what you mean."

"She never hurt nobody," he said. "She never hurt a soul."

"Mary Alice Redfield. Yeah, the multiple stabbing and strangulation." He shifted a cud-sized wad of gum from one side of his mouth to the other, pushed a lock of hair off his forehead and yawned. "What have you got, some new information?"

"Nothing. I wanted to find out what you had."

"Yeah, right."

He worked on the chewing gum. He was a patrolman named Andersen who worked out of the Eighteenth. Another cop, a detective named Guzik, had learned that Andersen had caught the Redfield case and had taken the trouble to introduce the two of us. I hadn't known Andersen when

I was on the force. He was younger than I, but then most people are nowadays.

He said, "Thing is, Scudder, we more or less put that one out of the way. It's in an open file. You know how it works. If we get new information, fine, but in the meantime I don't sit up nights thinking about it."

"I just wanted to see what you had."

"Well, I'm kind of tight for time, if you know what I mean. My own personal time, I set a certain store by my own time."

"I can understand that."

"You probably got some relative of the deceased for a client. Wants to find out who'd do such a terrible thing to poor old Cousin Mary. Naturally you're interested because it's a chance to make a buck and a man's gotta make a living. Whether a man's a cop or a civilian he's gotta make a buck, right?"

Uh-huh. I seem to remember that we were subtler in my day, but perhaps that's just age talking. I thought of telling him that I didn't have a client but why should he believe me? He didn't know me. If there was nothing in it for him, why should he bother?

So I said, "You know, we're just a couple weeks away from Memorial Day."

"Yeah, I'll buy a poppy from a Legionnaire. So what else is new?"

"Memorial Day's when women start wearing white shoes and men put straw hats on their heads. You got a new hat for the summer season, Andersen? Because you could use one."

"A man can always use a new hat," he said.

A hat is cop talk for twenty-five dollars. By the time I left the precinct house Andersen had two tens and a five of Mary Alice Redfield's bequest to me and I had all the data that had turned up to date.

I think Andersen won that one. I now knew that the murder weapon had been a kitchen knife with a blade approximately seven and a half inches long. That one of the stab wounds had found the heart and had probably caused death instantaneously. That it was impossible to determine whether strangulation had taken place before or after death. That *should* have been possible to determine — maybe the medical examiner hadn't wasted too much time checking her out, or maybe he had been reluctant to commit himself. She'd been dead a few hours when they found her — the estimate was that she'd died around midnight and the body wasn't reported until half-past five. That wouldn't have ripened her all that much, not in winter weather, but most likely her personal hygiene was nothing to boast about, and she was just a shopping bag lady and you couldn't bring her back to life, so why knock yourself out running tests on her malodorous corpse?

I learned a few other things. The landlady's name. The name of the off-duty bartender, heading home after a nightcap at the neighborhood after-hours joint, who'd happened on the body and who had been drunk enough or sober enough to take the trouble to report it. And I learned the sort of negative facts that turn up in a police report when the case is headed for an open file — the handful of nonleads that led nowhere, the witnesses who had nothing to contribute, the routine matters routinely handled. They hadn't knocked themselves out, Andersen and his partner, but would I have handled it any differently? Why knock yourself out chasing a murderer you didn't stand much chance of catching?

In the theater, SRO is good news. It means a sellout performance, standing room only. But once you get out of the theater district it means single room occupancy, and the designation is invariably applied to a hotel or apartment house which has seen better days.

Mary Alice Redfield's home for the last six or seven years of her life had started out as an old Rent Law tenement, built around the turn of the century, six stories tall, faced in red-brown brick, with four apartments to the floor. Now all of those little apartments had been carved into single rooms as if they were election districts gerrymandered by a maniac. There was a communal bathroom on each floor and you didn't need a map to find it.

The manager was a Mrs. Larkin. Her blue eyes had lost most of their color and half her hair had gone from black to gray but she was still pert. If she's reincarnated as a bird she'll be a house wren.

She said, "Oh, poor Mary. We're none of us safe, are we, with the streets full of monsters? I was born in this neighborhood and I'll die in it, but please God that'll be of natural causes. Poor Mary. There's some said she should have been locked up, but Jesus, she got along. She lived her life. And she had her check coming in every month and paid her rent on time. She had her own money, you

398

know. She wasn't living off the public like some I could name but won't."

"I know."

"Do you want to see her room? I rented it twice since then. The first one was a young man and he didn't stay. He looked all right but when he left me I was just as glad. He said he was a sailor off a ship and when he left me he said he'd got on with another ship and was on his way to Hong Kong or some such place, but I've had no end of sailors and he didn't walk like a sailor so I don't know what he was after doing. Then I could have rented it twelve times but didn't because I won't rent to colored or Spanish. I've nothing against them but I won't have them in the house. The owner says to me, Mrs. Larkin he says, my instructions are to rent to anybody regardless of race or creed or color, but if you was to use your own judgment I wouldn't have to know about it. In other words he don't want them either but he's after covering himself."

"I suppose he has to."

"Oh, with all the laws, but I've had no trouble." She laid a forefinger alongside her nose. It's a gesture you don't see too much these days. "Then I rented poor Mary's room two weeks ago to a very nice woman, a widow. She likes her beer, she does, but why shouldn't she have it? I keep my eye on her and she's making no trouble, and if she wants an old jar now and then whose business is it but her own?" She fixed her blue-gray eyes on me. "You like your drink," she said.

"Is it on my breath?"

"No, but I can see it in your face. Larkin liked his drink and there's some say it killed him but he liked it and a man has a right to live what life he wants. And he was never a hard man when he drank, never cursed or fought or beat a woman as some I could name but won't. Mrs. Shepard's out now. That's the one took poor Mary's room, and I'll show it to you if you want."

So I saw the room. It was kept neat.

"She keeps it tidier than poor Mary," Mrs. Larkin said. "Now Mary wasn't dirty, you understand, but she had all her belongings. Her shopping bags and other things that she kept in her room. She made a mare's nest of the place, and all the years she lived here, you see, it wasn't tidy. I would keep her bed made but she didn't want me touching her things and so I let it be cluttered as she wanted it. She paid her rent on time and made no trouble otherwise. She had money, you know."

"Yes, I know."

"She left some to a woman on the fourth floor. A much younger woman, she'd only moved here three months before Mary was killed, and if she exchanged a word with Mary I couldn't swear to it, but Mary left her almost a thousand dollars. Now Mrs. Klein across the hall lived here since before Mary ever moved in and the two old things always had a good word for each other, and all Mrs. Klein has is the welfare and she could have made good use of a couple of dollars, but Mary left her money instead to Miss Strom." She raised her eyebrows to show bewilderment. "Now Mrs. Klein said nothing, and I don't even know if she's had the thought that Mary might have mentioned her in her will, but Miss Strom said she didn't know what to make of it. She just couldn't understand it at all, and what I told her was you can't figure out a woman like poor Mary who never had both her feet on the pavement. Troubled as she was, daft as she was, who's to say what she might have had on her mind?"

"Could I see Miss Strom?"

"That would be for her to say, but she's not home from work yet. She works part-time in the afternoons. She's a close one, not that she hasn't the right to be, and she's never said what it is that she does. But she's a decent sort. This is a decent house."

"I'm sure it is."

"It's single rooms and they don't cost much so you know you're not at the Ritz Hotel, but there's decent people here and I keep it as clean as a person can. When there's not but one toilet on the floor it's a struggle. But it's decent."

"Yes."

"Poor Mary. Why'd anyone kill her? Was it sex, do you know? Not that you could imagine anyone wanting her, the old thing, but try to figure out a madman and you'll go mad your own self. Was she molested?"

"No."

"Just killed, then. Oh, God save us all. I gave her a home for almost seven years. Which it was no more than my job to do, not making it out to be charity on my part. But I had her here all that time and of course I never knew her, you couldn't get to know a poor old soul like that, but I got used to her. Do you know what I mean?"

"I think so."

"I got used to having her about. I might say Hello and Good morning and Isn't it a nice day and not get a look in reply, but

402

even on those days she was someone familiar to say something to. And she's gone now and we're all of us older, aren't we?"

"We are."

"The poor old thing. How could anyone do it, will you tell me that? How could anyone murder her?"

I don't think she expected an answer. Just as well. I didn't have one.

After dinner I returned for a few minutes of conversation with Genevieve Strom. She had no idea why Miss Redfield had left her the money. She'd received $880 and she was glad to get it because she could use it, but the whole thing puzzled her. "I hardly knew her," she said more than once. "I keep thinking I ought to do something special with the money, but what?"

I made the bars that night but drinking didn't have the urgency it had possessed the night before. I was able to keep it in proportion and to know that I'd wake up the next morning with my memory intact. In the course of things I dropped over to the newsstand a little past midnight and talked with Eddie Halloran. He was looking good and I said as much. I remembered him when he'd gone to work for Sid three years ago. He'd been drawn then, and shaky, and his eyes always moved off to the side of whatever he was looking at. Now there was confidence in his stance and he looked years younger. It hadn't all come back to him and maybe some of it was lost forever. I guess the booze had him pretty good before he kicked it once and for all.

We talked about the bag lady. He said, "Know what I think it is? Somebody's sweeping the streets."

"I don't follow you."

"A cleanup campaign. Few years back, Matt, there was this gang of kids found a new way to amuse theirselves. Pick up a can of gasoline, find some bum down on the Bowery, pour the gas on him and throw a lit match at him. You remember?"

"Yeah, I remember."

"Those kids thought they were patriots. Thought they deserved a medal. They were cleaning up the neighborhood, getting drunken bums off the streets. You know, Matt, people don't like to look at a derelict. That building up the block, the Towers? There's this grating there where the heating system's vented. You remember how the guys would sleep there in the winter. It was warm, it was comfortable, it was free, and two or three guys would be there every night catching some Z's and getting warm. Remember?"

"Uh-huh. Then they fenced it."

"Right. Because the tenants complained. It didn't hurt them any, it was just the local bums sleeping it off, but the tenants pay a lot of rent and they don't like to look at bums on their way in or out of their building. The bums were outside and not bothering anybody but it was the sight of them, you know, so the owners went to the expense of putting up cyclone fencing around where they used to sleep. It looks ugly as hell and all it does is keep the bums out but that's all it's supposed to do."

"That's human beings for you."

He nodded, then turned aside to sell somebody a *Daily News* and a *Racing Form.* Then he said, "I don't know what it is exactly. *I* was a bum, Matt. I got pretty far down. You probably don't know how far. I got as far as the Bowery. I panhandled, I slept in my clothes on a bench or in a doorway. You look at men like that and you think they're just waiting to die, and they are, but some of them come back. And you can't tell for sure who's gonna come back and who's not. Somebody coulda poured gas on me, set me on fire. Sweet Jesus."

"The shopping bag lady —"

"You'll look at a bum and you'll say to yourself, 'Maybe I could get like that and I don't wanta think about it.' Or you'll look at somebody like the shopping bag lady and say, 'I could go nutsy like her so get her out of my sight.' And you get people who think like Nazis. You know, take all the cripples and the lunatics and the retarded kids and all and give 'em an injection and Goodbye, Charlie."

"You think that's what happened to her?"

"What else?"

"But whoever did it stopped at one, Eddie."

He frowned. "Don't make sense," he said. "Unless he did the one job and the next day he got run down by a Ninth Avenue bus, and it couldn't happen to a nicer guy. Or he got scared. All that blood and it was more than he figured on. Or he left town. Could be anything like that."

"Could be."

"There's no other reason, is there? She musta been killed because she was a bag lady, right?"

"I don't know."

"Well, Jesus Christ, Matt. What other reason would anybody have for killing her?"

★ ★ ★

The law firm where Aaron Creighton worked had offices on the seventh floor of the Flatiron Building. In addition to the four partners, eleven other lawyers had their names painted on the frosted glass door. Aaron Creighton's came second from the bottom. Well, he was young.

He was also surprised to see me, and when I told him what I wanted he said it was irregular.

"Matter of public record, isn't it?"

"Well, yes," he said. "That means you can find the information. It doesn't mean we're obliged to furnish it to you."

For an instant I thought I was back at the Eighteenth Precinct and a cop was trying to hustle me for the price of a new hat. But Creighton's reservations were ethical. I wanted a list of Mary Alice Redfield's beneficiaries, including the amounts they'd received and the dates they'd been added to her will. He wasn't sure where his duty lay.

"I'd like to be helpful," he said. "Perhaps you could tell me just what your interest is."

"I'm not sure."

"I beg your pardon?"

"I don't know why I'm playing with this one. I used to be a cop, Mr. Creighton.

Now I'm a sort of unofficial detective. I don't carry a license but I do things for people and I wind up making enough that way to keep a roof overhead."

His eyes were wary. I guess he was trying to guess how I intended to earn myself a fee out of this.

"I got twelve hundred dollars out of the blue. It was left to me by a woman I didn't really know and who didn't really know me. I can't seem to slough off the feeling that I got the money for a reason. That I've been paid in advance."

"Paid for what?"

"To try and find out who killed her."

"Oh," he said. *"Oh."*

"I don't want to get the heirs together to challenge the will, if that was what was bothering you. And I can't quite make myself suspect that one of her beneficiaries killed her for the money she was leaving him. For one thing, she doesn't seem to have told people they were named in her will. She never said anything to me or to the two people I've spoken with thus far. For another, it wasn't the sort of murder that gets committed for gain. It was deliberately brutal."

"Then why do you want to know who the other beneficiaries are?"

"I don't know. Part of it's cop training. When you've got any specific leads, any hard facts, you run them down before you cast a wider net. That's only part of it. I suppose I want to get more of a sense of the woman. That's probably all I can realistically hope to get, anyway. I don't stand much chance of tracking her killer."

"The police don't seem to have gotten very far."

I nodded. "I don't think they tried too hard. And I don't think they knew she had an estate. I talked to one of the cops on the case and if he had known that he'd have mentioned it to me. There was nothing in her file. My guess is they waited for her killer to run a string of murders so they'd have something more concrete to work with. It's the kind of senseless crime that usually gets repeated." I closed my eyes for a moment, reaching for an errant thought. "But he didn't repeat," I said. "So they put it on a back burner and then they took it off the stove altogether."

"I don't know much about police work. I've been involved largely with estates and trusts." He tried a smile. "Most of my clients die of natural causes. Murder's an exception."

"It generally is. I'll probably never find

him. I certainly don't expect to find him. Just killing her and moving on, hell, and it was all those months ago. He could have been a sailor off a ship, got tanked up and went nuts and he's in Macao or Port-au-Prince by now. No witnesses and no clues and no suspects and the trail's three months cold by now, and it's a fair bet the killer doesn't remember what he did. So many murders take place in blackout, you know."

"Blackout?" He frowned. "You don't mean in the dark?"

"Alcoholic blackout. The prisons are full of men who got drunk and shot their wives or their best friends. Now they're serving twenty-to-life for something they don't remember. No recollection at all."

The idea unsettled him, and he looked especially young now. "That's frightening," he said. "Really terrifying."

"Yes."

"I originally gave some thought to criminal law. My Uncle Jack talked me out of it. He said you either starve or you spend your time helping professional criminals beat the system. He said that was the only way you made good money out of a criminal practice and what you wound up doing was unpleasant and basically immoral.

Of course there are a couple of superstar criminal lawyers, the hotshots everybody knows, but the other ninety-nine percent fit what Uncle Jack said."

"I would think so, yes."

"I guess I made the right decision." He took his glasses off, inspected them, decided they were clean, put them back on again. "Sometimes I'm not so sure," he said. "Sometimes I wonder. I'll get that list for you. I should probably check with someone to make sure it's all right but I'm not going to bother. You know lawyers. If you ask them whether it's all right to do something they'll automatically say no. Because inaction is always safer than action and they can't get in trouble for giving you bad advice if they tell you to sit on your hands and do nothing. I'm going overboard. Most of the time I like what I do and I'm proud of my profession. This'll take me a few minutes. Do you want some coffee in the meantime?"

His girl brought me a cup, black, no sugar. No bourbon, either. By the time I was done with the coffee he had the list ready.

"If there's anything else I can do —"

I told him I'd let him know. He walked out to the elevator with me, waited for the cage to come wheezing up, shook my hand. I watched him turn and head back to his office and I had the feeling he'd have preferred to come along with me. In a day or so he'd change his mind, but right now he didn't seem too crazy about his job.

The next week was a curious one. I worked my way through the list Aaron Creighton had given me, knowing what I was doing was essentially purposeless but compulsive about doing it all the same. There were thirty-two names on the list. I checked off my own and Eddie Halloran and Genevieve Strom. I put additional check marks next to six people who lived outside of New York. Then I had a go at the remaining twenty-three names. Creighton had done most of the spadework for me, finding addresses to match most of the names. He'd included the date each of the thirty-two codicils had been drawn, and that enabled me to attack the list in reverse chronological order, starting with those persons who'd been made beneficiaries most recently. If this was a method, there was madness to it; it was based on the notion that a person added recently to the will would be more likely to commit homicide for gain, and I'd already decided this wasn't that kind of a killing to begin with.

Well, it gave me something to do. And it led to some interesting conversations. If the people Mary Alice Redfield had chosen to remember ran to any type, my mind wasn't subtle enough to discern it. They ranged in age, in ethnic background, in gender and sexual orientation, in economic status. Most of them were as mystified as Eddie and Genevieve and I about the bag lady's largesse, but once in a while I'd encounter someone who attributed it to some act of kindness he'd performed, and there was a young man named Jerry Forgash who was in no doubt whatsoever. He was some form of Jesus freak and he'd given poor Mary a couple of tracts and a Get Smart–Get Saved button, presumably a twin to the one he wore on the breast pocket of his chambray shirt. I suppose she put his gifts in one of her shopping bags.

"I told her Jesus loved her," he said, "and I suppose it won her soul for Christ. So of course she was grateful. Cast your bread upon the waters, Mr. Scudder. Brother Matthew. You know there was a disciple of Christ named Matthew."

"I know."

He told me Jesus loved me and that I should get smart and get saved. I managed not to get a button but I had to take a couple of tracts from him. I didn't have a shopping bag so I stuck them in my pocket, and a couple of nights later I read them before I went to bed. They didn't win my soul for Christ but you never know.

I didn't run the whole list. People were hard to find and I wasn't in any big rush to find them. It wasn't that kind of a case. It wasn't a case at all, really, merely an obsession, and there was surely no need to race the clock. Or the calendar. If anything, I was probably reluctant to finish up the names on the list. Once I ran out of them I'd have to find some other way to approach the woman's murder and I was damned if I knew where to start.

While I was doing all this, an odd thing happened. The word got around that I was investigating the woman's death, and the whole neighborhood became very much aware of Mary Alice Redfield. People began to seek me out. Ostensibly they had information to give me or theories to advance, but neither the information nor the theories ever seemed to amount to anything substantial, and I came to see that they were merely there as a prelude to conversation. Someone would start off by saying he'd seen Mary selling the *Post* the afternoon before she was killed, and that would serve as the opening wedge of a discussion of the bag woman, or bag women in general, or various qualities of the neighborhood, or violence in American life, or whatever.

A lot of people started off talking about the bag lady and wound up talking about themselves. I guess most conversations work out that way.

A nurse from Roosevelt said she never saw a shopping bag lady without hearing an inner voice say *There but for the grace of God.* And she was not the only woman who confessed she worried about ending up that way. I guess it's a specter that haunts women who live alone, just as the vision of the flowery derelict clouds the peripheral vision of hard-drinking men.

Genevieve Strom turned up at Armstrong's one night. We talked briefly about the bag lady. Two nights later she came back again and we took turns spending our inheritances on rounds of drinks. The drinks hit her with some force and a little past midnight she decided it was time to go. I said I'd see her home. At the corner of Fifty-seventh Street she stopped in her tracks and said, "No men in the room. That's one of Mrs. Larkin's rules."

"Old-fashioned, isn't she?"

"She runs a daycent establishment." Her mock-Irish accent was heavier than the landlady's. Her eyes, hard to read in the lamplight, raised to meet mine. "Take me someplace."

I took her to my hotel, a less decent establishment than Mrs. Larkin's. We did each other little good but no harm, and it beat being alone.

Another night I ran into Barry Mosedale at Polly's Cage. He told me there was a singer at Kid Gloves who was doing a number about the bag lady. "I can find out how you can reach him," he offered.

"Is he there now?"

He nodded and checked his watch. "He goes on in fifteen minutes. But you don't want to go here, do you?"

"Why not?"

"Hardly your sort of crowd, Matt."

"Cops go anywhere."

"Indeed they do, and they're welcome wherever they go, aren't they? Just let me drink this and I'll accompany you, if that's all right. You need someone to lend you immoral support."

Kid Gloves is a gay bar on Fifty-sixth west of Ninth. The decor is just a little aggressively gay lib. There's a small raised stage, a scattering of tables, a piano, a loud jukebox. Barry Mosedale and I stood at the bar. I'd been there before and knew better than to order their coffee. I had straight bourbon. Barry had his on ice with a splash of soda.

Halfway through the drink Gordon Lurie was introduced. He wore tight jeans and a flowered shirt, sat on stage on a folding chair, sang ballads he'd written himself with his own guitar for accompaniment. I don't know if he was any good or not. It sounded to me as though all the songs had the same melody, but that may just have been a similarity of style. I don't have much of an ear.

After a song about a summer romance in Amsterdam, Gordon Lurie announced that the next number was dedicated to the memory of Mary Alice Redfield. Then he sang:

She's a shopping bag lady who lives on the sidewalks of Broadway
Wearing all of her clothes and her years on her back
Toting dead dreams in an old paper sack

*Searching the trashcans for something
she
lost here on Broadway —
Shopping bag lady . . .*

*You'd never know but she once was an
actress on Broadway
Speaking the words that they stuffed in
her head
Reciting the lines of the life that she led
Thrilling her fans and her friends and her
lovers on Broadway —
Shopping bag lady . . .*

*There are demons who lurk in the
corners
of minds and of Broadway
And after the omens and portents and
signs
Came the day she forgot to remember her
lines
Put her life on a leash and took it out
walking on Broadway —
Shopping bag lady . . .*

There were a couple more verses and the
shopping bag lady in the song wound up
murdered in a doorway, dying in defense
of the "tattered old treasures she mined in
the trashcans of Broadway." The song went

418

over well and got a bigger hand than any of the ones that had preceded it.

I asked Barry who Gordon Lurie was.

"You know very nearly as much as I," he said. "He started here Tuesday. I find him whelming, personally. Neither overwhelming nor underwhelming but somewhere in the middle."

"Mary Alice never spent much time on Broadway. I never saw her more than a block from Ninth Avenue."

"Poetic license, I'm sure. The song would lack a certain something if you substituted Ninth Avenue for Broadway. As it stands it sounds a little like 'Rhinestone Cowboy.'"

"Lurie live around here?"

"I don't know where he lives. I have the feeling he's Canadian. So many people are nowadays. It used to be that no one was Canadian and now simply everybody is. I'm sure it must be a virus."

We listened to the rest of Gordon Lurie's act. Then Barry leaned forward and chatted with the bartender to find out how I could get backstage. I found my way to what passed for a dressing room at Kid Gloves. It must have been a ladies' lavatory in a prior incarnation.

I went in there thinking I'd made a

breakthrough, that Lurie had killed her and now he was dealing with his guilt by singing about her. I don't think I really believed this but it supplied me with direction and momentum.

I told him my name and that I was interested in his act. He wanted to know if I was from a record company. "Am I on the threshold of a great opportunity? Am I about to become an overnight success after years of travail?"

We got out of the tiny room and left the club through a side door. Three doors down the block we sat in a cramped booth at a coffee shop. He ordered a Greek salad and we both had coffee.

I told him I was interested in his song about the bag lady.

He brightened. "Oh, do you like it? Personally I think it's the best thing I've written. I just wrote it a couple of days ago. I opened next door Tuesday night. I got to New York three weeks ago and I had a two-week booking in the West Village. A place called David's Table. Do you know it?"

"I don't think so."

"Another stop on the K-Y circuit. Either there aren't any straight people in New York or they don't go to nightclubs. But I was there two weeks, and then I opened at Kid Gloves, and afterward I was sitting and drinking with some people and somebody was talking about the shopping bag lady and I had had enough Amaretto to be maudlin on the subject. I woke up Wednesday morning with a splitting headache and the first verse of the song buzzing in my splitting head, and I sat up immediately and wrote it down, and as I was writing one verse the next would come bubbling to the surface, and before I knew it I had all six verses." He took a cigarette, then paused in the act of lighting it to fix his eyes on me. "You told me your name," he said, "but I don't remember it."

"Matthew Scudder."

"Yes. You're the person investigating her murder."

"I'm not sure that's the right word. I've been talking to people, seeing what I can come up with. Did you know her before she was killed?"

He shook his head. "I was never even in this neighborhood before. *Oh.* I'm not a suspect, am I? Because I haven't been in New York since the fall. I haven't bothered to figure out where I was when she was killed but I was in California at Christmastime and I'd gotten as far east as Chicago in early March, so I do have a fairly solid alibi."

"I never really suspected you. I think I just wanted to hear your song." I sipped some coffee. "Where did you get the facts of her life? Was she an actress?"

"I don't think so. Was she? It wasn't really *about* her, you know. It was inspired by her story but I didn't know her and I never knew anything about her. The past few days I've been paying a lot of attention to bag ladies, though. And other street people."

"I know what you mean."

"Are there more of them in New York or is it just that they're so much more visible here? In California everybody drives, you don't see people on the street. I'm from Canada, rural Ontario, and the first city I ever spent much time in was Toronto, and there are crazy people on the streets there but it's nothing like New York. Does the city drive them crazy or does it just tend to draw crazy people?"

"I don't know."

"Maybe they're not crazy. Maybe they just hear a different drummer. I wonder who killed her."

"We'll probably never know."

"What I really wonder is *why* she was killed. In my song I made up some reason. That somebody wanted what was in her bags. I think it works as a song that way but I don't think there's much chance that it happened like that. Why would anyone kill the poor thing?"

"I don't know."

"They say she left people money. People she hardly knew. Is that the truth?" I nodded. "And she left me a song. I don't even feel that I wrote it. I woke up with it. I never set eyes on her and she touched my life. That's strange, isn't it?"

Everything was strange. The strangest part of all was the way it ended.

It was a Monday night. The Mets were at Shea and I'd taken my sons to a game. The Dodgers were in for a three-game series which they eventually swept as they'd been sweeping everything lately. The boys and I got to watch them knock Jon Matlack out of the box and go on to shell his several replacements. The final count was something like 13–4. We stayed in our seats until the last out. Then I saw them home and caught a train back to the city.

So it was past midnight when I reached Armstrong's. Trina brought me a large double and a mug of coffee without being asked. I knocked back half of the bourbon and was dumping the rest into my coffee when she told me somebody'd been looking for me earlier. "He was in three times in the past two hours," she said. "A wiry guy, high forehead, bushy eyebrows, sort of a bulldog jaw. I guess the word for it is underslung."

"Perfectly good word."

"I said you'd probably get here sooner or later."

"I always do. Sooner or later."

"Uh-huh. You okay, Matt?"

"The Mets lost a close one."

"I heard it was thirteen to four."

"That's close for them these days. Did he say what it was about?"

He hadn't, but within the half hour he came in again and I was there to be found. I recognized him from Trina's description as soon as he came through the door. He looked faintly familiar but he was nobody I knew. I suppose I'd seen him around the neighborhood.

Evidently he knew me by sight because he found his way to my table without asking directions and took a chair without being invited to sit. He didn't say anything for a while and neither did I. I had a fresh bourbon and coffee in front of me and I took a sip and looked him over.

He was under thirty. His cheeks were hollow and the flesh of his face was stretched over his skull like leather that had shrunk upon drying. He wore a forest green work shirt and a pair of khaki pants. He needed a shave.

Finally he pointed at my cup and asked me what I was drinking. When I told him he said all he drank was beer.

"They have beer here," I said.

"Maybe I'll have what you're drinking." He turned in his chair and waved for Trina. When she came over he said he'd have bourbon and coffee, the same as I was having. He didn't say anything more until she brought the drink. Then, after he had spent quite some time stirring it, he took a sip. "Well," he said, "that's not so bad. That's okay."

"Glad you like it."

"I don't know if I'd order it again, but at least now I know what it's like."

"That's something."

"I seen you around. Matt Scudder. Used to be a cop, private eye now, blah blah blah. Right?"

"Close enough."

"My name's Floyd. I never liked it but

I'm stuck with it, right? I could change it but who'm I kidding? Right?"

"If you say so."

"If I don't somebody else will. Floyd Karp, that's the full name. I didn't tell you my last name, did I? That's it, Floyd Karp."

"Okay."

"Okay, okay, okay." He pursed his lips, blew out air in a silent whistle. "What do we do now, Matt? Huh? That's what I want to know."

"I'm not sure what you mean, Floyd."

"Oh, you know what I'm getting at, driving at, getting at. You know, don't you?"

By this time I suppose I did.

"I killed that old lady. Took her life, stabbed her with my knife." He flashed the saddest smile. "Steee-rangled her with her skeeee-arf. Hoist her with her own whatchacallit, petard. What's a petard, Matt?"

"I don't know, Floyd. Why'd you kill her?"

He looked at me, he looked at his coffee, he looked at me again.

He said, "Had to."

"Why?"

"Same as the bourbon and coffee. Had

to *see*. Had to taste it and find out what it was like." His eyes met mine. His were very large, hollow, empty. I fancied I could see right through them to the blackness at the back of his skull. "I couldn't get my mind away from murder," he said. His voice was more sober now, the mocking playful quality gone from it. "I tried. I just couldn't do it. It was on my mind all the time and I was afraid of what I might do. I couldn't function, I couldn't think, I just saw blood and death all the time. I was afraid to close my eyes for fear of what I might see. I would just stay up, days it seemed, and then I'd be tired enough to pass out the minute I closed my eyes. I stopped eating. I used to be fairly heavy and the weight just fell off of me."

"When did all this happen, Floyd?"

"I don't know. All winter. And I thought if I went and did it once I would know if I was a man or a monster or what. And I got this knife, and I went out a couple nights but lost my nerve, and then one night — I don't want to talk about that part of it now."

"All right."

"I almost couldn't do it, but I couldn't *not* do it, and then I was doing it and it went on forever. It was *horrible*."

427

"Why didn't you stop?"

"I don't know. I think I was afraid to stop. That doesn't make any sense, does it? I just don't know. It was all crazy, insane, like being in a movie and being in the audience at the same time. Watching myself."

"No one saw you do it?"

"No. I threw the knife down a sewer. I went home. I put all my clothes in the incinerator, the ones I was wearing. I kept throwing up. All that night I would throw up even when my stomach was empty. Dry heaves, Department of Dry Heaves. And then I guess I fell asleep, I don't know when or how but I did, and the next day I woke up and thought I dreamed it. But of course I didn't."

"No."

"And what I did think was that it was over. I did it and I knew I'd never want to do it again. It was something crazy that happened and I could forget about it. And I thought that was what happened."

"That you managed to forget about it?"

A nod. "But I guess I didn't. And now everybody's talking about her. Mary Alice Redfield, I killed her without knowing her name. Nobody knew her name and now everybody knows it and it's all back in my mind. And I heard you were looking for me, and I guess, I guess. . . ." He frowned, chasing a thought around in his mind like a dog trying to capture his tail. Then he gave it up and looked at me. "So here I am," he said. "So here I am."

"Yes."

"Now what happens?"

"I think you'd better tell the police about it, Floyd."

"Why?"

"I suppose for the same reason you told me."

He thought about it. After a long time he nodded. "All right," he said. "I can accept that. I'd never kill anybody again. I know that. But — you're right. I have to tell them. I don't know who to see or what to say or, hell, I just —"

"I'll go with you if you want."

"Yeah. I want you to."

"I'll have a drink and then we'll go. You want another?"

"No. I'm not much of a drinker."

I had it without the coffee this time. After Trina brought it I asked him how he'd picked his victim. Why the bag lady?

He started to cry. No sobs, just tears spilling from his deep-set eyes. After a while he wiped them on his sleeve.

"Because she didn't count," he said.

"That's what I thought. She was nobody. Who cared if she died? Who'd miss her?" He closed his eyes tight. "Everybody misses her," he said. "Everybody."

So I took him in. I don't know what they'll do with him. It's not my problem.

It wasn't really a case and I didn't really solve it. As far as I can see I didn't do anything. It was the talk that drove Floyd Karp from cover, and no doubt I helped some of the talk get started, but some of it would have gotten around without me. All those legacies of Mary Alice Redfield's had made her a nine-day wonder in the neighborhood. It was one of those legacies that got me involved.

Maybe she caught her own killer. Maybe he caught himself, as everyone does. Maybe no man's an island and maybe everybody is.

All I know is I lit a candle for the woman, and I suspect I'm not the only one who did.

The employees of Thorndike Press hope you have enjoyed this Large Print book. All our Thorndike and Wheeler Large Print titles are designed for easy reading, and all our books are made to last. Other Thorndike Press Large Print books are available at your library, through selected bookstores, or directly from us.

For information about titles, please call:

(800) 223-1244

or visit our Web site at:

www.gale.com/thorndike
www.gale.com/wheeler

To share your comments, please write:

Publisher
Thorndike Press
295 Kennedy Memorial Drive
Waterville, ME   04901